An Audience with the King

Kat Caldwell

A note from the author

The characters, peoples, towns and kingdoms have names that the author made up out of thin air. If there is any resemblance to real names, it was not done on purpose. The characters, places and events are fiction.

There are several words from different languages from around the world woven into the story. That was done on purpose. While the author understands that language is rich and complex and direct translation from one language to another doesn't always fit correctly, she thought it would add more to the characters if the reader could hear them speak another language. The author sincerely hopes the reader will allow her the fun of using other languages mixed in, even if perhaps the grammar of those languages isn't always perfect. A lexicon of the meanings and which language the words are from is located at the end of the book.

Chapters

1.   masking unease
2.   the sargarisees
3.   free will
4.   an audience with the King
5.   to dine with the King
6.   leaving Niebo
7.   feeding Krimaltin
8.   touring alone
9.   black nails of sorrow
10.   a purpose
11.   meeting Zanderi
12.   one's place
13.   dirty beggar
14.   words that wound
15.   love and mercy
16.   awakening from the daydream
17.   stones of shame
18.   a baby from a rock
19.   new wine skins
20.   home again
21.   a final blessing

To my beautiful girls.... Always remember to see yourself as the King sees you.

Chapter 1

masking unease

Nelia shivered as she stepped through the green arch. Each room was more exquisite than the last. With each item more beautiful than the one before, she lost her ability to feign disinterest. Instead, her eyes widened more and her open mouth hung lower.

When she had first arrived at the palace, she had been determined not to look around in awe. She didn't want to seem uncouth. Mother had done a good job of instilling a minimum amount of pride in her. The last thing she wished was to give the impression that she never saw fine things in her life. Perhaps her faded dress screamed that gold chairs should impress her, but Nelia was single-minded in not giving the palace staff any reason to pity her. She had come for so much more than the luxury; she had come for answers. And truth. Her quest was noble, not petty. To prove it, she had thought it best to act aloof and just keep her focus on not messing up too much. But she was failing miserably. There was no hiding the fact that everything about the palace mesmerized her. The gold, the silver, the jewels, the crystals. She couldn't imagine a more magnificent palace.

Who was she to feign boredom at gold moldings along the ceiling when her ceiling had bacterial mold and cracks from a shifting foundation?

That troublesome feeling that crept over her when out of her natural habitat was fighting to take control of her legs, turn her body and run. *Who was she to snub marble floors? Who was she to act as though velvet-covered couches were normal? Who was she…? Who was she…?*

That distress could grow to an overwhelming size if she allowed it to; if she didn't fight it with each step she took. Pretending she had the right to be indifferent helped keep her flight instinct at bay. She couldn't have imagined there existed a beauty that pushed away every emotion except awe. It was a quagmire. If she allowed the awe to overwhelm her senses as it wished to, she was afraid she might fall to her knees and weep. Either way, she would ruin the visit – ruin her one chance to see the King.

After silently filling her lungs with air, Nelia locked her mouth shut, deciding to sacrifice her jaws instead of her dignity.

"Over here, Nelia," her attendant said, ushering her closer to a divider wrapped in green silk with dark, green emeralds lining the border. Nelia followed immediately, determined to look ahead, as a queen might.

But even in her imagination, Nelia was no queen. The gleam of the ceiling pulled her gaze up, even before she could catch herself. Mother had always said she had a weak character. She felt that her own gasp of wonder at the seaside scene – which was so delicate, so lifelike that she could almost hear the laughter of the little girl depicted – confirmed Mother's judgement to be true.

"Isn't it beautiful?" the woman asked. "Sometimes I come in here and lie down on the floor just to stare for a little while. I like to pretend I'm right there, in a place as pretty as the picture, though I've never been to the sea."

The admission brought down some of Nelia's defenses, which had sprung up the moment the attendant spoke. Perhaps if she, looking so very comfortable in this grand space, was still in awe of the palace, then – just maybe – it was acceptable for Nelia to show admiration. Though that would also mean Mother might have been wrong, which was a terrifying prospect.

Neither Mother nor her uncanny ability to always be right was something Nelia was willing to ponder at the moment.

"I've never seen anything so beautiful," she whispered, though her eyes were now on the screen lined with emeralds. Instinctively she reached out to touch the cool green stones before pulling her hand back, alarms ringing in her head at her actions. The deep flush in her skin oozed over her just as she saw the air take on a pink tinge in the large mirror behind the screen.

Instead of admonishing her, as Nelia had expected, the attendant laughed.

"Go ahead – touch them. They won't come off. I tried to steal one the first time I came in when my attendant wasn't looking."

Nelia couldn't stop her mouth from almost hitting the floor. The woman put her hand up, palm out.

"Scout's honor," she said, her eyes sparkling. "Try as I might, I couldn't get them off. After working here for a time, I felt so overcome with guilt that I finally admitted it to the King one day. Just blurted it out. It was my birthday, and he had thrown a party for me, as he does for every worker in the palace. The King invited me to a waltz, and he looked at me so kindly that I almost vomited from the guilt. When I told him what I had tried to do, do you know what the King did?"

"Fifty thrashes?" Nelia guessed, it being the regular punishment in her village.

"No. He laughed."

The woman giggled at the memory as she pulled out a bright yellow dress, along with a fur cloak, from a hidden closet in the silk-papered walls next to the mirror. This movement gave Nelia a moment to recover from the shock of a strange new image of the King that was forming in her head. She dared to glance about, and a vanity dresser carved from one piece of soft white stone caught her eye.

The gleam of the stone touched the short-term memory button in Nelia's head. Ivory was the name of the woman escorting her. Though she had tried her best to remember it, her nerves had gotten the best of her within minutes of being introduced. So far, she had gotten away with deliberately not speaking the woman's name, but now she could finally relax. Unless she managed to forget it again.

As she repeated the name softly under her breath, Nelia stepped closer to the vanity. The color was warm and cozy, inviting one to sit and gain warmth from it. Nelia ran her fingers along the length of the vanity, finding it to be cool to the touch.

"Ivory," she whispered one more time, satisfied that she knew the name. She tapped her fingers against the dresser and smiled. Maybe it was the fake ivory they used sometimes to fool those who didn't know what the product truly looked like. She had seen real ivory once, carved into a statue, before they had outlawed it in her town. The statue had been of a woman, and it had been so lifelike that Nelia had had a hard time understanding it had once been an animal horn. So much warmth and light had radiated from the statue. She had expected it to feel like soft butter, able to be molded into shape from a simple touch. When she had gotten up her nerve to reach out, she had found it to be warm, though perhaps that was due more to the statue sitting in the sun than the material itself. To this day, she related ivory to softness and heat.

"Put these on," Ivory said, holding up the dress and new undergarments.

The request brought Nelia's heartbeat to an angry pace. Her head snapped back to reality. Only three words, and her chest was constricting as though caught under a heavy weight. Anger pressed down into her thighs, screaming at them to run.

"I'll wear my own clothes, thank you," she bit out, her voice cracking against the walls with emotion. The words were so brittle and brown that she watched them disintegrate into dust once they hit the walls. The sight caused her to stop her indignant tirade cold. Aaron had warned her about her tongue before she left.

"Bite it until it bleeds if you have to," he had said.

"These are your clothes," Ivory said, seemingly unruffled by the venom in Nelia's voice; she softened her eyelids to keep it from shooting out from her corneas. Ivory went on. "The King had them made for you the day you became a citizen of the kingdom. See? Here is your name."

"I became a citizen at eight years old."

"Yes, you did."

At once Nelia's defensiveness dissipated in exchange for confusion. She looked Ivory straight in the eyes for the first time, finding them to be a warm, deep black. The taller woman looked down at her with a small, kind smile, still holding out the dress in mid-air.

"As a citizen grows, so does their dress. Or suit, in the case of a man."

Patience, the color of budding lilacs, floated in the air around Ivory's shoulders. It oozed from her, wrapping around her like a woolen shawl. But her voice was not like that of Mrs. Duffle, who huffed and puffed, always muttering about Nelia's lack of intelligence or creativity. Every year Mrs. Duffle won a plaque certifying that she was the most patient woman in the town. And every year Nelia wondered what connection there was between Mrs. Duffle and the town board.

In contrast, Ivory acted as though she had all the time in the world to spend with Nelia, as though she had the answer and yet was willing to wait for Nelia to figure everything out for herself. And she neither huffed, puffed, nor muttered under her breath.

Nelia had seen glimmers of this kind of patience. Those who made a yearly trip to the palace came back with it, although Nelia found that theirs was short-lived in most cases. Some people like her mother and Aunt Velma found such patience each year, making the trek to the palace as though in need of a fill-up. At the palace, they would eat up their portion of peace and come home ready to take on all the children and demands of life. It still came with a sort of jaw-clenching to it, and only lasted a month or less. They always blamed the loss of it on their children or the harsh life they all lived.

Only old Mr. Zehner and the young Miss Patinski who taught the kindergarten class at the local school held the same patience that Ivory seemed to have. Nelia remembered that Miss Patinski had never yelled and always explained things, again and again, never tiring of Nelia, even when her young mind would confuse the letters and numbers. The day she had graduated from kindergarten, Nelia had sobbed. She had known that she was not only losing a teacher, but losing love from her life. She had managed to sneak back to Miss Patinski during the first and second grade to ask for help, though many of the other students had found out and hidden along the path to ambush her with half-eaten fruit or pinecones. But no amount of pinecones hitting her flesh would keep her from an embrace of love. Even Nelia had been smart enough to understand that exchange.

Miss Patinski was the one who had discovered Nelia's dyslexia. She had even tried to convince her mother to get her tested. Mother never had, of course. But that hadn't deterred Miss Patinski from doing it herself and getting Nelia an official letter, with the hopes she would go to high school and then college.

Old guilt crept over her in a slow yellow slime when she remembered how disappointed Miss Patinski had been when Nelia didn't even finish high school. Funnily enough, the guilt couldn't seem to stick this time. As quickly as it tried to overtake her, the slime fell away.

"Are you ready to get dressed now, Nelia?" Ivory asked, interrupting her thoughts.

"I – well, do I get to keep it?" she asked, the words blurted out before she could stop them. Ivory laughed, a deep, melodic laugh – the kind that attracted Aaron. He called it an honest laugh, in contrast to the kinds of giggling fits girls in the village had around him.

"It's yours. You can do what you wish with it. Some leave it, and some take it."

"What does the King recommend?"

Ivory's eyes widened slightly, her brow lifting. Her smile shortened, though it was still warm.

"The King," Ivory intoned, reverently, her voice almost a whisper, "always has them made for the person to keep and wear. But he will not force you to keep it. Some tell him they have no place to wear it to. Others say they do not deserve it. There are others who tell the King they prefer their own clothes. Many times, I've heard the excuse that they don't wish to get it dirty. They do not believe him when he tells them that it cannot get dirty."

"It can't get dirty? How is that possible?"

Ivory's smile turned mischievous.

"With the King, anything is possible," she said with an air of mystery. "I do not understand the science, but I do know that this dress I'm wearing is the same one I received when I first came."

"Ah," Nelia said. "It is a way to save resources. Like recycling. He wants to keep you in the same dress. Of course, that means he doesn't hire any laundry women."

"No laundry women," Ivory answered. "None here. But you are wrong about saving resources. There is no shortage of resources or dresses. I have a dress in each color of the rainbow, but today I chose to wear this one. It's still my favorite, no matter how many others I receive or buy."

Nelia took a good look. The dress was a deep teal: the same color the pond had at Helestau Mare when one stood on the diving rock high above the water and looked down. Well into fall and winter, Nelia would go to that spot, sitting out as far as she dared on the diving rock, looking deep into that cavernous teal circle and wondering what it would be like to touch the bottom. Only once had she dared to jump from the rock, but she hadn't had the courage to open her eyes and look underneath the foamy blue water. Instead of the peace she had sought, and so many others had told her she would feel, a desperate need for air had attacked her. Panic had invaded her every pore. She had kicked at the water as hard as she had ever kicked before in her life, reaching the surface out of breath and paralyzed with the fear of sinking to a blue, watery grave. For a few wonderful seconds, she had seen the world above the water, but had soon sunk back down again into the water. It was Aaron, realizing she was about to drown, who saved her. That was also the first time they had ever spoken to one another. Despite the panic and embarrassment that the whole moment had caused, the place above the water called to her each time she needed comfort. After all, it was the place that had brought her Aaron.

Ivory turned slowly, the teal dress rippling as the water at the pond would on a windy day. Nelia took a good look. The beautiful material elegantly hugged Ivory's hips, was generous in the bust to make room for her bountiful chest, and had no sagging or pinching anywhere. There were no stains and no rips and no tears. Nelia looked down at her own skirt, instantly able to see the spots around her middle and along the left side that were faded and threadbare from scrubbing out grease stains. There was also a stitched-up tear down the side of her right thigh and the fact that her left sleeve had no cuff. She had gotten too close to the stove one night. Thankfully, only her cuff had been burned off.

"I will put the dress on."

The moment the words were out, her skin pricked at the idea of soft fabric sliding against it. That meant, of course, that she would have to take off the old dress so she could put on the new one, which would mean being naked in front of Ivory. She had never been naked in front of another woman since she had been a girl. And then it was only on washing days with all the women gathered around to wash all of them. No one really even paid attention. They merely wanted the dirty clothes and the dirty children scrubbed at the same time.

But Nelia was now convinced that she couldn't approach the King in this raggedy dress. Not when she had an opportunity to be properly attired. There was nothing to do but simply get it over with. If she was careful to keep facing Ivory, perhaps the woman wouldn't notice her underwear sagging without elastic and the fact that her bra only had one hook, instead of two.

As though reading her thoughts, Ivory turned slightly and Nelia took a deep breath. Quickly she pulled off her dress, then stood as still as a statue, waiting for the beautiful yellow dress to bunch up in front of her and cover her spindly legs. But instead of the dress, Ivory daintily held up a hanger with brand new underwear.

Pure shock and wonder lifted Nelia's hand to take the beautiful silk garments. She was still rubbing the fabric in wonder when Ivory stepped out of sight, calling over her shoulder for Nelia to advise when she was ready for the dress.

Nelia stopped rubbing the silk with her rough fingers when her callouses almost pulled a small thread out. Even without any charts or math knowledge, she understood the market value for these items. Never again would she question the right for the stores to sell them at such unattainable prices. The fabric was like cream sliding over her body. Not even her dry, hardened skin pulled on the fabric, unlike the fake stuff sold at the Under 2 Klinous shop, where everything was 'priced to disappear'. A one-time purchase of fake silk there had been all she'd needed to learn from her mistake. After one wash, the pretty material had snagged and torn in two places.

Right now, the feeling of beauty was priceless. The instantaneous change within her was comparable to the time Aaron's cousin had painted her nails for their wedding. She remembered staring down at them all day long, barely touching anything for fear that the color would chip off before the wedding ceremony. But this time the feeling went deeper than just her fingernails. This time she might be worth looking at.

A rumbling in her stomach interrupted the moment. Nelia looked up to check the time, but there was no clock fixed to such beautiful wallpaper. And if the palace people were smart, they wouldn't place an ornate clock anywhere someone could steal it. Which is why there was none on the vanity. That was her thought, anyway.

"I'm ready for the dress," Nelia finally said, her voice cracking.

Just like you – never enjoy a moment for the moment's worth.

That was her grandmama's voice chiding her in her head. It was true, but Nelia shook it away. The urgency of time had come over her enough to prick her skin with panic. The truth of the matter was that it would be just like her to spend all of her time gaping at silk undergarments only to lose all of her time with the King.

Though she hadn't owned a watch since selling hers three years before to cover their rent payment, Nelia still looked at her wrist. There was no magical time written there.

Dawdler! Nic nie robić! Mother's voice cracked in her head.

The rumbling in her stomach turned to nausea. She was about to miss her appointment with the King. Nothing would make Aaron laugh harder than if she were to tell him that. And Kendra would click her tongue and chastise her for having wasted the King's time in the first place. How dare she keep a man like that waiting? For underwear!

A thin sheen of sweat covered her skin. She could not fail to see the King. If she did, she could never face the embarrassment at home.

"What time is it?" she asked timidly as a bundle of yellow cloth finally approached her, hiding Ivory.

"You have plenty of time, Nelia, don't worry. Worrying isn't allowed here in the castle. Things always work out."

"I don't want to keep the King waiting," Nelia answered, her voice muffled as the smooth, cool fabric fell over her head.

"Don't worry, Nelia," Ivory repeated. "We plan the time for each person to get dressed. You are well ahead of schedule."

"Will you be taking me to the King next?"

Kind hands placed themselves upon her waist, turning her to face the mirror, but Nelia was too agitated to look up. Instead, she looked at the smooth stone floor while holding her hair away as Ivory laced up the back of the dress. In place of ties, there were tiny little pearl buttons that Ivory hooked through loops one by one. Something about the rustling of the fabric sent a tingle of excitement through Nelia's spine in anticipation and nervousness at how ludicrous the dress might look on her. Would it enhance how she had no right to be dressed in such exuberance?

"Ain't no Raddford worth a kostspielig like that." Mother's voice rang in her head. *"We's workin' people. We dress like workin' people. Ain't no use gettin' on any high horse, Nel."*

All that speech solely because Nelia had dared to express her desire to one day have a white, satin wedding gown. The knot in her stomach twisted up tighter. Pushing away any thoughts of her mother would be best. They usually left her feeling empty and worn: not a feeling she wished to have just before seeing the King. This was a once-in-a-lifetime opportunity. She would not allow her mother to invade it.

"The material is so exquisite," Ivory said, breaking up the dark thoughts. Nelia sighed both in relief and agreement.

It was a dress Nelia might see on the cover of magazines, worn by women with blown-back hair or flowers floating through wavy tresses. Even for her wedding, Nelia had not worn anything remotely close to this dress. That day of joy had brought with it a frost-covered ground and a dress borrowed from her cousin, who had found it at a second-hand shop. Many uses had worn away the brocade and there had been small moth-holes in the folds, though everyone had claimed they never saw them.

Aaron had admitted just last year that he had seen them, but said he'd thought they were little crystals. Which had made her laugh. When would they have been able to afford crystals on anything, much less a dress? Even the stone in her own wedding ring was glass. This she had found out one night while scrubbing the floor only a few months into their marriage. In a very tender moment, Aaron had presented her with a small, polished stone from the river a few weeks later. Probably her many tears over the shattered 'stone' had confounded him enough to push him into action. She remembered watching his large hands work their magic, the tiny swell on her belly that would leave her in an angry torrent of blood and pain only a few weeks later shaking with joyous laughter when he managed to fit it into the empty prongs of her ring.

"Look up, Nelia," urged Ivory as she stepped away, looking satisfied with her task.

Obedient as always, Nelia lifted her head and found a strange image staring back at her through the mirror. Starting from the top of her head, Nelia seemed to be glowing. Her hair, which a moment before had looked tired, worn and in need of coconut oil, now seemed to glimmer healthily in the sunshine.

Her eyes narrowed. Surely the mirror was playing tricks. Or perhaps the bright yellow dress combined with the sunshine was causing her hair to look different.

At six yesterday morning she had plunged into the frigid water that Aaron had left in the metal bathtub for her the night before. He was not a particularly warm man, nor was he prone to understanding the complexities of women, but the small gestures he made let her know he still loved her. The other night had been one of those moments. Though her heart had proved to be quite deadened since Zayzay's death, love had welled up in it when she'd caught him bathing outside, pouring water over his head to get rid of the absurd amount of bubbles he had created. His own beliefs about the King he kept to himself, but he wouldn't deny her the opportunity to meet the King.

Aaron knew the Prince, having fought with him, but Nelia had never heard him say anything much about the King. The only time he had ever mentioned him was when Nelia and her mother had been complaining about a law they thought unfair; Aaron had warned them to think deeper, because such things were always more complicated than appeared on the surface. Whatever his thoughts, by leaving her clean bath water she knew that her husband understood her nervousness and anxiety.

Nelia stepped closer to the mirror to get a better look, to find the girl she knew was still behind that image she saw. The dark freckles caused by too much sun seemed to have faded almost completely away. And instead of the flecks of dry scales that normally caught her eyes, she saw a faint glittering, as though her skin was covered in that powder the girls at the pharmacy had tried to convince her to buy last year during Christmas.

Nelia stepped back in surprise. No, shock. The distance between her and the mirror widened, allowing her a better look at herself. And Nelia couldn't pull her eyes away.

Right in front of her, with the same eyes that looked back at her every morning, was not only a dress that could be on the cover of a magazine, but a woman who could equally be featured there. There were no black rings under her eyes. There were no lines of strain around her mouth. Her skin shone as though it had been pampered all its life; her eyes sparkled and carried none of the usual daily cares they normally did. Her thin body looked vigorous instead of suffering from poor nutrition. When a breeze rustled through the window in the ceiling and the sunlight changed, Nelia saw her skin give off glittering rainbows across the wall. Most strange of all was that something akin to peace settled upon her shoulders.

"I – I don't understand how I look like this. You didn't put makeup on me. Look, even my wrist is now straight. It hasn't been straight since I was seven. What did you put on me? What is inside this dress to make me look... like this? I look rested and calm and... strong. You're bewitching me. Or this mirror is. Is it a magical mirror?"

Ivory giggled, her eyes dancing with glee. She held up a small mirror for Nelia to hold while she combed out what now looked like rich brown tresses.

"Do you prefer the ponytail, or would you like me to style it differently? You could also leave it down."

"What does the King like more?"

"He likes you to be more comfortable."

"Then maybe a half-up, with part of it down to hide my shoulders, as I know they will shake."

Ivory laughed again, touching her shoulders lightly.

"I feel no shaking," she said, the pins in her mouth impeding her speech slightly.

"Truly, Ivory, how did you do this? Is it a trick of the lighting?"

Ivory placed the last pin into Nelia's dark brown hair before meeting her eyes in the mirror and answering.

"You now see yourself as he sees you."

"As he will see me? So this is a trick? You still see my sunspots and yellow teeth and broken wrist and dry, unruly hair?"

Ivory scrutinized the woman in the mirror before answering.

"I see you as a beautiful young woman full of energy and creativity."

"Creativity? I haven't done a creative thing in my life. I work a farm with my husband and his people."

"You also fix furniture, and you used to make beautiful gifts out of the bits and pieces of scraps you would find on the road and around town."

Nelia blinked once. Then twice. She blinked until her blank mind produced the image of a wooden box sitting before her on the kitchen table in her parents' home. Formerly the home to a bottle of wine, the box at that moment was covered in bits of lace, dried flowers, and pieces of colored paper. Black ink still gleamed as the weak sunlight took its time to dry the letters. It had taken intense labor on her part to write those letters in cursive, surrounded by tiny flowers and leaves, just as she had seen embossed in fairytale books. In the center of it all was the old picture of her grandfather. The only one Grandmama still had that was in focus and not eaten by moths, sun or damp. Nelia remembered the look of joy on Grandmama's face along with her mother's misty eyes as they looked at the box.

Those two distinct looks of delight had fed her through the tumultuous next year.

"How do you know about that?"

"The King told me. He said you would have made more, if the hard years that followed hadn't been so dark. The way he said it made it seem like you fell on very hard times. He remembers the box very well. He says it is one of your talents. Oh! The Prince will be here soon."

"I haven't seen that box in years," Nelia mused, unable to hear anything else but her own thoughts. "I guess it must have gotten thrown out."

She felt herself float off into her own thoughts, teetering on the verge of going to memories she had no business visiting right before meeting the King. Though she had no makeup on to smear, she certainly didn't want puffy eyes or splotchy skin when meeting him either.

Suddenly aware that Ivory was looking at her, patiently waiting for her to put herself together, Nelia sat up straight.

"I'm sorry. What were you saying?"

"No need to apologize, Nelia. This is an exciting moment, and it brings up many emotions in people. I was just wondering if you missed your grandpapa. I'm told you loved him very much."

"Yes," Nelia said, her voice cracking as she pushed her tears away again. The walls within her stomach tightened, threatening to pull up all of its contents. "He was like a father to me – the person I could run to for refuge. The only person who ever called me beautiful, though Mother scoffed at the words. Grandmama once told me that something happened to Mother when she went away to the city, something that made her angry. Seemed to Grandmama that Mother focused all her anger on men, no matter who they were. Even Grandpapa. He called her his Valentine – my mother, that is. She never told him to stop, but she would always bristle at the words. Like she couldn't accept the love they held."

Ivory smiled, her skin pulling back as smoothly as a child's. A small child whose cheeks were still swollen with fat.

Like a four-year-old.

Nelia bit her tongue to stop the tears from forming. *Zayzay.*

Chapter 2

the sagarisees

Nelia had promised Aaron she wouldn't bring up little Zayzay. She had promised *herself* not to bring up Zayzay. The very topic of him would ruin the entire day.

"Nelia, what's wrong?" Ivory asked, her eyes intensely compassionate as she grasped Nelia's hands in her own.

Before Nelia could speak, a majestic presence entered the room. A royal presence. No fear came with it, but it did instill immediate awe and reverence, much like entering the grand cathedral every Christmas and Easter. Nelia had only ever been permitted to sit in the balcony section, but from there she could see the elaborate ceiling and all the people below who paid more dues each year so they could sit closer. The acoustics of the cathedral were perfect for hearing the sermons on giving more than one received and working hard to be a better, more moral person. This was done in exchange for being accepted into the King's presence, as far as Nelia understood.

Every Sunday at the Champs Parish these same sermons were delivered, though softer in tone. In the sermon last Sunday the pastor had talked about how only those pure of heart would be accepted into the King's presence, causing Nelia's spine to stiffen. She felt cold with shock at the sudden thought: was all of this just a test in humility?

That would mean she had already failed, then, standing here and presenting herself as pure of heart enough to face the King when even she knew that was a lie. There were days when she woke up hating everything and everyone around her. About once a month she tried to change her focus from herself to those in need, but she had so little and so much had been taken away from her. The sermons about giving in order to receive only depressed her. While she did try to improve her attitude, her outlook on life, her confidence, her love for Aaron, she failed consistently.

Now she was about to embark on her biggest failure yet: to know from the beginning that she was too lowly to come to the King's castle. She was a dunce. There had been so many signs along the way, and she had missed every single one. The invitation had been a mere test in humility and she'd failed. Just as she had every math test in school – the main reason Mr. Dunbury had pleaded with her to drop out altogether so that her grades would not bring down the rest of the class. That was the year they had had a chance at the regional championship. But only if their average stayed up.

Mother's only comment had been that she knew Nelia would drop out at some point. No reason for a stupid girl to spend time at school. Everyone had a purpose, and the purpose of a stupid girl was to work.

"Make way!" sounded a powerful voice. "Here enters Prince Pokoj: Minunate, Rechter, Chansagwan, Bapa Kekekalan, Sostenitore, Umeluleki, Frälsare, Joh-Eun Muwaja, Jumala Mwenye Nguvu!"

The voice was so deep, so grave, so powerful that it sent a zap of golden electricity through the room. Nelia watched it zip past her, then zip by in the reflection of the mirrors.

"Your highness," Ivory murmured, her deep curtsy snapping Nelia out of her thoughts. Panic shot through her like lightning.

The muscles in Nelia's frozen, stiff back sent out warning messages of pain. At the same time, the corners of her eyes filled with tears. Ivory must be in on the whole ruse. At any moment she would recount Nelia's self-righteous attitude and lack of humility. And how would she defend herself? There was no time to get out of this mess she'd placed herself in by being so prideful. Just like always, she was too late in figuring out the puzzle.

"Ivory," said a deep voice as shoes clipped across the stone floor. "So nice to see you again. Is this Nelia?"

The royal presence was directly behind her now; she could feel it. The essence of the room completely changed because of it. Though the cologne that wafted her way was pleasant and the voice speaking was smooth and calm, Nelia could not turn around. Fear froze her to the spot. She saw Ivory's lips move again, her smile radiating as though direct sunlight touched it, but Nelia didn't hear the words. All her mind seemed capable of was chiding herself over and over for being stupid enough to think her invitation to the palace had been genuine.

And now it was too late to run and leave. Now the Prince was here, and he would surely bring her out to the balcony to humiliate her in front of a crowd eager for a good laugh. That was what Mayor

Billisborth would do. He'd done it several times over the last few years. Pride was punishable with twenty lashings in Overge.

As she battled with her emotions, Nelia searched desperately for an escape route but found none. Shoes clipped along the stone floor again, the essence shifting in front of her. Within a few seconds two black, shiny shoes presented themselves before her eyes. Nelia swallowed past the lump in her throat. She knew she had to look up. There was no other option but to pay respect to the Prince. Continuing this behavior might only get her into more trouble.

The Prince stood tall, straight-backed, with a smile playing on his lips. Nelia dared not look from his mouth up to his eyes, where she expected to see a glimmer of frustration or cruel mockery. Perhaps he was well-trained enough to keep a smile pasted to his lips while serving punishment, but never had she seen anyone show insincere warmth in their eyes. She tended to keep her own averted; that way she would not see the true feelings and thoughts people had of her.

Two warm, gentle fingers lifted her chin, asking her to move her eyes up to his. Nelia didn't dare defy the request. She obeyed.

His smile widened, creating small creases at the corner of his eyes. Amazingly, the stress of ruling over a large kingdom did not show on his face, save for those creases.

"Nelia," the Prince said, his rich, smooth voice filling the entire room. "I am so glad you've come to see us today. We have waited a long time to meet you."

"Your highness," Nelia croaked, dipping her torso into an awkward curtsy. That curtsy harkened back to her one semester of dance class, a required course for every fifth-grade girl in Overge. Madame Cavalliere had told them it would probably be their only reference on how to act if ever they were lucky to be near the King. She had been right, though the possibility had seemed laughable at the time. What would the King want with a bunch of poor, barefooted girls?

"Would you like to take a walk with me?" the Prince asked. "My father is eager to visit with you, but he asked me to spend some time with you beforehand."

"A walk?" Nelia stammered, glancing at Ivory, who stood smiling softly at her. Nothing had changed in Ivory's kind demeanor. There was no darkness, no hint of judgment. Still, Nelia was unconvinced that it wasn't all a hoax. Surely this walk the Prince was speaking of would be a walk straight to the high court to be mocked. Or worse, punished.

Who did she think she was to come to the palace and meet the King? Not even her mother had dared to take her own invitation seriously when she had received it. Grandmama admitted that she had gone to visit the King when she was very, very small, but Mother had dismissed that claim with the wave of a hand and another accusation of Grandmama becoming senile. Her mother's pilgrimages to the kingdom had taken her as far as the outer boarding houses, with daily trips to the cathedral services. She said people like them shouldn't demand anything more.

"Come, Nelia, have you seen the gardens? There is a path that leads along the tulips and eventually gives way to a fantastic view of the mountains. It's one of my favorite places. Would you like to see it?"

"Yes, your highness," Nelia answered, her voice barely audible as she placed her hand into the Prince's. She couldn't help but notice that her long fingers appeared dainty in his palm. While the Prince did not seem as imposing as some men, he certainly was not small. Nelia guessed that he was likely taller than her Aaron, who was the tallest man in their village at the moment. His build was slighter than Aaron's, though, probably because he did less wood chopping at the palace.

The Prince asked about her journey as they walked, and with each short but polite answer, the burden on her chest slowly dissipated. No one came to mock her. There were no crowds at the windows. The servants bowed their head as the Prince passed, but none sneered at her.

With each step along the smooth, green cobblestone path, Nelia felt able to breathe better and think more clearly. The tulips were indeed blooming, though she couldn't understand how. Nothing was blooming in her village. Aaron said it was because of the chemicals running down from the factories two villages over, but Nelia wasn't certain that was true anymore. Once the had message got out that the flowers would die, everyone had stopped planting them. Little by little, everyone had turned their flower beds into other things; more practical things. And now their village seemed full of concrete and wood.

Full of dead things instead of living.

Sun rays floated down to them, kissing her cheeks and keeping her warm despite her bare shoulders. She noticed that the Prince walked with steady strength, a man confident in his own skin and palace. The sheathed sword at his side clanked in rhythm with his steps, creating soothing music.

Nelia's limbs and heart finally relaxed. The stress that had haunted her since the war had started, that unrelenting doubt of any surety of safety, melted away in that moment with the clanking sword and sweet mountain air. But something about it was wrong. Instead of allowing herself to enjoy the moment of wellbeing, her forehead pinched in thought at what was wrong with the picture. Small gray bubbles circled her. The mountain. The palace. The Prince. *The sword.*

Fear washed over her in a cold rush, the bubbles turning from gray to black. And then the sword clanked one final time as the Prince stopped near the small garden wall, and her body again relaxed.

Perhaps the fear was gone, but her confusion was only just beginning. Nelia stepped closer to the Prince, still washed in security, and almost laughed out loud. The idea of a sword being soothing instead of terrifying shocked her. Mayor Billisborth had banned them in her village three years ago with the notice that the Prince no longer believed in carrying one. The common refrain ever since had been that just the sight of a sword could send shockwaves over a person, possibly killing them.

It was a bold lie – she could see that with her own eyes, though Mayor Billisborth lying did not come as a shock. There was something about the thin lips and oily eyes that made her distrust him. Plus, he had once pushed her into a corner during the spring festival and managed to get his dirty hands under her dress before she could get away. With most of the husbands away to war at the time, rumors had flown around town to stay far away from the mayor in any circumstance.

At first, the men had protested giving up their swords, but they had been told that to complain meant they only cared about their power rather than people's safety. The men countered that they had all grown up with swords and worse, and yet none of them had died.

Those arguments were ignored, usually with long sighs and much head-shaking, as though the men who had just won a long war were stupid children who couldn't understand the nuances of life. The only response to any reasoned counter-argument was that the Prince no longer wore his sword.

When Aaron had cited the giant bear that had terrorized them all a few years ago, the council laughed and shouted away his words. Nelia found it bizarre that no one cared anymore about the threat nature brought them every few years in the form of coyote packs, bears, and other dangerous animals. Swords would help them stay safe, but Mayor Billisborth said that the men were more dangerous when armed than bears. Many of the women had agreed.

And with that, rationality had seemed a thing of the past. Now school taught the boys that they were weapons in and of themselves and so had to learn to tamp down their strength in order to not hurt others. Aaron, though he didn't truly believe the King or the Prince to be their protectors or responsible for their town at all, had wondered aloud what they would think of these strange new laws trying to bend people into something they had never been since the beginning of time.

Wouldn't the King pass an order, were He to want them to change their nature so drastically? Aaron had wondered such things aloud on several occasions – sometimes in the middle of town where others could hear him. Nelia had shushed him, for fear that someone would report his dissonance.

"What are you thinking about?" the Prince asked, his smile kind yet amused. "You seem very far off."

"I'm very sorry, your highness," Nelia answered as her heart pounded against her ribcage. "I was noticing your sword. My husband would be quite jealous."

"Ah, yes. Mayor Billisborth banned them from the men in Overge, did he not?"

"Yes, your highness. About three years ago. Aaron still wears one around our land, especially when he goes into the forest."

Aaron had handed in his army sword and one knife. Nelia remembered watching him stand back and cross his arms, almost daring the rail-thin confiscator to challenge him. There was no challenge given, so the other five swords and knives stayed in their hiding places.

The prince smiled again, but said nothing.

"Are you in agreement with our mayor?" Nelia asked, the words out before she could check herself.

"I smile, Nelia, not because I agree, but because I admire your husband. My father does as well. I would like to visit your village soon and speak with him. There is something great in the future for Aaron."

"For Aaron?" Nelia asked.

They stepped up the short flight of stairs and came into view of the majestic mountains surrounding the palace on the north side. They seemed to float along the balcony along with the crisp, fresh air that hit her lungs stole her train of thoughts.

"Do you know what meek means, Nelia?"

She looked at the Prince in surprise. Pastor Kento used the word quite often in church to describe how they should act as people in this Kingdom. Since Pastor Kento was such a small, soft-spoken man, prone to jumping at the sound of a mouse, she admittedly envisioned *him* as meek.

"I am meek, Nelia," the prince said, his voice stronger and deeper, as though trying to implant something important within her. "I am meek, and I see Aaron as meek."

"Oh," Nelia answered, noticing that her name had not been mentioned.

"Someone with a sheathed sword," the prince said, turning to look her fully in the face. "'Meek' was never meant to mean someone with no courage, someone who will go along with the crowd. Somehow it divulged into this meaning after the story of how I didn't fight the Sagarisees, but instead spoke them into peace. The men who wished to fight and kill those who wished us harm went home angry, misunderstanding my purpose at the Battle of Balertone. Soon stories were told of how the Sagarisees had put me under a spell to trick me, or how they had seemed too strong for me to fight. The truth was that my father had decided well before we headed to the fight that he wished to show the Sagarisees compassion. He saw many good things in the people, and wished for them to live peacefully among us."

Nelia squirmed, as she tended to when the conversation turned to the Sagarisees. Her great-grandmother had been a Sagarisee – a fact that had caused her isolation and a few unfair punches at school. The people were still angry that the Sagarisees had been granted amnesty in the land, forgetting that they had brought with them the knowledge to build machines which made all of their lives easier.

"After we signed a peace treaty with the Sagarisees, those who follow me felt they needed to defend my actions. Unfortunately, instead of going back to the root of why we decided not to wipe out the Sagarisees, they accepted the stories that I was weak. They felt that the only way to go was to try and make being weak a virtue. Suddenly, not fighting was a virtue. The word 'meek' changed even more over time, coming to mean someone who is weak of character. But Aristotle describes it as 'having one's resentment under control'. If we were to go back to the Greek meaning of the root word 'pra' we would see that it means 'strength under control'. I controlled my strength that day, choosing to do as my father advised and not kill every Sagarisee, but to look into the future and see the good of having such intelligent men and women live among us. Have their inventions not made your lives easier?"

There seemed to be a fire in the air behind him, distracting her from answering. Though it billowed no smoke, the light it created was intense. Nelia wished to see what was causing the light, but felt unable to move from the spot where she stood. Peeking around the Prince was not what a grown woman would do. Instead, she stood still and absorbed the information he gave, her meager education challenged to the limits by this man in front of her.

"That day at the Battle of Balertone, I stood with the authority of the King and all of his mighty armies behind me. The leader of the Sagarisees saw that might and immediately dropped his own sword, signaling mercy. Only those closest to me saw this. I did not even need to wave my sword at the man who was leading what was left of his people away from the land that suffered under the worst famine in the history of the world. Xersuses stood with his oldest son at his side when he confronted us, ready to fight us for the right to stay in this land. Though his son, Ferontu, was slight from lack of nourishment, he stood with fire in his eyes, at the ready of his father's command."

"What did you do when you saw them?" Nelia asked, transfixed by the imagery of the story. The fiery light was still behind the Prince, but she focused all her energy on the story.

"As I said, I went intending to offer them peace. It was what my father wished. As you might have heard, I only do what my father tells me to do. I do not sway from his will. There is no reason to do so, since he has never gotten anything wrong."

"You trust him so implicitly?"

"Yes. And though I wish my people had not damaged my reputation or spread lies about me in this manner, I'm quite happy I listened again to my father and did as he asked me to do. Sometimes it's difficult to follow him, since only he knows what his plans will lead to, but every time his plan is good. For me and for his people. Look at you, for example: had we killed every one of the Sagarisees, we wouldn't have you exactly how you are."

"Me?"

"Of course, you," the Prince replied. His smile crinkled the corners of his eyes. "Your great-grandmother would have been dead somewhere instead of helping to raise your grandmother. My father thought of you and the others born from Sagarisees as a reason to be persuaded to let you live out your lives over there in the valley."

"He doesn't always see that, though. There have been many wars where you have killed every soldier."

"There was also the one where the other soldiers ended up killing themselves," the Prince said, smiling with amusement.

"Yes, that was the year that Aaron was part of the army. He's told me the story before. You used sound to confuse them."

"The suggestion was made by a Sagarisee, who understood the complexity of the echo in exactly the right place to make the noise. My father granted me permission to try it. It was fascinating to watch it work."

Nelia studied him. The urge to mock him, mock his ideas of fighting, rose strongly within her, but she tamped it down. Nothing good would come of taunting the Prince. Besides, she wasn't sure she disagreed. Mocking was such an ingrained part of her education that she tended towards it whenever she felt challenged or out of place. During the last few years, though, she was noticing it to be a worthless weapon against someone stronger in mind than herself.

"The armies we fight are ones who have made it clear that

negotiating would be a waste of time. I travel often, and most of my travels involve convincing those who threaten us to back down."

"But no matter what happens you can always come back here, where you would be safe. No one has ever taken over the palace," Nelia pointed out, leaving off the accusation that he was safer than her or anyone else living outside the walls, though she thought her tone probably implied it well enough. "But the kingdom used to be much bigger. We hear news of many sections of the kingdom that are being taken over by other armies. The stories we hear are awful, though Aaron always warns me about believing everything the messengers say. It seems the invading armies prefer to kill everyone or take them as their slaves."

The fiery light behind Prince Pokoj instantly dimmed, and it was then that she realized it was *his* light that glowed around him. Nelia watched as a dark wave of sadness rolled over the Prince at her words. She had not seen that kind of sadness since the day her grandfather had died. It had rolled through Grandmama for weeks afterward, and it had taken hard work to rid the house and Grandmama of the sadness once it stopped rolling and sat on her chest. But Nelia noticed that the sadness could not hold on to the Prince. It was not oily nor sticky, as the sadness that haunted Overge was. Instead, it was like small drops of dew which evaporated into a puff of smoke once he rolled back his shoulders and drew up his spine.

Chapter 3

free will

Though amazed by the sight, never having seen sadness puff away like that, Nelia's mind was too busy working out what her consequences for saying such things to the prince would be to ponder the phenomenon. Her mouth was her downfall in school, at home and surely it would be her mouth that would get her into trouble here. The Prince could shut down Overge for her insults, just as his father had rejected Hanature. And that rejection had resulted in the entire region of Hanature being overtaken by the Bruins. Those not slaughtered had been taken away as slaves, never to be heard from again.

Perhaps it was unkind of her to bring up his shortcomings. He was the Prince, after all. And most powerful. It was unquestionably unwise – but that was a fleeting thought, overpowered by her anxiety in trying to keep a reign on her tongue. But once her tongue started, there was no stopping it.

"If you are the almighty Prince who never loses in battle, why did you not go to fight for your kingdom in those sections? Do you not care that they were overtaken? Is it because those sections are poor? Or did you have revenge to take against one of the mayors?"

A strange noise gurgled in the Prince's throat at her questions, but other than a small movement of his cheek muscles he showed no signs of agitation.

"It's easy to blame me, Nelia, but let me ask you something. Have you ever thought that perhaps it is not my fault, but the free will of those regions?"

"It's their will to be overtaken?"

The Prince smiled, but this time Nelia felt a familiar tickle of annoyance on her skin. A smile for a child. Though the tickle urged her legs to march haughtily off the terrace as she would do in her own village, this time she was stuck. Her words had gotten her into trouble before, but even she could not imagine the pain the Prince could inflict on her for such foolish comments. Luckily, he seemed more bent on having his say than calling for punishment.

"There was a referendum a few years back," he began. There was a sharpness, a vigilance, in his tone that caused her hands to shake in fearful anticipation. "You would have been much younger then, when the outlying sections asked for more autonomy. They wanted to have their own judges instead of bringing their issues here to the palace. They said it was too far to travel, and they didn't want to wait for the King and my yearly visit. We offered to send a permanent representative, but they again said no. They claimed they needed to make their own laws, because they were becoming so different from the people here or even those sections close to here. It pained the King, but he has always wanted everyone to be as free as possible and always maintained that if a section did not wish for any protection or blessings from him, he would consent to it. So, he consented. And within a year those sections had withdrawn completely from any communication with us. When we heard of the armies rising to take them over, I personally went with my army to offer our services, but they refused us."

"But why were they so foolish?" Nelia asked, perplexed by the new information. Her legs still tingled in relief that she was not being tortured. That small voice in the back of her head chided her for carrying a conversation with the Prince as though he cared to explain himself to her. "I'm sorry. I ask too many questions."

The Prince continued, almost as though he didn't mind talking to her.

"In the case of Hanature and Cumberstein, they had told their village that the King had initiated the withdrawal to keep the people from revolting or voting against leaving the kingdom. When they saw us coming, the mayor and his people realized that they were trapped in a lie. The only choice they had was to confess the truth to their people, or send men to stop us from approaching. We had to leave."

"Even though you knew that women and children would die?"

"And men, Nelia – thousands of men."

"Why didn't you stay and push your way into the fight to save the villages?"

"My father's law doesn't allow us to push our way into any fight. The villages said they didn't want us. Even people from the villages, thinking we had abandoned them years before, came out to jeer at us. They wanted us gone. We could not help them with their eyes clouded in lies. I knew that if they didn't prepare for the incoming armies, they surely would lose. Though I didn't think they had much of a chance of winning, no matter how much they prepared."

"But the town of Twinure won. Mayor Rinfold and his men took the Pancheloux army captive."

The Prince answered with silence. Again, the words had come out before she could stop them. Perhaps it hurt his ego to remember the fact that a section had won a battle without the help of him and his army. If one region could win against a formidable army, then perhaps all of them could. Perhaps the need for the King and his son was exaggerated.

"Rinfold won, but at a great price. A price that breaks my heart to see."

"What price?" Nelia asked, the prickling of her skin now gone. Her confidence seemed heightened by his obvious compassion in overlooking her insulting words, though the small voice in her head didn't stop scolding her. Perhaps this was the freedom of speech so heralded by Aaron when he spoke of his days in the Prince's army. "Our papers say they are quite prosperous."

A quiver at the corner of his eyes. It was the smallest of movements but one that sent wavelengths through the air, hitting her chest like a hammer. Her lungs expanded with fear, and suddenly she didn't want the answer at all. It was dark. She could feel it before he spoke. But the Prince's lips moved before she could breathe. The answer was out before she could close her mind.

Hard labor camps meant to kill. Women as breeding machines. Schools that twisted a child's mind until they conformed. Kids informing on parents, killing them in their sleep for speaking the wrong words. The mayor getting fat while those he disliked starved and died. The plague wiping out thousands because the mayor refused to import the medicine.

"But Overge scraped together money for the poor to have medicine!" Nelia protested. Days and nights spent knitting, washing, and peddling to other towns. Raising the red flag, calling on everyone to help. Partly it had been selfish; the town didn't want the plague coming to them. But partly it had been genuine, since many in Overge were distantly related to the people of Twinure. "They didn't get the money?"

Of course. Mayor Billisborth would not have given it away. He was a selfish man, only interested in his perpetual movement up the social ladder, although he had seemed sincere when throwing his coins down into the bucket.

"Your mayor sent the money, Nelia," the Prince said, her thoughts not hidden from him. Though the words were not written in the open air, the nature of her thoughts hung there before the wind took them away. A fascinating sight – one that reminded her of her grandmother's tales of old. "But Mayor Rinfold used the money for himself. He wanted a gold-plated sword, though it is worthless in battle. It sits above his desk."

Her throat closed in on itself at the words. The rage inside her bubbled so furiously that she thought she might faint.

"200,000 people died for a gold sword?" she whispered. Her own child, beaten down by the plague, was one of those numbers. Many, though, said the number must be higher, for the streets of Amhune, a town between Twinure and Overge, were practically empty.

"After the plague left the town, Rinfold gathered all the surviving women and put them into the East wing of the palace. Their children are now brought up in closed schools while the women are used to breed. He needs the population to grow."

"Why do they not refuse to do this? Is the sheriff on Rinfold's side? How could he have become so powerful?"

"Those who try to escape have their legs cut off. They can still breed without legs."

Nelia opened her mouth to breathe. Her knees buckled, though she kept standing.

"And the men? They are fine with their wives and daughters being used like this?"

"If they resist, Rinfold's soldiers kill them. Most who live there have only known this tyranny, so they believe it is their duty to do as Rinfold says. Most don't realize there is any different way to live."

"They do not know you or your father?" Nelia asked.

"There are a few, but most don't believe we exist. Believing in anything other than Rinfold is forbidden. He has set himself up as a king above all others. Knowing a king like my father would bring the people the idea of freedom. Rinfold cannot, will not, allow that to happen. He must keep a tight rein on his region, what he calls his kingdom, in order to survive."

"Will you ever invade it?"

A bagpipe echoed against the mountains, emphasizing the Prince's hesitation.

"Why ever not? Why do you not invade and save the people?"

"We cannot go unless invited. We cannot go unless people believe we are there for their good. If my army were to go now, the people would want us dead and it would end with the slaughter of hundreds of thousands. The problem with free will, Nelia, is that sometimes children pay for their parents' choices. Would you have me send

Aaron to a town where the people will want to kill him because they believe everyone from the outside wishes them dead?"

Nelia shook her head, trying not to remember the day Aaron had come home limping up the road. He had left a young man, a boy in most regards, and come back a soldier. Broad shoulders, chiseled features, strong legs that could run with 50 pounds carried on his back. When she had run to him, more grateful than ever in her life to once again have protection around, he had plucked her from the ground as though she weighed nothing. On their wedding night, they had laughed when he staggered while trying to carry her across the threshold. The day he came home from the war he had carried her the rest of the way home, limp and all.

"No; I would not have Aaron going away again."

The Prince nodded. He smiled gently at her as they took a moment to listen to the bagpipe. The music soothed the images of Rinfold and what Twinure must be like out of her mind until they were like wisps of dry leaves blown away in the wind.

"Are you ever frustrated by those who claim to believe in you and the King?"

"What do you mean?"

"Do you ever regret the free will that you give to us? For I know of many who claim to love and respect as you do, and yet their actions say differently. There seem to be more poor examples of your followers in real life than good ones."

"Do you not hear of good followers?"

"I hear stories of people, but I do not see them with my eyes. Stories can be categorized as fables. They can be easily set aside as not all true. What I see is something different."

"You see the black magic, don't you, Nelia?"

She snapped her head back to his gaze.

"Yes. I see the black magic. It's everywhere."

"Have you ever entered a place where the black magic can't work?"

Nelia opened her mouth with a quick retort of the impossibility of such a place, but stopped short of speaking: a rare moment of self-discipline that filled her with a fleeting pride. Then she saw her grandfather in her memory's eye. Inside his house, bare though it had been of material things, there had never been black magic. He wouldn't allow it. Summers spent with him had been carefree, light, full of laughter and music. When Nelia's mother had come back from her pilgrimages, there had been no black magic on her and it had stayed away for weeks afterward. There were a few houses in her village where the black magic seemed to pass over and a few people who, even in the midst of the plague, had seemed healthy and steady on their feet. There were also those who had lost people in the plague or to the day-to-day grind of farm or mine work, and yet they never allowed the black cloud to sit on them. Then there were those who wrapped themselves in it, like a dark shawl covering them completely. And the more they spoke of its hold on them, the darker it seemed to get.

"I have seen such places and people," Nelia admitted. "What does it mean?"

"Those are the people you speak of wishing to know. Not everyone will be known in history for their great faith. Not everyone gets stories told of their bravery. For most, bravery is done one day at a time. Most bravery goes unnoticed by the people around them and never told round campfires."

"What bravery?"

"That of caring for your family, even when they care nothing for you. The bravery of pressing on with faith after losing a child or spouse. That of losing everything except for the hope and knowledge that the King loves you and will help you. That of coming here in person even when everyone tells you it is foolish. That of trusting a King known for his love and might rather than the ideals people around you push for you to believe in more," the Prince answered, holding his elbow out for Nelia to take. "Unquestionably, there are stories of brave men and women on battlefields or taking noble, heroic actions against tyrannies. There are good stories of men killing bears or lions who come to eat their children. There are stories of women traveling across the earth in search of cures for their towns. And these are good stories. But my favorite stories are of the day in, day out acts of courage that people take. For it takes courage to live truly in this world of free will and pain. It takes courage to stand in quiet faith against the wagging tongues of society. It takes courage and faith to come here, Nelia."

When he spoke her name, the sound touched her ears as smooth velvet would. She allowed herself a minute to feel the warm, silky air wrapping around her, soothing away her doubts and anxiety. Just as the words he spoke wrapped their velvet persuasion around her, she opened her eyes. The air gleamed golden around her. It was the same color as the sparkles that always used to come back with Mother, though there were many more around her right now.

"Ask me, Nelia," the Prince said, seeing her thoughts swirling about. "Ask me now so you will not regret not knowing the answer."

"What question?" Despite the comfort and beauty she felt with the Prince, there was still that burning question she had had since the time she was a child. Since the first time her stepfather had struck her. "Do you know what I want to say?"

"I do not see the words until you speak them, but I see how important the question is to you."

Nelia pulled her hand from his elbow, unable to touch his warmth. If she were to ask this question, she would need to face him, not prance about the terrace on his arm, pretending to be a fine lady of means. With the last note of the song taking its final echo against the green mountain, Nelia turned to face the Prince, looking him straight in the eyes. Soft, golden-brown eyes that waited patiently. And a smiling mouth that claimed no judgment towards her.

"Why is it…" Nelia started, her voice soft, halting. It would take more courage than she had thought to form the words. She started again. "Why is it that people who follow you, people who follow your example of love, are still capable of hurting others? But I don't mean by accident – I mean they hurt others as though they have never heard any of your teachings. Or perhaps it's certain people who they don't even think to treat in the way you teach to treat people. I don't know how to say it, other than that I have lived my life surrounded by both people who believe in you and your way of living, and those who think you are a myth and try to live their own type of morality. Both groups of people have let me down, hurt me, disappointed me and even pushed me to the side."

"Both groups have loved you and hoped for the best for you also," the Prince answered, his eyes so clear and deep that Nelia felt no defensiveness at his remark, and yet her honest answer shocked her.

"Some people in both groups have wished me harm and no success or joy. Some people have even wished for me to not exist."

A brief sadness flashed across the Prince's eyes. Nelia felt that if she stared long enough into the depths his eyes held she might find the essence of his heart, but the Prince looked away before she could dive deep enough. He watched the mountains in silence, and she joined him. Typically, she pushed for answers immediately, but peace hung in the surrounding air, curling its way around her as well. This peace allowed her to take in the large, purplish mountains and the majesty they contained without pushing for more than silence.

"The majesty of these mountains does not compare to the majesty of my father," the Prince said, nodding towards the distance.

Nelia looked again.

Majestic. Regal. Beautiful.

In her village, there were no mountains, just large rocks and forest and the creek that pooled into the pond. She had only ever seen mountains in photographs. Two days ago, when they had risen higher than the road, she had stopped to take them in – much to the aggravation of her guide.

More majestic was the King.

The Prince turned to her, his eyes as warm as they had ever been.

"Have you ever thought of what majesty is?"

This question perplexed Nelia.

"Isn't majesty what makes the King a king?" she asked, her obvious lack of knowledge flushing her cheeks.

"One measures a king's majesty in his strength, true. He has shown great strength in battles."

"I do not know of any the King has not won."

"If the King fights, he wins. That is certainly true. But as we spoke of before, not everyone wishes for my father to fight with them."

The complexity of what they had spoken of began to hit her. It was senseless to not want a King who had never lost to fight with you. Except for pride: something she saw often. Pride was what seemed to have brought Twinure to a place of hell.

"Even on smaller matters than war, there are those who do not want my father's help. He sends out a letter to each region every month. He has done so since the beginning of time. Yet there are those who never read the letter. There are those who find the letter quite annoying."

Nelia flushed again. Each month on the 28th there seemed to be the same conversation to be had: those who read the letter tried to get those who had not to read it. There were scoffers and beggars and ultimately shouting matches. Hardly ever was there a change of sides.

"Do you know what is in the letters each month, Nelia?"

She stuttered slightly, then looked away when her blush burned her cheeks.

"Do you, Nelia?" he asked again, walking around her to raise her chin.

"I don't regularly read the letters. They were difficult for me to understand when I was younger. They told me I—"

"Was too stupid to understand them, and so you stopped trying."

Nelia moved her chin from his warm finger. Those soft brown eyes were too intense.

"In those letters, you will find the answer to every question the region is asking."

"Not true."

Rashly said, yes. But if that were true, then everyone would read them.

"Yes, Nelia. The reason that people do not read the letters anymore is because many times they must work for the answer to be fully revealed, and the leaders don't want to do the work. One letter told Mayor Billisborth that the answer to his need for a science teacher was for him to teach it. But he deemed that impossible with his job being mayor. And so he wrote back saying that the King must be mistaken, for being mayor was a much grander job than being a teacher and that he, Jean Billisborth, was not about to give it up. He implied – quite indelicately – that the King was trying to unseat him."

"Doesn't surprise me none. Mayor Billisborth is more concerned with his status than anything else."

The Prince laughed. A clear, joyful laugh. Nelia had forgotten how she had used to make Aaron laugh when they were younger. The sound pierced her heart with a deep ache. She hadn't realized until now how much she missed Aaron's laughter.

"What is more important? Being the mayor or being a teacher?" the Prince asked, drawing her back to the conversation.

"Why could he not have done both? He doesn't seem to do much as mayor, always standing about in the plaza day after day."

The Prince tapped her nose lightly, his warm eyes sparkling.

"But he didn't wish to do both. That was the last letter he read. He has to allow the letter to have public viewing if he wants our protection, but I have seen the efforts he makes to persuade the public from reading them. They have been effective, have they not?"

Nelia blushed, feeling the criticism piercing her directly through the heart – though she had to admit that his tone lacked harshness.

"So why would Billisborth do this?" he asked. The lesson could not dissolve into the air, though she wished it to. After swallowing hard, Nelia could finally answer. An answer she knew all too well.

"Pride."

"Pride," the Prince repeated. "Not the kind in having done a good day's work, but the kind that will keep you from the good future the King has for you and for those around you. In this case, for the good of your village. There is little water and the need for an engineer is great; there isn't one trained in your town because there has been no science taught in Overge for over a decade. Now Billisborth cannot employ a local, so he must pay the price of hiring outside. All due to his own foolishness."

There was a moment of silence as the information sank deep into her understanding. Overge could have avoided the water shortage.

Nelia understood this type of pride well: a sense that it was possible to do everything without help. She knew more people who scorned help than those who welcomed it in her village. Now that they had to campaign to hire someone from outside the village the availability of fresh water was becoming political, fractioning families and friends into groups with their own arguments for and against the mayor. All with no real solution, it seemed to her.

There was a crack. A pink lightning bolt slashed through the air, pointing back to what Prince Pokoj had been saying earlier.

"Majesty is also the strength in a king's love and mercy," he said, his graceful transition not unnoticed by Nelia. "Do you believe our King, my father, is strong in kindness, love, and mercy?"

"I have heard tell that he is," Nelia answered.

The Prince nodded once.

"But what do you believe?" he asked. "Do you believe that I am strong in love and kindness? Do you believe that *I* am majestic?"

Nelia tried not to squint her eyes at him, but the muscles at her temples contracted anyway. There was a strange, strong desire within her to tell the truth: that she did believe him to be majestic. He had only shown her kindness, and a love she had never thought could be real. But there were other words running through her head as well.

Rich… easy life… overblown ego… typical male self-confidence.

The Prince's steady gaze held no contempt while Nelia struggled with her thoughts. A tug-of-war was going on inside of her, and she wasn't yet certain which side would win: that which she used to hold to be true, or that which she was seeing to be true. It was not so easy to change habits.

His lips curled slightly at the edges as he noticed her struggle.

"You believe I am being overly egotistical?"

"If you were my husband, I would mock you," Nelia said without thinking. Then she clamped her hand over her mouth.

"And why? If he asked you if he was a good man, would you sneer at him? Is he not good to you?"

Nelia weighed the question, not wanting to answer flippantly again. The Prince seemed always measured with his thoughts and words. Surely he had more practice with that than she did, but still. At the moment, self-control seemed almost an impossibility for her.

"He isn't a perfect man," she began, but the Prince interrupted before she could continue.

"I didn't ask if he was perfect. I asked if he was good to you."

Confusion threatened to bring tears to her eyes. The Prince seemed to turn everything upside down, and yet it was true what he said. Only, if she ever did talk about her husband with other women, she always found a way to tell them that Aaron wasn't perfect.

Was there a perfect?

"Aaron is good to me," Nelia said, measuring her words carefully and slowly. They felt strange coming out her mouth, and she suddenly realized that it might be the first time she had ever admitted such a thing, though it was true. Aaron was good to her. Normally. Not that he was perfect. There were moments like a few weeks before leaving to come here. Or that night he had thrashed at her with the whip when she'd followed him to a secret meeting. He had told her to stay home, but she'd thought it was a trap. The fear she saw in his eyes when he realized she was following him was something she had never seen in him before or since. Still, him being afraid for her safety wasn't enough for her to forgive him right away for snapping the whip at her.

Nelia shook the memories violently out of her head. Rehashing them in the presence of the Prince was unacceptable.

"Yes," the Prince said, turning back to the mountains in the distance. "He is good to you. He provides for you, works alongside you, never forgets you. He held you as you mourned your son's death, and he finds small ways to tell you that he loves you."

"Does he love me?"

Again, the bagpipes started in the distance.

"If you doubt that, should you not ask your husband directly?" he asked, starting towards the doors again.

They strolled in comfortable silence. The bagpipes sang, their music echoing out over the hills and mountains. A long time had passed since she felt this kind of comfort: that deep, inner warmth that made her want to snuggle into the moment and not let go.

"Regarding your question earlier, Nelia," the Prince said, interrupting the warmth. "*That* is free will. It is your decision whether to ask your husband or to simply assume. It is other people's free will that guides their love for you and others. If they speak words to convince you that they are like me in their love for justice and truth, then their actions must match accordingly. If their actions do not match, then it is up to you to either follow that check in your spirit that tells you they are false prophets, or to close your eyes and ears and follow them despite their wrongdoings. Sometimes it is our duty to speak the truth even when it is easier to stay quiet."

"You would have me confront them?"

"I would challenge you to think on whether you should. What if there is a chance that they will teach others to act as they do, deceiving them in wrongly thinking it is true justice and love?"

Nelia looked into the distance as she walked alongside him. There was too much information in her head for her to speak more.

Chapter 4

an audience with the King

The dining hall was a grand room with tall, narrow windows that peaked at the top. The thin strips of iron that held the stained-glass pieces together glowed softly when the sunbeams touched them.

It was impossible not to hear the melodic echo of her heeled shoes when entering the grand room. The sound brought her back to when she had been sixteen and worn high heels for the first time. She'd felt so grown up that day, tapping the heels against their small porch as she waited for Aaron to fetch her for the summer fair. The shoes had been Mother's, from the time she'd spent in the big city. She had found them only two days earlier while rummaging in the shed. After polishing them, Mother had presented the shoes to Nelia when she came in from finishing her chores. She hadn't felt that kind of excitement zip through her since waking up for Christmas as a kid. Not only was one of the most handsome young men in Overge taking her out, but she wouldn't have to wear her farm boots under her patched-up dress. Even Mother had laughed as Nelia danced around the porch, her skin and hair scrubbed to a polish, that pleasant clicking sound enveloping all of them.

Unfortunately, times had only gotten harder, and Mother had later sold the shoes in exchange for meat. Nelia had recently become engaged to Aaron at the time; she'd cried when she found out. Her tears had so angered Mother that she had refused to give Nelia any of the meat. "Hunger will make you grateful next time,"

Mother had said, though Nelia wasn't certain of the truth of that statement. She had been hungry often while growing up, even when she hadn't been ungrateful.

The clicking now, years later, was still pleasant to hear, even if the memories were not. Nelia wondered if everyone had such memories to contend with. She was beginning to realize just how many different people and experiences there were in the world, not to mention just this kingdom. She did not want to move away from her town; it was her home and always would be. But while traveling here she had started to understand the basis for which people had their conception of life. Aaron often mused that more people in their town should travel to foreign lands and it used to annoy her, mostly because she couldn't understand what traveling would do. But even this short trip was like a peephole beginning to open in her mind. People were different. And that wasn't bad. It wasn't… anything. It was just that their culture and language and traditions were different.

Not everyone lived in a field and mine-studded region. There were some towns where factories billowed smoke or where large universities produced lofty-headed youngsters sipping coffee and narrowing their eyes at her worn-out dress. There was even a town she had passed where it had seemed most everyone made just about the same income, though they also were strangely transparent in skin color, with little difference amongst each other. She hadn't dared pass directly through that town for fear they would find her too strange. But now that she thought of it, perhaps she hadn't passed through because she found them too strange.

Overge had rich and it had poor, with a small group of people in between climbing their way to the side of the rich. Those who were rich, meaning Mr. Billisborth and a few others, seemed to be the ruling class, and yet they didn't dare pass laws that would restrict people from moving where they wished to go. An insurrection of the working class was what Billisborth feared the most. But there were other villages along the way from there to here where the residents were clearly locked up more. These villages had looming walls. No one was allowed in, and the almost non-existent movement at the gate told her that few ever left. She had watched this all from afar, fearing that if she got too close, they would grab her and not let her out either.

Click. Click. Click.

"Stop!"

Nelia stopped pacing as her voice echoed three times over

the beams. She needed all thoughts of her village and those she had seen on her way here to leave her mind.

"That is enough of that," she said to herself. "Look around, Nelia. Take in your surroundings. When is the last time you will be somewhere like this? Gather memories for when you are old, as Grandmama used to say."

The long dining room held a grand table that must have been the length of two elephants – or, more appropriately for her education, about the length of three Doon houses. The houses that almost everyone had in her village, built in the days when they'd thought they might break loose from the King and set up Cunsh as king. As Aaron liked to say, "Thank the bloody sun they had enough sense not to do that."

Nelia shook the thought out of her head again as she stepped up to the table. It was made of heavy wood, the borders of it painted in cream with ancient script written in it.

Síochán was the only word Nelia recognized from her grandmother's schooling. *Peace.* She dared to trace the word with her fingers, the cool surface warming almost instantly at her touch.

After looking for another word she might recognize and failing, Nelia noticed there were no place settings set out on the table. A strange thing, since she had thought she would be eating with the King. Farther down there stood a high-backed chair with what looked to be rubies set into the top of the wood. It stood out from the other chairs. Not that they were less magnificent, but because it was about a foot taller than the rest. Behind it was a giant fireplace from which a warm glow now came. Nelia stepped closer, her awe compounding. What glowed was a chunk of wood about the size of Aaron's torso. And it glowed brightly, having caught the flame with perfection, right in the middle.

The warmth now surrounded her, and she no longer felt so frightened of her impending lunch with the King, though there was a lingering… excitement? Perhaps nervousness. She knew nothing of what was to happen. Would she be with just the King? Or would she be one of many guests? On one hand, she wished to be alone, since her manners were no match for anyone who had ever eaten in a noble place. On the other hand, she would be responsible for all the conversation if she were the only guest. Which embarrassment would she like to endure? That of being judged by those in the court, or by the King himself?

Trumpets called. A bagpipe roared.

Nelia straightened her back at the foreign sounds. No

trumpet had called in her village since the King had come to visit. Her grandmother had told her the story of that day many times.

There were marching sounds as well, with another trumpet blast held for longer than Nelia would have thought possible for a human. She rushed to one of the tall windows to catch a glimpse of what might be happening. War? News from afar? Was it a good sign or bad? She tried to see in between the delicate iron lines in the windows, but couldn't find one spot that didn't fragment the scene below.

As the marching came closer, a slight panic gripped Nelia. Surely someone more educated than her would understand what to do, what this all meant.

Taking a deep breath as her grandmother would have instructed, Nelia suddenly connected two thoughts: the trumpet and the coming of the King.

The King was coming.

Nelia ran to the middle of the floor, in between the large dining table and wall where enormous scenic paintings hung. She hadn't noticed them before, but prudence snapped her head to look down in reverence. Now was not the time to get distracted. The noises were coming closer; the trumpet blew again and though it seemed nearer, it also seemed more muted. The marching came closer and closer, but Nelia dared not look up at the wide doorway for fear she would look straight into the King's eyes. She must look humbled and meek, though after her conversation with the Prince she was no longer certain if that was a word to apply to herself anymore.

A chorus of voices rose up from somewhere outside. Somewhere close. Nelia resisted the urge to pull open the tall glass doors and see what was going on outside. Instead, she kept her head lowered, her knees bent in a constant curtsy. Even when pain shot up and down her calves, Nelia did not rise.

The marching faded, and the trumpets with it. People outside still sang and shouted. It sounded as though some wept as well, but no one had yet come into the room where she stood. A few minutes later, when the silence continued, Nelia stood straight up and looked around. The room was still empty, save herself and the table and chairs. A clock she could not see ticked away some seconds before Nelia could register the situation. Just as anxiety at having messed up somehow gripped her, a shadow darkened the door.

"Nelia," a voice called from the doorway. It was Ivory

again. "Time to go now. Did you think you were meeting the King in the dining hall? No, everyone meets him in the throne room, then you will be escorted back here. I just had to drop you off here for a bit. The King had some business to finish. And no one is allowed to wait in the throne room."

"Why not?" Nelia asked, immediately closing her eyes at her impertinence.

"Just one of the rules. And it must be respected, because the King is worthy of respect. He is the best King we've ever had; don't you agree?"

Nelia was starting to, though she kept her mouth shut. Ivory didn't wait for a response, anyway. Already her high heels were clicking down the polished hallway floors. The stones glistened so much Nelia thought she might slip, but when that proved impossible to do in the shoes made for her, she began to relax her shoulders and walk quickly to catch up with Ivory.

Had she not been in a hurry to keep up, Nelia would have lingered in the hall. It was one she hadn't yet seen, and it was just as magnificent, if not more so, than the others. Some paintings spanned from ceiling to floor. The floorboards were not made of wood, but gold. The windows glistened as though made of crystal and there were small, sparkling crystals in the frames of the glass. Like diamonds. Through them came rainbows that danced up and down the walls.

It was quite a magical place, just as every other room in the palace was, but Ivory was getting further ahead and Nelia didn't wish to be late.

For the first time, Nelia entertained the idea of staying at the palace to work. Word in the village was that anyone could apply to stay and work at the palace. It seemed strange that just anyone could ask and be granted a position, but that was what one woman had said. Though her companion had laughed because, according to her, "It wasn't like the likes of them would ever dare to ask in the first place."

"True," the first woman had agreed, shifting her basket of bread rolls. "I's gots enough sense to know my place, like."

Nelia had finished paying for her bread roll and chewed on the words of the woman along with the two-day-old bread. She had agreed with them at that time. Knowing one's place was of utmost importance in Overge. Lives were lost in rebellions and uprisings and even in misunderstandings, because of people not knowing their place.

But now, for some strange reason, she felt able to entertain the idea that perhaps knowing one's place wasn't truly that important to the King. It seemed, in fact, that the King had perhaps found that certain utopia of classless workers, bringing peace to Niebo between tradesman, laborer and nobleman.

Ivory stopped outside two giant doors made of silver. From behind the doors came music as though an entire orchestra was playing just for the King. Nelia opened her mouth to ask if that were true, but Ivory placed a finger to her lips. Instantly Nelia complied, shutting her mouth. As much as she liked to rail against authority in her mind and in small actions, she was always quick to comply with demands.

The music softened as though on cue. Ivory turned to look at her, arranged her curls in specific ways, gave her a bright smile, then turned to the door and waited. Nelia placed her eyes directly on Ivory's heels, though she longed to look up. Gawking at the throne room certainly wasn't how she wanted to appear when entering.

Anticipation snapped in the air, like those popping firecrackers that Grandpa used to love. Nelia could even see the small sparks bursting around her. Her fingers lifted to touch them, but a shuffle from behind the door brought them back down. Ivory bounced on her heels, then quieted herself by shaking out her wrists. For a moment, the contents in Nelia's stomach threatened to come up, but she avoided that messy ending through soft breathing.

Then the trumpet blared one time. Nelia thought her bones and skin might have reversed themselves. She braced her teeth against each other and waited. Another longer blare. There was stillness, and then the doors started to open.

In such tomb-like silence, Nelia heard her heart clamoring for oxygen, desperately trying to keep her extremities alive with blood. Peace and power poured from the giant room behind the doors as they opened. Nelia felt her lungs contract, wanting, no, needing to fill themselves with more of the sweet air. Ivory moved forward and Nelia followed. She dared to look ahead, though still towards the floor, and saw a man standing just inside, where the sweet air surely filled his lungs at every breath. Ivory stopped and murmured to him while in a deep curtsy, and when she rose a trumpet blared. It was closer, and yet the noise somehow did not pain Nelia's ears. Still, the noise caused her nerves to rise as though on points.

"Nelia Bitrovia of the village of Overge."

Ivory stepped aside, and Nelia knew it was her moment to step forward. She did not know how she managed to move, for she felt at a loss for command of her body. But somehow her legs were drawn towards the center of the room, as though by an outward force.

Strangely, fear had no grip on her. Without being told, she knew this was a place where the black magic held no power. Though she dared not look up, she was not shaking in fear. Instead, awe filled her innermost being. Every desire in her was to show his Majesty her utmost respect.

Finding herself almost at the edge of the long carpet, Nelia stopped. By some magic, she had walked the entire length without tripping or stumbling, and she heard no murmurs of disapproval. Perhaps that was due to some sort of rule. Or perhaps choosing to wear the dress from the King kept whispers away. The reason didn't matter. It was a relief not to hear giggles directed at her.

But there was no time to dwell on the magic of arriving without making a fool of herself. It was time for her to curtsy. Another minute passed as she carefully placed her feet into position without stepping on her long skirts. Then she plunged into the deepest curtsy she could manage, complete with wobbling legs. Luckily a hand reached out to hers when it came time for her to rise.

That hand belonged to Prince Pokoj. He smiled at her as she pressed her weight into his hand to help her get back to a standing posture. Making a spectacle of herself was once again diverted.

"Come, Nelia Bitrovia. Come and meet the King, my father," he said, his voice deep with sincere compassion and friendship. It was easy to see why so many men were loyal to him. And most any women that ever met him. Grandmama had forever been loyal to the Prince. She wouldn't put up with anyone saying anything against Prince Pokoj.

To ready herself, Nelia turned her head and allowed her eyes to rise past a foot in front of her shoes. Stretched out in front of her she saw the lush red carpet give way to a floor made out of a material she had never seen before. It resembled wool and gold at the same time. She lifted her eyes farther and found the feet of the throne, carved directly from emeralds. There her eyes stayed until a long finger tapped her chin and lifted it up ever so slightly, ever so gently. Nelia did not resist.

Though the King settled back into the emerald throne, he

did not take his eyes from hers. Nelia couldn't help sizing him up, realizing he was taller than she had ever imagined him and not as old. His head was crowned with thick, gray hair that seemed to dare not fall from his head. The skin on his face was smoother than perhaps other older men, but then he did not spend his days in the fields as her grandfathers had. The corners of his eyes crinkled, though, and along his mouth as well she saw signs of his age.

He looked at her straight on. Held in those eyes the color of the clay her aunt used to create plates and bowls, Nelia's heart melted instantly. There was no sense of fear, no anxiety, no nervousness. Surely those plagues would not dare enter this King's throne room. He sat strongly, with his shoulders back and his head held high. The strength of his mighty shoulders did not scare her, nor did the proximity of his knees. Peering back into his eyes, Nelia saw no lust, nor sniveling contempt. In its place, she found compassion, love, and pride. He looked at her as Grandfather once had. As a man who thought her worthy of honor and sacrifice.

The weight of the feelings in his eyes caused Nelia to stagger back. Suddenly every pore in her body seemed to understand where she was. But stepping back caused her to see the King in a better light. The Prince glanced at her, his hand steadying her at her lower back as though worried she might run off. She could not have run off even if she wished to, which she did not.

The King sat on his magnificent throne, watching her with curious and compassionate eyes that never roamed her body nor lost interest in her. There was a kindhearted air about him, as though he would welcome dozens of children in to sit on his knees and listen to stories if he had time for such things. Nelia had loved her grandfather dearly and felt the safest when near him, and it was precisely that same feeling of safety that she felt with the King. She suddenly felt that leaving him and the palace would break her heart. With that feeling came a wave of tears she had to fight back.

"I've been waiting to see you, child," the King said. "I'm so very glad you came to visit me. Have you had a good afternoon on the terrace?"

"Yes, your majesty," Nelia stammered, unable to fathom that she was not in a dream. "It is a lovely view up there."

The words did not seem like enough when, quite literally, it would be a day she would remember for the rest of her life.

"The Prince was very kind to me."

The King smiled. "Pokoj is rarely anything but kind, especially to pretty women."

Nelia felt her entire face flush with heat. Aaron was a kind husband, but he rarely complimented her on her looks. She had always thought it was because she wasn't much to look at.

"Come, child, let us sup together and have a bit of a talk."

The King stepped down and gave her his elbow, which she found to be as strong as his son's. It was true that he did not seem to age, for he must now be about four hundred years old. That is, if her grandmother was correct. He was at least older than Grandmama, since she claimed only to have ever known him as King.

Of course, the Danjunites, the lineage Grandmama was from, were known to live longer than most – though only if they were not killed by rocks falling on them in the mine, or ground into dust in war, or taken by a wasting disease. Nelia's grandmother had lived until one hundred and fifty, having given birth to Mother when she was eighty-five. But Mother did not capitalize on her Danjunite genes. She drank too much dzin to live a long life, and when a sickness swept through the town she was not strong enough to fight it. Nay, she did not even bother. Instead, she accepted her fate and drank away the fear.

These thoughts caused Nelia to almost run her elbow into the large doors as they exited the throne room. It was the King who maneuvered her away so as not to be bruised. He smiled gently, without a trace of malice, as Nelia tried desperately to swallow away her embarrassment. She did not wish to ruin her walk back down the beautiful hallway with thoughts of her dead mother. There was always time at home to think of her and all the others these last hard years had taken away from her. Right now was not the moment.

"I hoped Aaron might make the journey with you," the King said, breaking the silence.

Nelia's words tumbled out in a jumbled noise before she clamped her mouth closed again. This King, who everyone claimed knew everything, was asking for Aaron. Aaron, who had served with Prince Pokoj but who had lately admitted he was not so certain about the King's authority or sovereignty. How was it that the King asked for him?

The King leaned his head down slightly to whisper in her ear without being heard by others.

"You just tell him what you see here, what you experience. Describe me to him, and he will realize who I am. Soon after you do this, he will have another dream, as he did when he was a lad."

"A dream?" Nelia asked.

"Yes," the King said, rainbows from the diamonds in the windows running across his face as they approached the dining hall. "A dream. Don't worry about what it means. Just report back to him and allow the dream to come."

"Yes, your majesty," Nelia replied, her bewilderment keeping her tongue in place.

Chapter 5

to dine with the King

They entered the dining room, where the long table was now laid out with a place setting for each chair. At the end of the table, the King stopped them and gently pulled his elbow away. With a deep breath, Nelia steadied herself, daring to breathe in and out slowly instead of fainting into a heap or running away. As a footman pulled the large, ornate chair away from the table for her, Nelia squeezed out a silent prayer that she would not do anything embarrassing. With her fists clenched together, she reminded herself to pay attention.

She would *not* act shamefully, as her mother had claimed she always did.

The moment Nelia sat on the chair, she alighted closer to the table. It was a wonder, but the small footman had picked her up, along with the chair, so that it would not scratch the floor. But she had no real time to wonder at the magic of that. There were forks and spoons and two glasses to worry over. How a small lad had lifted her taller frame was not worth fretting over.

Another look at all the silver surrounding her plate overwhelmed her senses. It was easier to look up at the others who would join them for lunch, hoping to find an ally to watch and imitate. She was pleased to see Prince Pokoj sitting across from her and Ivory at her left side. Besides those two, there were four other couples. One couple who looked to be nobility from some exotic place, two couples who seemed as enchanted and new as she felt, and yet another couple who wore working clothes and looked both delighted and very out of place.

"A toast, my child, to you coming to see me, for it makes my heart light to meet with my children," the King said, tipping his goblet to her. At her widened eyes, he laughed. "I call all of you my children, for I love each one as my own. It truly pains me that there are those who believe otherwise. Also, a toast for Isabel and Roberto, Minh and Boon-Nam, as well as Thimba and Matvly. Ivory, it is always wonderful to see you. A toast to all of you. Thank you for coming."

"Long live the King!" came a shout from near the doorway. The guests repeated the shout with their goblets raised before sipping the sweet wine.

Nelia had thought it impossible that her heart could grow bigger with sentiment for this man, but grow it did. Her inner core swelled with love, pride, and sheer pleasure at being in the same space with him. It was the first time she had felt such emotion since seeing Zayzay learn to walk.

"Thank you, your majesty," she managed to say, tipping the wine slightly to drink. She did not wish to be rude, but too much wine tended to make her foolish. Also, it always made her tired and there would be no time to take a nap after lunch. No place to take one, really. She had no money to stay at a hotel, and she found the notion of napping in the sun in the city too scary. One could do those things in the countryside with little chance of being bothered, but the city had so many people milling about. When entering Niebo she had noticed that there was no yelling or bawdy laughter, and no women screaming at the carts roaming through the streets as there always was in the center of her town. Everyone had seemed to be exceptionally nice to each other. Even so, she wouldn't take the chance.

"And how did you leave Aaron, Nelia?" Prince Pokoj asked, interrupting her thoughts as a large white plate was set before her, filled with duck confit and a tall mountain of mashed potatoes with melted butter running down the side.

"Aaron? He is well, your majesty."

"My father once offered him a job here at the palace – remember, Father?"

The King nodded with a smile.

"I heard of his ability to tell the truth without offending. I could always use men like that around here."

"Yes," Prince Pokoj agreed, nodding as he smiled at Nelia. "But he politely rejected the offer. He said he felt more comfortable in his fields and that he had a beautiful wife to get home to."

Nelia blushed. She was almost certain the Prince was exaggerating Aaron's statements for her benefit. Not in all her years together with Aaron could she recall him calling her beautiful. It wasn't for malice; it was because she was not a beauty and they were too frank a couple for flowery compliments that were untrue. Aaron called her 'strong', 'determined', 'sincere' and a few others. He always kissed her nose and took pleasure in her breasts, but beautiful? That sounded nothing like her Aaron.

"My husband is very gifted in his fieldwork, your majesty," Nelia answered, watching Ivory out of the corner of her eye pick up a certain medium-sized fork; she followed suit. "He has grown quite a bit more than others, even throughout the drought. He advises others, but many won't take it because he is unschooled. There was a group of men who came to the village a few years ago that set up workshops and sold us many chemicals and gave a great deal of advice, none of which Aaron took. I tried to convince him to invest in the chemicals because I believed the men, but it turns out Aaron was correct. Perhaps people would listen to him if he had gone to school, but it doesn't seem to bother him."

"It bothers you, though," Prince Pokoj stated. It was a statement. Not a question even hinted. Nelia blushed again, the air closest to her deepening into a darker hue of pink. She waved the pink fog away by bringing her napkin to her mouth in an exaggerated gesture. It was certainly obvious to anyone watching, but she only cared for the pink to go away.

"Yes, my lord, a little."

"I do not understand this insistence on pride in some people," the King said. "I built the universities for some, but not all have to go there to receive their knowledge. Many people have knowledge that can't be contained in a classroom or a book."

Nelia searched for something witty or candid to say in reply but couldn't find anything. Her mind seemed blank, other than retorts that wouldn't have been appropriate for the occasion. To keep her tongue from saying something that Aaron would be ashamed of her for, she picked up her wineglass and, with shaking fingers, brought it to her lips. She barely sipped it before setting it down again, but as careful as she wished to be, her nerves betrayed her even further by causing her to spill the contents.

Someone heaved across the table. Before Nelia could turn her head to see who it was, she felt a slight wind of calm move from the King down the table. Within a second of the wine pooling around her glass, a servant was already stepping forward. He dabbed up the ring of red with a smile and a quick pat on Nelia's back.

Of course, the servant would feel sorry for her. Even in her village, the lower class stuck together. Though the pat on her back felt good for a moment, she couldn't bring herself to lift her head. There were whisperings down from where the sigh had come from. Her hands began to shake more. Taking up her fork to give herself something to do was now out of the question. It would surely fall from her clumsy fingers and clank onto the plate, possibly breaking it outright. And she certainly could not afford to pay a debt that large.

"Nelia." She heard her name being called through the fog in her head. "Nelia. Look at me."

It was the Prince calling to her from across the table. With her fingers digging into her thighs to steady herself, Nelia obeyed. Who could not obey the Prince? Even if he was going to kick her out of the dinner.

"Nelia," he said in a gentle voice.

Nelia swallowed hard, preparing her body to rise as nimbly as it could with every muscle shaking, and to leave at least with a modicum of honor. But before she could even prepare her body to stand properly, Minh stood.

"I would like to apologize, Nelia. I'm still working on my impatience, and it was rude of me to sigh so heavily at something that could have happened to anyone. The last time I was here even the Prince, who was very animated in his speech, made the entire glass of wine spill across the table."

"I can't say you were too pleased with me that time," Prince Pokoj said with a light-hearted smile.

"No, I can't say that I was. But now I appreciate you encouraging me; for believing I can learn more patience. I am sorry, your majesty, for breaking up the peace of the meal."

Nelia's insides turned to stone. How the blame had moved from her to Minh, she didn't know. And yet the word 'blame' did not seem to appropriately describe what was going on. In response to Minh, the King bowed his head with a smile, made a strange circling motion with his hand and blew softly towards Minh. At once a sparkling, translucent ball appeared to the side of her plate. The smile of joy on her lips turned her face into one of a young girl. Nelia almost expected the grand lady to clap and jump for joy.

Instead, Minh curtsied towards the King and sat down

again, jubilation emanating from her.

Nelia turned her head to face the King, her eyes still wide in disbelief.

"I… I'm very… very sorry."

But before she could continue her hand was covered by the large, warm hand of the Prince. Her eyes registered the King smiling at her gently, picking his crystal goblet up and out towards her.

"Here we do not cry nor apologize over spilled milk. Or wine. Accidents are bound to happen. Luncheon with the Prince and the King can many times cause one to become nervous or to feel out of sorts."

Nelia nodded her relief at his words, but still sat as though made of stone.

"Please, Nelia," the Prince said, squeezing her hand gently. "Accept Minh's apology."

It took more force to turn her head, but she managed, and soon faced Minh's expectant, earnest face.

"I'm sorry, Nelia. It has more to do with me than with you. Imagine my poor children, as they have been on this journey with me from the beginning."

"Or her poor husband!" Boon-Nam said with a laugh. "Sorry, your majesty. I'm not poor, but I do suffer!"

The King roared with laughter, a sound that awakened Nelia's bones to soften. Then her lips loosened enough to smile. And finally, her neck became flesh again, allowing her nod towards Minh. With that her tongue was released from its stony prison.

"I accept your apology, Minh. I'm more confused as to why I'm not being disciplined than wishing to make you feel bad."

"It is a shame that many of our villages and people do not remember that one of the first laws made was to give grace. It comes with loving each other and thinking the best of each other. The King's wish is that we think how each situation is affecting each person around us more than how it is affecting ourselves," said Prince Pokoj.

"It's a shame that our nature is to think more of one's self than of others," said Thimba. "It takes almost an entire lifetime just to learn self-discipline."

"Exactly," the King said. "But before I go on, Nelia, please, will you take a sip with me? My goblet becomes heavy."

The table laughed good-naturedly at the surprise on Nelia's face and her subsequent blush. Surprised to find her fingers no longer trembling, Nelia lifted her glass with no effort and delicately tapped the King's goblet. His smile sent a wave of warmth and peace over her body.

Suddenly she wished for Aaron to be there with her. To experience this with her. The feeling was intriguing and new, at least for the past few years.

"As I was about to say, Thimba, self-discipline takes a lifetime: that is true. But it brings you the most satisfying life, do you not think?"

"Absolutely," Matvly said. "It takes much work and effort, but Thimba and I often recall how our lives were before we started looking inwardly. We have concluded that when you start on the journey of self-discipline, at first you may feel dismayed at how much work you see you need, but if you continue and do not give up, you will develop more compassion for each and every person who crosses your path."

"In other words," Thimba added, "you will see that, since you are not perfect and have so much to work on, the imperfections in others do not bother you as much. Because you see it is a trouble with everyone, not just them."

"Hmmm," agreed Ivory, her fingers delicately replacing her fork. "Also, I have found that the more grace I can give myself, the more I can give to others."

"Yes!" exclaimed Isabella. "Perhaps that is what I was trying to put together in my head. I was once very upset with all the things I felt I needed to change, but as I learned to follow the ancient commands and to walk in love with my fellow man and woman, I saw more potential in people, whereas before I would only see their faults. I was so consumed with the faults of people a few years ago."

"That is a perfect statement," Minh agreed. "Perhaps it is more as women, but I also found it more difficult to see the beauty in people and the good in people when I was demanding perfection of myself. I was demanding perfection in my works and therefore saw only the imperfections in myself and others. Which eventually left me too empty, too powerless to love."

Women dominating the conversation would never happen in Overge. Of the few banquets Nelia had attended in her village, all she remembered was being hushed. Not that she had spoken barely a word, for no one in her village wanted to hear her opinion, but even the women who held positions within the village were not always permitted to speak. If too many women spoke at once, the mayor would visibly roll his eyes and his assistants would make snide remarks on not being able to get a word in with all the chatter. The lower-class women were hushed into unequivocal silence by the women of the upper class. They would not allow the lower-class women to 'use up the patience of the men with drivel'.

That was an exact quote from Mrs. Crumly, who was married to the richest man in the village. She was known for treating everyone as children, no matter what their age. Nelia tried her best to avoid Mrs. Crumly at all costs. Of the times she was ever caught near the woman, she was made to either help carry packages so Mrs. Crumly could spend her time striking poses for the people who were not bothering to watch her, to hold open doors for Mrs. Crumly and her simpering rich friends, or to be the brunt of her jokes, which were only laughed at because her friends were afraid of becoming her enemy.

A footman changing the first plate for another woke Nelia from her thoughts. She smiled back at Prince Pokoj, who was watching her.

"Ivory, how is your son getting along in school?" Minh asked, taking full opportunity of the short stall in conversation.

A dreamy smile spread over Ivory's face as she began to tell stories of her little boy attending the local school.

"He is marked for leadership," Ivory said, her pride contagious. "But at the moment he is more concerned with being funny. He will sacrifice obedience to get a few boys to laugh."

"To be fair," Boon-Nam said, "he is quite funny."

"And quick-witted," laughed Isabella. "It is the way that he says things that always makes me laugh."

"He means no disrespect, I know," Ivory said, visibly happy that others found her boy to be funny as well. "But being the clown in school can be quite exasperating for the teacher. I fear that his good marks will get him only so far with his behavior."

Boon-Nam started to laugh, his food almost choking him in the process as he recalled something Ivory's boy had done recently. As best he could, he described the little boy marching through town to put on a one-man show in the square because he wished to. On his march, he had imitated the known people in the town or even those on the street in such a way that no one was offended, and everyone was laughing.

"It's a gift, Ivory, that a boy can do such a thing without any adults taking offense."

"I'm not sure there is any way to do such a thing in my town without someone feeling offense," Nelia ventured to say.

Thimba nodded, his eyes sympathetic.

"I grew up in a town like that. Of course, living in Niebo people are most likely to be of good humor. They understand more of the blessings they have been given and the black magic is less able to stick to them."

"Do you have children, Nelia?" Minh asked.

It was a question that Nelia dreaded each and every time she was with people who did not know her. It always came up, especially with women. What was funny was that, as much as the question now annoyed her, she still asked that very same question to women she didn't know.

"I had a son," she answered, swallowing hard before going on. "But the plague swept through our town and he fell to it."

"The plague came to you?" Matvly asked, his voice earnest. "Was it as bad in your town as in Twinure?"

Nelia shook her head, her throat too constricted to speak. She looked towards the Prince and saw him studying her. Just like in the garden Nelia saw small streams of color, her pure emotions floating around her.

As she struggled to find something to say, Nelia felt her hand being enveloped again into the King's strong hold.

"There will be a time when you will see Zayzay again, my dear Nelia. For now, he is safe."

"There are times still when I do not wish to be here, but to be with him," Nelia admitted.

"This is how I felt for a long time after my first wife died," Matvly said. "Sometimes I still feel an intense longing just to see her for a moment, though I know she is well, and I know I will see her again soon."

"Life is difficult sometimes," the King said, his voice heavy with emotion. "But there is hope."

"Is there?" Nelia asked. Her spirits rose at the sight of the King's kind eyes on her. Usually, when she thought of Zayzay she fell into a thick, black cloud that might keep her in bed for days or weeks. That was the reason Aaron had told her not to speak of him while on her trip. His eyes had betrayed his grave concern that she would fall into that black cloud while traveling and not be able to get back home. And who would care for her? Most people, if they were like those in Overge, would leave her in the cloud, ignoring everything about her until she shriveled up, too weak to travel again. She might disappear completely if she were to enter that cloud while so far from Aaron's care. At least while at home Aaron would make sure she had some broth or some tea to keep her in some strength until the day she was able to see the sun again and eat.

Before the King could speak again, a string quartet came in playing the most beautiful music Nelia had heard in her life. She turned to watch them enter, the lead violinist so lost in the music that he almost ran into a servant carrying away the plates. The young man behind him playing the violin-cello side-stepped the almost disaster with a nimble hop and skip, his animated face telling the dinner guests he was quite used to such happenings. Again, the good humor of people in Niebo surprised Nelia. Though sometimes they laughed in Overge, their sense of humor was muted and gray in comparison.

The quartet continued into the room without further incident. The fire now roared in the ornate fireplace, though there was no smoke and the heat was not too intense. The air filled with an aroma of spices and oak as an island of meringue floating in cream, the afternoon's desert, was placed in front of her. Another servant put down a delicate cup of coffee. Never in her life had Nelia liked the taste of plain coffee, but she was too shy to ask for cream. Not wanting to be rude, she picked the porcelain cup up to sniff the rich aroma coming from it. Once it was near her mouth, she realized she should sip it. If someone pointed out to her that she had merely sniffed the coffee, even if only in jest, her humiliation would be profound.

Her throat muscles contracted, expecting a hideous taste to assault her tongue, but quite the opposite happened. The warm liquid burst onto her tongue tasting of chocolate and some dark, exotic spice she couldn't quite name. The experience with the first coffee she had ever liked convinced her to try the desert. It didn't disappoint.

The vanilla cream and crispy meringue created a melody with the dark coffee. Had she been at home, Nelia would have groaned in pleasure. The food, the music, the rise in her spirits – all of it combined to lift her into almost an aura she had never known. She felt drunk with pleasure and peace.

"Nelia," came a deep whisper through the music.

She opened her eyes, surprised that they had been closed in the first place, to find Prince Pokoj standing beside her.

"Yes?" she asked, her cheeks flushed, her eyes seeing pink from being caught in a bubble of full self-indulgence.

"Would you dance with me?"

Nelia sat back in surprise, looking around to find everyone dancing except Thimba, who drummed enthusiastically on his thigh. For the first time, Nelia noticed that he was missing his right leg from the knee down.

"Nelia?" the Prince asked again, holding his hand out.

Slowly Nelia placed her hand into his, finding her long fingers looked small against his strong hands. The Prince pulled her to her feet, a patient smile on his lips as one song faded and another one started.

"I... am not the best dancer."

The smile on the Prince's lips widened, displaying perfect white teeth. They were such a stark contrast from the teeth she was used to seeing that Nelia couldn't help but take a second to look. She also couldn't help but compare the general air around them, another vibrant contrast to anything she had seen in Overge, even the Christmas parties. The atmosphere literally sparkled with good humor and enjoyment.

"Relax, sister," Prince Pokoj said, shaking her shoulders gently to get them loose. "What you must remember is to trust the man who is leading you, whether it be me on the dance floor or Aaron in your life."

Nelia narrowed her eyes, though she made it a point to loosen her shoulders.

"I did not tell you to blindly follow them and do whatever it is they tell you to do. You were given a brain for a reason, Nelia," the Prince said, laughing at her unspoken disagreement. "Do not be blind, but do not refuse to trust simply out of sexism."

"Sexism?" Nelia said with a laugh. "Is that not more men towards women?"

"Can it not be both?" the Prince asked, taking up her now loosened arms and gliding her with ease across the floor.

Nelia felt as though she were flying. And at first her muscles tensed in fear, but when the Prince brought her focus to his eyes by staring deeply into hers, Nelia found herself laughing. Sheer joy burst forth from her, wrapping her in glittering splendor, and suddenly she felt her trust of the Prince deepen.

"That's it, Nelia," he said, twirling her across the floor that seemed to lengthen where the Prince went, unbound by laws of physics. "Trust me, for I will not fail you. Nor will I let you go or fall."

"I trust *you* to dance well," she said between giggles, "but I have not taken a class since I was eleven."

The Prince's hand tightened slightly against the small of her back. He, too, laughed as they sailed across the floor.

Nelia closed her eyes, unsure of how her feet were moving so quickly, but unconcerned with the thoughts of whether they would keep it up or not. It seemed that the more she released herself to the arms of the Prince, the better she danced. And so, she let go. There was no reason to keep hold of it at all.

"Nelia, open your eyes," the Prince said, slowing their pace.

She obeyed and saw that the King stood by, waiting for his turn to dance with her.

Prince Pokoj stopped her directly in front of his father and gently placed her hand into his. With a bow and smile, the Prince stepped up to Minh and asked her for a turn about the room.

Nelia, left alone with the great King, gave a shy curtsy. Her knees wobbled, almost knocking her down, at the idea of dancing with the great man.

"Nothing else gives me more pleasure than to dance with one of my daughters, no matter how old they are," the King told her with a wink. Then he pulled gently on her hand to have her step forward, gracefully placed his left hand on the middle of her back, and stepped forth at the precise moment the next song started.

"They wrote this song for my birthday, did you know?"

Nelia shook her head. While she was trying to let go as she had done with the Prince, the pressure to not let the Great King down was too great. Unfortunately, the more she concentrated on her feet and their steps, the more she tripped over imaginary obstacles.

The King turned her as the dance demanded, and Nelia now faced the fireplace alongside him. At the last second, she remembered to dance the tiny steps required on her toes, but she had no time to breathe a sigh of relief at her quick mind before he twirled her around to face him again.

"Dance with me as you would have your grandfather," the King suggested, slowing his steps a bit. "I know that Prince Pokoj is a bit more graceful than me in his steps, but I have more experience."

"The only time I ever danced with my grandfather," Nelia said with a laugh, "I danced standing on his feet."

The King slowed to a stop and stuck out one foot as an offering. Nelia laughed from the pit of her stomach, but did not take the offer.

"I thought it was worth a try," the King said with a shrug as he pulled her back into the music. "There you go, now. That laugh was all you needed to loosen up. Now, off we go."

Nelia and the King danced around the room in swirled and skips and hops as the quartet started playing the Skutta Snurr, an energetic dance that Nelia hadn't participated in since her sixteenth birthday. The music was spirited, encouraging the dancer to hop side by side faster as each turn about the room was completed. For as old as she knew the King must be, he certainly showed no signs of slowing. As the end neared, the two violinists were playing with such speed that a few of their strings had snapped. Nelia's feet, too, were moving so quickly that she thought they might crumble within themselves, bringing her to the floor at any moment. Everyone around them clapped in time to the music, but Nelia only saw blurred faces as she and the King danced faster and faster. Her laughter bubbled out of her, but the sound was too slow to get to her ears before it faded away.

Again, they repeated the hops and skips and twirls until every string on the violins snapped and the music came to an end, too suddenly for her and the King to stop at the same time. Thankfully, the King was still in control, as he always must be, and with his strong hands holding her she felt gently led to a slower and slower speed until her head was no longer spinning and she could hear her laughter surrounding her.

"Bravo!" shouted the Prince.

"That was beautiful!" Ivory added, her golden laughter echoed by the others who stood to clap their appreciation.

Nelia laughed, gasping for small bursts of breath as she curtsied to the King and then to the other guests. The King gave an elegant bow, lifting his head with a wide smile.

"That was quite fun," he said. "I am so very glad that you came to visit me, my dear. You will come again soon, will you not?"

The atmosphere, though still light – though the speckles of sparkles still floated about them – became slightly more sobering. Nelia was finally able to breathe, and felt herself suddenly swallowing back tears.

Her time with the King was ending.

"Do not cry, my daughter," he said gently, running his index finger under her eyes. "I am so happy to have met you face to face. And you are welcome to come here any time."

"I almost wish to ask you for a station here so that I might stay."

The King smiled brightly, but shook his head.

"As you may know, I give positions to anyone who asks, but I have marked you for something else. There will be a time when you will be freer to come here and find a station, but right now Aaron needs you by his side."

Nelia struggled not to cry. With her emotions finally under control, she dared to glance around and found that she was alone now with the King in the great dining hall. The only other people in the room were the two guards at the doors, and they were too far away to hear anything she said.

The King bent his head down to kiss her lightly on the cheek.

"You miss your grandfather greatly?" he asked, half question, half statement.

"Yes."

The King lifted her chin, just as he had a lifetime ago in the throne room, and looked deeply into her eyes. The world turned within his eyes: all the situations that required his attention and all the people surrounding his kingdom, both those who loved him and those who hated him.

"I will miss you as well," Nelia said, trying to be earnest in whatever last moments she had with him. "I feel so carefree here. The very idea that you care enough to eat with me, listen to my thoughts, and think me capable of following the conversation of others is quite incredible. And dancing with you, your majesty, it was... quite exhilarating."

The King smiled, then took her hand and led her to a window. There he opened the latch and thrust the stained-glass upwards, allowing them to see the view of the mountainside.

"I miss every one of my children who do not come to see me very often."

Nelia turned her attention to the jutting rocks, marveling at the splendid view.

"It's impossible for me to come see you more than once a year. And I'm not certain I will get back here next year, even," she said. "I would like to come with Aaron one day, but I'm uncertain how long it will take to convince him."

"You do not have to make the long physical journey each day to spend time with me," the King said, turning to face her, away from the mountain.

"How would one see you or know you if they do not come

here? You know that my village has followed the order to destroy their direct lines as well as free their falcons long ago. Almost everyone canceled their mode of reaching someone from overseas or even across the way. I didn't agree with it, but no one really asked us commoners," she said.

The King's soft laughter indicated that she had missed something, perhaps something he had said that she hadn't listened to. With determination, Nelia shook the gray cloud of frustration off herself and placed every bit of her attention back to the King.

"My voice is in the cool breeze, Nelia," he was saying. And this he was saying earnestly and seriously. Though Nelia's knee-jerk reaction was to scoff, she instead strained her ears and mind to work better. The King continued, "Just walk with the breeze in the cool of the morning or evening; speak into it, and your words reach me. Listen carefully, and my words will reach you. Also, read the letters I send each month, as I told you before. The words there will reaffirm what you believe you hear in the breeze."

Nelia tried hard to comprehend it all. There were a few times in her life when she had thought she heard words whispered in the breeze of the evening, but whenever she had said it to anyone they'd laughed at her.

"Yes, my child. You heard me correctly, just as you heard me correctly when you heard me in the breeze as a child."

"I remember," she whispered. "I heard: 'You are beautiful. You are secure. You will mother well.'"

"Yes."

Nelia shook her head.

"I cannot mother again. Zayzay is gone and my womb is dried up. The doctor said there was no use."

"Not from your womb, my child, but from a rock. Keep your eyes peeled all around you as you walk home, and you will find what you are searching for."

The doors opened before Nelia could open her mouth to ask what the King meant, and two men cloaked in deep hues of purple and green stepped in.

"Excuse me, your majesty," the one in green said, giving a deep bow of reverence. "It is time for the calling."

The King gave Nelia's hands a gentle squeeze. She swallowed hard against her tears before quickly daring to kiss his cheeks.

"Goodbye, my dear child," the King said. "Know that I love you and think of you often."

Nelia could only sink into a deep curtsy as tears of sorrow streamed silently down her cheeks. Before she stood, the doors closed with a thud and she was left alone in the great dining hall.

Chapter 6

leaving Niebo

"Would you like to wear your dress home?" Ivory asked.

They were once again in the room where Nelia had changed earlier that morning. After the King had left her in the dining room, Ivory had come to fetch her. Together they had toured more of the palace, meeting more of the people who had stayed to work there. From the balcony of the South Garden Wall, Nelia had caught a glimpse of the little boy whose humor had caught the attention of the people at luncheon. Ivory had waved back and forth from the balcony, calling out to her son, who turned and looked once the wind carried down the noise. His friends playfully punched his shoulders, teasing him about his mother, but the boy didn't seem to care. He shrugged away their guffaws, opting to climb one of the low walls that lined the streets and complete a perfect cartwheel.

Ivory had gasped, her jaw clenched, the skin on her knuckles stretched until every vein was visible. Together they had watched her boy land first his hands on the stone, then his feet. At the very moment that Ivory let out her breath and relaxed her grip, the boy unexpectedly tumbled down, completed a series of somersaults and turns, causing the other boys to run after him shouting, then suddenly jumped up, grasped onto a low-hanging branch, drew himself up and again tumbled out of the tree before sticking his landing.

Nelia couldn't help but clap and exclaim aloud. Even the other boys laughed and applauded, though one boy couldn't help shouting over and over that he had known Tiyant was only joking.

Ivory shuddered a gasp, muttered under her breath, then burst out laughing when he bowed gracefully towards her. The other boys shouted in her direction, clearly cheering Tiyant on to do another trick, but the boy shrugged them off. He must have challenged them to a race, for within a few seconds they were scampering away at full speed.

"Do you see what I mean?" Ivory asked, her heart still visibly pounding hard in her chest. Nelia laughed until Ivory finally joined her. They had stumbled back into the palace with their laughter echoing off the stone walls, but now, as she stared at herself in the mirror, the memory faded into a grainy, gray sadness. She tried to imagine Zayzay that age, doing the same things with other boys, but the image was too elusive.

Ivory snatched at the air, taking the grayness in her fists and throwing it aside. It dissipated in one fell blow against the wall. Nelia watched with widened eyes. Ivory shook her head behind her in the mirror.

"No space to be sad here, Nelia. You should know that by now," Ivory said as she took hold of Nelia's hair and plaited it into one long braid at the side.

"Don't I have reason to be?"

"Not in the least. There is a mission for you, do you not remember? And you cannot complete that mission unless you go back home. Plus, you would miss your husband if you were to stay here."

Nelia's lips moved, releasing a vacant sound of disappointment and acknowledgment of truth.

"Will you wear the dress home then?" Ivory repeated.

Nelia studied the dress in the mirror. Despite having been in the dress for over six hours, there was not even the least minimal change in her appearance. Her skin still glimmered as gold dust scattered over bronze would, her black curls were shiny and healthy, her cheeks glowed, and her eyes were afire. Even the lines around her lips were gone. And though Ivory had never put any makeup on her face, she looked fresh and ready for a ball.

"Does the magic ever wear off?"

Ivory looked up at her, meeting her eyes in the gilded mirror.

"It isn't magic, Nelia. Do you not understand yet? In the presence of the King, you see yourself as He sees you. I see you as He sees you."

"But He is not here now."

"His presence is everywhere," Ivory said with a shake of her head. "It's in the air, in the walls, on the floor, in the ceiling. It is everywhere He steps. And so everywhere around here you and everyone else will see you as He sees you."

"You mean to say then that the closer I get to my village, the more I will look as I always do?"

The disappointment of that thought sent her heart into a marathon of beats. It seemed the most obvious answer, and yet Ivory shook her head, a sly smile touching her lips.

"If you accept the idea that He is everywhere, then you will always see yourself as He sees you. If you accept that He loves you as you are, you will always see yourself as you do now."

"But no one else will."

"Those of us who stay on are able to because we choose to see each other as He sees all of us. There are those who do not see others in this way. But that is a choice. Free will. Do you see?"

"But... sometimes it's hard to see people as He sees us," Nelia said. "He always sees the best of us and we do not always act the best that we can act. It is hard to think the best of others when their actions and words contradict those thoughts."

Ivory smiled, her hand dropping from Nelia's shoulder to tuck in a bit of her own hair. Ivory's hair shone like spun gold.

"I used to want that color hair," Nelia said, watching the light reflect from the silky strands. "Your hair is so yellow for you being Aziatischin."

"My father was Aziatischu and my mother was Clovendin. It is from my mother that I get my hair. But honestly, I always thought my hair was unoriginal. There are many with this same color, though most of them are six years old and with light-colored eyes. That copper color that my son has? That's the color I always wanted. That is the color my mother had, and I always thought she was so beautiful. Anyway, I guess it's true that we always want what we can't have."

A breeze entered through the open window, bringing with it a shift in the room's atmosphere. Nelia sighed, knowing it was time for her to go. She didn't want to leave, but if she waited too much longer, the sun would set and darkness would cover her path. It wouldn't be the first time she had slept alone in the dark wilderness, but not having liked it the first time, Nelia wished to avoid it altogether. And she absolutely didn't have the money to stay another night in the dingy motel outside of Niebo.

As it was, the day was stretching out as she had never seen it do before. Her mother used to tell her of the stretching days that followed her back home from Niebo, but it was quite a sensation to actually experience one.

"I must go," Nelia said. "I will wear my old dress. But I would like to take that one home with me. And I will try to start seeing myself in my mirror as He sees me. Perhaps then, as Mihn said, I will start seeing others as He sees them, and I will have more compassion for them."

"Compassion is good," Ivory said with a smile. "Grace is better."

Together, the two of them carefully peeled the delicate dress from

Nelia's body. She stood by herself behind the silk divider, seeing herself again in the new underwear and feeling as though she might cry and yet jump for joy. The energy within her was so strange, so divided, that all she could do was stand and stare.

"Here is your dress," Ivory said, handing the old dress back over the top of the divider.

"But I thought you said there are no laundry women in the palace," said Nelia as she took it.

"Things go back to how they were created to be when in the presence of the King, Nelia," Ivory said, her singsong voice like that of a teacher. "Things go to order and away from chaos."

The stains had disappeared, and the fabric was no longer discolored more in one spot than another. Since Nelia had never seen the dress new, though, she couldn't say for certain that it looked as such. What she did know was that it looked better, as though she had had a farthing to her name to spend on a new dress. Tears ran down her face as she picked up the familiar, yet new, fabric and rubbed it between her fingers. Now she could enter church without trying to cover up the more worn-out spots with a shawl, even in the smoldering summer.

But there was no time for emotions. The time to leave had come. In one swoop Nelia had the dress back on and was once again staring at herself in the mirror. Still, her skin shone, and her hair looked slick and healthy. She smiled at the sight, glad to find that the fear of not looking still as the King saw her had no grip on her in the palace. Perhaps that was why she still saw herself as worthy of this visit.

"Ivory?" called a voice from the doorway.

"Yes, my lord?"

Nelia froze, though she had hardly been moving before hearing his voice. She had already given her goodbyes to the prince and, though she would do anything for another walk around the garden, the idea of saying goodbye to him again seemed unbearable.

"Is Nelia ready? I've finished all my meetings today and since I thought to go in the direction she is going, I've decided to accompany her on the journey."

"I believe she's almost ready, my lord," Ivory answered, just as Nelia scrambled out to face the Prince in her cotton dress.

She watched his face intently, though by now she no longer expected any judgment from him. She was correct. There was not one raised eyebrow, no flinch of his eyes nor twitch of his lips. Just like a man it was, as though she hadn't changed at all. And in this case, she found that reaction comforting.

"Would you allow me to accompany you, Nelia? I thought I might visit with Aaron."

Nelia narrowed her eyes slightly. She was not as well-trained as the Prince in her facial expressions.

"Not to convince him to go to war again, my lord?"

The Prince laughed.

"No, not for anything of the kind. I only wish to speak with him, laugh with him again, see how he is getting on."

They set out in silence, except for the march of the six guards that would accompany the Prince.

"I never go anywhere alone. Not really," he said with a smile. "Though soon you will neither hear them nor see them."

"But they will still be around?"

"Here and there," shrugged the Prince. "They have various assignments from my father which they must do, but they are always nearby."

As they crossed under an archway Nelia heard an echo of names being shouted out.

"That sounds as though it is coming from the palace."

The Prince stopped to listen, then smiled. He didn't answer right away, but rather held her hand to escort her around a puddle.

"That is my father calling in his sons and daughters who have fallen away. He calls each one by name every day."

"Each one?" Nelia asked, trying not to sound incredulous. Everything in this place was both believable and unbelievable; possible and impossible.

"Each one. Remember, time stretches here. Horizontal time does not constrict us as it does in your village, though it will once we cross over into Croizante."

"Are we going through Croizante? I wished to see it when I was coming here, but it looked quite far away. Won't it make our journey longer?"

The Prince stopped to take the reins of a royal horse standing by for him. Nelia, not expecting to stop, almost ran into a cart full of vegetables, driven by such a short man that only his hat was visible from the front.

"So sorry," Nelia gasped, pulling herself in as much as possible so she would not disturb the produce.

The little man tipped his hat to her with a toothy grin.

"No harm done, m'lady," he said, then turned to concentrate on moving his cart through the semi-crowded streets.

Never having been called 'lady' before, Nelia was momentarily stunned. Air and time wafted around her as she slowly looked down at her dress – the day dress that she wore everywhere and to everything and for everything except for harvesting and cleaning the toilets. Yes, it was revived, but so much?

But then she remembered the way she had looked in the mirror at the palace, and her heart settled enough to hear the noise of the street again. Magic or not, Nelia felt as though she were walking on air at what she considered to be the finest compliment she had received to date.

"Nelia?"

Nelia looked up to find the Prince standing next to the horse with another man standing at the ready. They both watched her expectantly.

"Will you mount?"

Nelia stepped back in surprise.

"I have ridden a donkey before, but never a horse. I will not know how to tell it where to go."

"Do not worry about that. This little lady, Igna, will follow my horse with no difficulty whatsoever. She has never thrown a rider. Ever. She is the gentlest, sweetest horse we have, isn't she, Tanek?"

The young man standing at the ready, dressed in the finest livery clothes Nelia had ever seen, nodded eagerly, patting the dark brown horse lovingly.

"She really is, my lord. Come, miss. I'll help you up and adjust the reins so that Igna feels comfortable. Then all you will have to do is let her do as she has been trained to do."

Taking a deep breath, Nelia stepped forward. Prince Pokoj took her hand and raised it to the horse's nose, allowing the mare to take a deep breath of her scent. Igna gave her approval in a stuttered exhale, then lowered her head a notch for Nelia to pet the soft spot between her eyes. The softest, finest fur met her fingertips. Their donkey had been an ornery one with stocky legs and fur that pricked when touched. Nelia could not say she had been sad when Aaron had sold the beast. Not after the donkey had stuck her head through the open kitchen window and eaten their dinner. Twice.

"Do you prefer sidesaddle or dressage?"

"With my dress?" Nelia asked. "I don't think I should straddle the horse. Her middle is bigger than I thought it would be."

Prince Pokoj nuzzled the horse's nose and laughed as the great beast snorted while pawing the ground.

"No, love, she isn't calling you fat. You're just stronger than she thought."

The hair on the back of Nelia's neck pricked upwards at the tease, but when the Prince looked up at her with twinkling eyes, she let go of her breath and relaxed. It was difficult to rid herself of all her normal tendencies. Teasing was something not done with wit or charm in her village. Teasing was to cut a person down to their place. Or at least to the place the other person thought they should go. There hadn't been a day in high school that she hadn't been put in her place of poverty, ugliness, and stupidity. When she'd dropped out Nelia had thought she would leave behind teasing all together. Little did she know that grown women continued the practice, just with sharper words and lifted eyebrows. The most poised women she ever saw were the ones who could cut another down the quickest.

So, when Prince Pokoj did it with love in his eyes, the type of love she had seen in the eyes of the King and in the eyes of her grandfather when yet he was alive, it forced Nelia to reconsider the very way in which she thought of teasing. Perhaps that was the way that Aaron had meant it when they first were married. He hadn't dared to tease her about anything since the day he had pulled on her braids and asked if she was six. The first plate flying at his head had surprised him. It must have been the second plate that told him not to say such things to her again, because he never did. When next she had taken up the scissors and cut both braids with two great snips, the look of horror on Aaron's face had never left her. Even then she had known she went too far, but since he had never teased her again, Nelia had assumed she had won the argument. Yet it didn't feel like winning. Not when she was left with the memory of his shock and silenced laughter. Her heart sank as the reality sank into her for the first time. It was not winning when you lose a small part of your husband.

"Place your foot here," said Tanek, offering his interlaced hands. "That's right. And give us a small jump. Just like that."

Next thing Nelia knew, she was sitting sidesaddle atop Igna. She was uncertain whether she had flown there or if her body somehow, in some way, had known what to do.

"There y'are now," Tanek said with a smile and dip of his head. "Have safe travels, my lord."

"Thank you, Tanek. You are a great help as always," Prince Pokoj said, jumping onto his white horse with ease.

To see him atop the beautiful, tall stallion, one would think it was his second home, Nelia thought.

"Have the guards left already?"

"About five minutes ago, my lord," Tanek said.

"We're off as well, then. See you soon, Tanek."

The young man stood to attention as the Prince turned his stallion and started off in the direction of the gate. Nelia watched him go in a slight panic, but just as she was about to ask Tanek what to do, Igna started off behind the Prince. All Nelia had to do was hold on.

Chapter 7

feeding Krimaltin

Orange and pink was smeared across the horizon with a dash of golden sparkle, though Nelia assumed the sun wouldn't fully set at all that day. Her mother had once said that the sun never dared to set on Prince Pokoj or the King. Aaron had confirmed her mother's claims, in a way. When she asked him, after he returned from the war, he had said that there was always light around the Prince. At the time she had assumed that meant her mother was correct, which both irritated her and made her proud. Anything that had to do with her mother was always more complicated than it ought to be.

Riding behind him, gazing into the beautiful sky, she wondered why Aaron always had to leave out key details.

"Come up here, Nelia," the Prince said. "We are coming close to Croizante. Do you see the famous bridge?"

In the distance, tiny poles poked out of the earth before swirling into a strange, modern art project in the air. The closer they got, the clearer Nelia could see the spokes twirl and move around each other. Once they were about half a mile away she finally saw the full magnificence of the bridge: the movement of the planks that swayed from side to side, playing music as they went.

"Will they become firm when we approach, as the legend says?" Nelia asked, already noticing that the large planks were transparent and porous. It was the wind moving through the holes that made the music.

"Don't you worry, Nelia. Just follow me and watch."

Nelia obeyed, for there was no way for her to stop Igna from continuing. But she also couldn't help holding her breath as her brave horse stepped onto what seemed only semi-solid. Once her head registered the clack of the horseshoes hitting a hard surface, Nelia let out a small bit of air. When they continued forward, neither one of them plunging into the raging river below them, Nelia slowly breathed all the way out and in.

"You are fine, Nelia," Prince Pokoj called out to her.

Much to her surprise, she *was* all right. No black magic clung to her, taunting her into a deep fear as was custom when she was at home. Looking down into the moving, blue water, Nelia swallowed hard but forced herself to face what was below.

"I'm fine," she repeated, until she could look in awe at the whole scene around her instead of in trepidation.

Almost too soon, Nelia found herself safely across the bridge and stopped in front of the great gate of Croizante. It was made of solid river rock and bordered by emeralds and gold dust.

"Do you find it as magnificent as the stories say it is?"

"More so," Nelia answered, her eyes taking in the details of the scene etched into the river stone. It was the story of Croizante: the town that had once worshiped the sun and thrown their babies from the top of the mountain into which they carved their palace.

"Is that you, right there?" Nelia asked, pointing at an image of a strong man in the stone who held a spear, both hands wide open. "Did you really approach them with your arms held open like that?"

Prince Pokoj smiled, almost shyly.

"When I approached, separated from my men due to a thick fog that covered miles of road, I approached the city at the same time of year that they would present their children to their sun god, Krimaltin. Each month, they placed the names of any baby born into a large pot like this one here. See? It was made of iron, with the opening depicting the open mouth of Krimaltin. For two years the name stayed in the pot, and each month the priestess of Krimaltin stirred the pot to move the names around. Then, on the second Tuesday of November, the priest would pick five names, remove the babies from their home and offer them as a sacrifice. Many of the surrounding towns complained about how horrible it was, but they spoke about it in a way that said they believed the people were horrible for doing it, but that it wasn't something anyone could change. No one was willing to speak up and tell the people of Croizante that it wasn't right to sacrifice their children to the sun."

"But wasn't that because the one person who tried was burned at the stake while hanging over the mountain?"

"A bit of an exaggeration," the Prince said. "The last person to enter the city walls soon afterward became the bloodiest priest in their history, claiming that the reason the crops were failing was that they weren't sacrificing enough babies. He demanded they choose ten names in November and ten in December. And on December 21, he demanded that they choose three boys of fourteen years of age to fight to the death as a tribute to Krimaltin."

"But unless you have many babies, you might kill off most of the coming generation."

Silence replied. They both looked at the carved story etched in the gate's frame. A profound sense of gratitude for not having been born in Croizante sank into Nelia. She would never have been able to place the name of her baby in the pot. She would have run away – though where to, she didn't know.

As Prince Pokoj looked at the door, his eyes filled with tears. Nelia followed his eyes to the corner, where the stone depicted baby after baby falling from the highest balcony of the city.

"The year I arrived, just the day before they had thrown down eight babies. They would throw them down over the edge and then burn them once the ceremony was over. Those who survived the fall—"

"Some survived?"

"Very few, but some. Those who survived would be burned in a separate fire and require that another name be pulled from the pot. Not dying the first time meant that the child was rejected by Krimaltin."

The contents of her stomach tried to revolt at the thought. She steadied herself on Igna, breathing in and out through her mouth, unable to stop staring at the door, unable to stop listening to the story.

"When I arrived, I saw something falling from above and knew it must be the second Tuesday of November. I realized it was time to tell the people that more was expected of them. That they could be so much more, do so much better, but that their yoke could be lighter if they chose to take direction from my father. My arms were outstretched to catch the falling baby who screeched and wailed as they stripped him of all his clothing and dropped him over the balcony. According to their tradition, not even the priest could watch the baby fall. They only come to look when the ceremony was finished. I believe it's because the spirit within humans knows when something they do is terribly wrong, even if they cannot explain the reason that it is."

Nelia released her breath life a hiss.

"You were able to save one?"

Prince Pokoj smiled.

"For an innocent human, I can do just about anything. That day a wave of holy anger surged within me and I was able to catch all of them.

"Then they came out, the people of Croizante, to see if Krimaltin had accepted the blood they sacrificed. The more mangled the body of the baby was, better, for it signified that Krimaltin had chewed it for a longer time and was satisfied. They came down chanting and wailing out their prayers to Krimaltin and I stood waiting for them with my feet parted, trying to calm my heart from the anger I had. There was one baby that I almost didn't reach, though I caught him by the ankle, which snapped with the pressure that I had to exert to catch him. Just before the parents came down, I had set the bones of the little one, who was almost two years old, and was holding him in my arms. The pain had made him pass out long before I had to set his bones, which was a blessing for me and him.

"As I heard the people coming, I started to pray harder, not wanting to say anything in the flesh, out of anger, for I didn't want to give one person a reason to try to defend their actions. I wanted them to see, to open their eyes. I wanted them to look at every single baby. Each one a precious gift. How do people stop believing that there is a plan for each one of these precious children?"

"We are strange like that," Nelia said, shrugging her shoulders. She was trying hard not to envision babies being thrown down the high cliff she couldn't take her eyes away from now. "But we are also strange in that we will hold tight to traditions even if they hurt us, just to not be wrong. How is it they accepted you? Though I can't imagine sacrificing my own child, I'm surprised that they didn't resist you and the change that you came to bring them."

"Oh, they resisted," Prince Pokoj said, stepping up closer to pull the thick rope hanging next to the door. "Some were furious. But you know that fiery spears cannot come near me and hurt me. I walk in the power of my father."

"They threw fiery spears?"

"And darts. That is how they start the fire for the sacrifice. When they saw all eight babies sitting or lying down near me, the priest decided to burn us all up," he said with a wry smile. "You should have seen the black magic that day. The priest's anger was so fierce he could have set fire to the city with it. But, of course, the fire went out immediately once it came near me. That is when a woman stepped forward screaming, 'This is the Prince! The one in the prophecy!' I could see that she was drunk with the wine that Croizante was known for."

"Cineranha? I've seen people who take that," Nelia said with a shudder.

"Her eyes were wide with fright, though I do not know if she really saw me or another being. I felt my father's presence in the wind, so I knew that he was working in the background. I know that he has intervened at times when a person's mind is being lost through drugs. A few people have told me of seeing my father or some of his

Guardians when they are far away from their right mind. Perhaps she saw something more, but what is true is that she saw me and knew who I was. Her screams stunned the entire crowd. Even the priestess, who was hissing and screeching in an effort to rouse the people, stopped."

Nelia stroked Igna to control the nervous energy those words sent through her spine.

"What did you do?"

"I told them I was Prince Pokoj and that I was there on that day to show them a better way. Then I turned to the priest and told him that if he could get to me and tie me up, then I would allow him to continue with the sacrifice. But if they couldn't tie me up, then they would have to stop the sacrifices altogether and return to being part of my father's kingdom. As you can see, they could not tie me. The ropes kept breaking or falling apart. Soon some women crept forward towards their babies, weeping with gratitude that they were saved. It took until the drugs started to wear off before they could understand truly what was happening."

"I would have taken them from the women. I can't believe they would sacrifice their own kin and then cry as though they had nothing to do with it," Nelia said coldly. Imagining herself there on that day, on the side of the Prince, Nelia felt no sympathy for those women. They shouldn't be given babies just to throw them away.

Prince Pokoj turned to face her.

"It's strange to me that many times women don't want to take responsibility for what they decided to do," she said.

"I have heard that statement or a version of it many times before," Prince Pokoj said, mounting again as the great door started opening. "But the meaning of long-suffering is not gritting one's teeth. Long-suffering means to be willing to wait a long time for a person or people to change. And it's part of my father's commandments."

"Like patience?" Nelia asked.

"Almost," the Prince said, nodding to the people poking their heads out of the shops to see who it was that was visiting. Suddenly, in the middle of the cobblestone road, a boy appeared. His eyes lit up with pleasure at the sight of Prince Pokoj, then, as though coming to his senses, his body jolted and off he ran up the steep road, shouting. He shouted in a dialect Nelia could not understand, but she assumed he said something to the effect that Prince Pokoj was there, for everyone the boy passed stopped what they were doing to dip into a curtsy or bow. "Long-suffering means to see the person in the light of who the father sees them as, and to be willing to encourage them as long as they take to see themselves in the same way and to change."

"Is anyone able to do that except for you? Or really, is anyone willing? Seems to me that most people are not willing whatsoever."

"That is because the people of your town have hardened their hearts considerably to the King and his word. But if you were to read his word and get to know him a little better, you would find that he's a good King and that all of his commands are there to make your life better. He simply knows best because he knows you better than you know yourself."

Before Nelia could answer, the sound of a drum filled the street. Boom, boom, boom. Its rhythmic sound echoed against the shop walls. Igna perked up her ears and began to prance. Then came the trumpets. Nelia looked at Prince Pokoj, who sat with a wide grin on his face. Down the hill the same boy came running back now, his face lit up with expectation. When the Prince motioned to him, the boy made a beeline straight towards him. Nelia gripped Igna's mane, hoping her horse wouldn't spook at the energy of the boy, but there was nothing to worry about. Not only did Igna ignore the boy, but the Prince reached down, scooped him up and plopped him at the front of his ornate saddle.

"How are you doing, young Suring?" Prince Pokoj asked.

But the boy could hardly answer. He was too busy waving to the townspeople he knew; those he wanted to see him there, atop the Princes' horse.

They proceeded towards the trumpet and drum sounds, the last coherent words Nelia heard being, "Not again! Why does Suring always find the Prince first?"

The boy ignored the complaint and continued to pretend to direct the horse towards the castle. The precession was long and slow, with more and more people filling the street with every passing sound of the trumpet. Soon there were people from one side of the stores to the other, barely allowing passage to the horses. The air resounded with buzzers and flutes and makeshift drums. They used anything to announce to the world that the Prince had come back.

Chapter 8

touring alone

For what seemed like another hour they sat atop the horses, watching the people and waving. Soon enough Nelia couldn't help but wave along with Suring. She knew no one cared about her being there, but the joy radiating from the crowd was enough to elevate her mood. When women and children waved at her, she waved back. The mayor of Croizante came out, bowing deeply to the Prince before stepping up to the microphone to give a short speech in honor of his visit. Nelia noticed that two of the guards had somehow slipped in before them and were now standing at attention around a certain door.

Once the mayor finished speaking, the crowds dispersed to the outer courts, where they were given a banquet. Two men from the castle guided Prince Pokoj and Nelia toward the door where the guards stood at attention. Soon afterward, Nelia found herself in a luscious apartment of velvet cushions and lacquered wood, attended by three young maidens.

Nelia took a deep breath, watching her reflection in the mirror. It had taken her a very long hour to convince the three attendants to leave her alone. They didn't believe her at first, or at second, that she wasn't a lady. Her pleas that she was just a farming woman went unheard for a long time. Having come into town with the prince convinced them she was someone to pay attention to. It wasn't until one of them asked for a tip, and Nelia admitted that she had nothing to give them, that they understood.

A cool breeze blew through the open palace window, cooling Nelia from the strange embarrassment she still burned with. At the same time that she had been arguing to convince the attendants who wouldn't stop attending to the most minute thing she could have wanted, there had been a strange voice in her head, one that sounded almost like the King, that told her she deserved the royal treatment.

Which was absurd. She was nobody, and this was no longer Niebo. This was the real world, where people were expected to act their station.

A loud knock at the door startled Nelia, her thoughts dispersing into a thick, grey cloud tinged in yellow. Shame. The emotion surprised her, not having seen it in the last twenty-four hours.

"Not here, though," she muttered with a sigh, seeing the yellow heighten when the large door creaked open and a short, stocky man walked through. Nelia scrambled to come off the high window ledge as gracefully as possible, but she ended up barely missing her backside hitting the floor. In all the commotion, the man stood silently. When Nelia finally straightened herself out, he did not bother to meet her eyes. Like a good servant, he kept his gaze up towards the corner of the ceiling.

"Dinner will be served in one hour. There are a few visitors from around the kingdom come to visit. His lordship Romanztrup and her ladyship are here, as well as Mayor Doongr and his wife."

"I'll take my dinner in my room," Nelia answered before the poor man ran through the entire list. She had already heard it from the maidens, as though it should impress her. She had never heard of anyone on the list before now and she had no intention of meeting them, certain that her name was making no impression on them at all.

The short man opened his mouth in silence once, showing his surprise, but quickly recovered.

"Very well. As you wish, my lady."

With that, he snapped his heels together and vanished.

Nelia picked up the woolen shawl left for her by the light-skinned maiden and wrapped it around her head and shoulders. She was not about to sit around her room like a rich woman who needed to rest before dinner. Wives of farmers did no such thing. If she were at home, there would be a million things to get finished before she could sit down for dinner. She was not at home, but she was still a working woman. And as a woman used to walking and doing chores about the house and farm, her legs ached from not being stretched and moved all day long.

Her thoughts were so occupied upon leaving her big, luxurious room that Nelia didn't at first notice she had gone straight in the direction of the servant stairwell. She hesitated. First, she couldn't understand how she had arrived there at the servant's staircase. A small voice in her head taunted her about working women's intuition and knowing where she really belonged. Nelia shook the voice away and turned towards the direction of the grand staircase, but found herself unable to move forward. The whisper in her head that told her she had no right to be in this palace except to be a servant grew stronger. Alas, instead of dreaming of being a grand lady tiptoeing down the grand staircase, all she could dare to dream was herself in a glistening staff uniform. And even that dream vanished as soon as it appeared. Nelia couldn't help but doubt they would even take her.

Two young men dressed in butler's uniforms passed her as she descended. They raised their eyebrows slightly but didn't dare to say anything.

As she passed by the kitchen, Nelia slowed to watch the motions. Fish cooking in butter sauce wafted through the air. The chef with a dark, trim beard and large round belly bellowed out commands, though no shouting seemed necessary. A young man teased a chambermaid with bits of a buttery biscuit while two young boys sat scrubbing the mud away from shoes and chatting amiably.

"Might I be able to help you?"

The voice was unexpected. Nelia had assumed she would be invisible, more or less, to all these people – but of course, they must assume that she needed something if she was a guest and deemed it necessary to come downstairs to the bowels of the palace. Nelia schooled her expression into one of indifference, a look she saw constantly on the rich women in her town, before turning. She faced the housekeeper, who was dressed all in gray with her hair pinched back into a tight bun. Nelia had expected the woman to have a sour face, but the woman was smiling softly.

"Would you like a biscuit to take with you on your walk? I could put a bit of ham into it."

"With mustard?" Nelia asked in wonder. She hadn't had ham in years.

The housekeeper's smile broadened, and it was then that Nelia's mother spoke to her from the grave, chiding her for showing how lowly and poor she was. Even to a housekeeper, who surely came from almost as lowly a place. But the words were out, and the fingers already snapped. The same young man who had been teasing a young maid just moments before now set to work to slather mustard onto a fluffy biscuit and carve away a slice of ham from the bone set on the cutting board in front of him.

"Warm from the oven," the housekeeper said.

Nelia took the steaming bundle from the man. Then he gave a slight bow, turned on his heel and left with a wink.

"Thank you. It smells delicious."

"Will you be back in time for your dinner, Madame Nelia? Or

would you prefer that I keep it warm for you and bring it up later?"

Never in her life had she so many choices.

"Later," she answered, barely able to control the water in her mouth as she smelled the sandwich in her hands. "Thank you very much."

The housekeeper dipped her a curtsy but before she could leave, Nelia called after her.

"Is there a post nearby where I can send a message?"

"There is one near the Place de Merville, on the way to the Place de Pokoj. Take a walk through the park, my lady. It is beautiful this time of year. I highly recommend it."

Nelia gave her thanks, then made her way to the back door. Finally, out in the evening light, she sank her teeth into the buttery, savory sandwich. It took quite a bit of control for her to not gobble it as a starving child would. Though she had eaten nothing since lunch with the King, she hadn't realized just how hungry she was.

Looking out over the palace gardens, Nelia blinked back her alarm. Lunch with the King had been that very same day. Or perhaps several days, what with the stretching of time and all. She wasn't sure. What she did know was that she hadn't yet slept, so that made it the same day for her.

It seemed impossible.

"A most interesting day," Nelia murmured to herself. "And I'm not yet even tired."

She licked the butter lingering on her fingers, uncaring if anyone saw. She wasn't about to let good butter go to waste. Perhaps rich women had to keep themselves from eating to guard their waistline, but she was going back to a place where she would look for anything to keep the fat on her and Aaron's bones, for that was what seemed to help people stay alive once winter came.

Pulling her shawl closer around her face, Nelia stepped out of the protected area of the palace gardens and into the town proper of Croizante. The streets were not quite as busy as before, but there were still couples lingering about, children running with hoops through the streets, and peddlers calling out their goods. It was a prosperous town, Nelia had seen that right as they entered, but now that she had time to look closer she could see that even the beggars looked better fed than anywhere else she had seen.

What a dynamic change must have taken place for this town to change in only three generations. She turned right, following the town signs, and found herself on a street lit with small lights overhead and flowers gracing every balcony. Small chairs and table were set about outside of the restaurants, with people sitting outside as they ate. Laughter filled the air, and somewhere not too far an accordion was playing.

Nelia felt as though she had stepped into an oil painting, like the giant ones hanging at city hall where Mayor Billisborth had set up his office and eventually attached his house. When people dared to complain about the rise in taxes to build his house into the structure, the mayor had told them they would eventually save money due to him not needing a police escort to work.

They had yet to see any lowering of taxes, though. Somehow the people working within the city hall had found something that needed the money.

Nelia scoffed to herself. Now that she and Aaron had no children, the tax office had sent them a notification requiring them to pay more. The new idea was that those without children should pay for the school as a sort of investment for the day they did have children. Never mind the obvious injury to insult that created for all the parents who had lost their children to the plague, or the hunger that came afterward.

All around her in Croizante people seemed to smile. Children ran about happily, carts watched out for others on the road, women smiled and waved as they passed one another, and men kept watchful eyes without seeming to impose their strength on others.

It was hard to believe this village had used to throw its children over the mountainside to be burned.

"Good evening, madam." An old man greeted her as she stepped into the pigeon post. "Wish to send a message to someone?"

"Yes. To the town of Overge, to the outskirts, really. There is a landing post at the crossroads of North Standing Passage and Dinny Road still, though it hasn't been used in a long while. Do you have a pigeon that will know to stop there?"

The old man allowed a slow smile to spread over his face, revealing three empty spots along the gums. Nelia noticed now that he also had at least four or five days of beard on him, and his clothing seemed to have known better days.

"Who ye sending a note to, madam?" the old man asked as he hobbled slightly, due to a slightly shorter left leg. "A young man, perhaps?"

Heat rose to her cheeks, along with a dim pink fog. Would she be sending a note to a young man? She was already thirty-three, and Aaron five years past her. That was half their life gone.

Half their parenting lives gone, anyway.

"To my husband," Nelia answered. "He'll be wondering what is keeping me. I don't want him to worry about me."

"Aye, he would be missing a young lass such as yourself," the old man agreed, with a strange twinkle in his eye.

Nelia curtsied her thanks before stepping over to the tall table which held small pieces of parchment paper and dark, black pencils with oily tips. It took a few minutes to come up with something believable. That was the trick; she didn't want to sound too fantastic, though it was hardly plausible that she was in Croizante with Prince Pokoj. Still, she didn't want Aaron to worry about her safety or her fidelity. And since he would probably go up to his mother and father's house for dinner, which would bring a whole new conversation around an old subject, Nelia didn't wish for him to have any reason to agree with his mother on her age-old lecture of why Nelia wasn't good enough for him.

Tafneya, her mother-in-law, had been happy at first when Nelia had told her she was going on a voyage. All she could talk about for two weeks was the time she had made the journey herself, making a point to add on her thoughts of how the journey would help Nelia dig her way out of her depression or 'whatever was going on with her moods'. Tafneya said it would be 'refreshing' for her spirit. Anything that was good for the spirit was all right with Tafneya.

But when Nelia had mentioned that she would stay a night away, Tafneya had thought it was a joke and laughed. When she'd realized Nelia was serious, Tafneya stomped away to yell at her son, making no attempt to keep her opinion from being heard by Nelia, just around the corner of the house.

Nelia staying a night away? Ridiculous! What for? Staying a night away was equivalent to abandoning both Aaron and her duties to the house.

It wasn't until Tafneya brought Zayzay into the mix of reasons that Aaron cut his mother off. They hadn't discussed the topic again, at least not in front of Nelia. Nelia shuddered at the way the discussion about her might go tonight. She could nearly hear her mother-in-law as though she were standing in front of her: *"She went to get her spirit refreshed, did she not? To see the King and be blessed by Him, did she not? Is this now a vacation? When is she coming home? How many more days will she abandon my son and her duties as a wife and farmer? I can't take up all of her chores just so she can go gallivanting about the countryside. Do you think I never want to take a vacation? I would think that your father and I deserve a vacation before her. We haven't been on a trip since before you were born! And Croizante! She'll erase anything good the King gives her by going to such an evil place!"*

It didn't matter that Tafneya had never traveled to Croizante. She knew the stories, and that was enough for her to pass judgment. When the pastor had spoken one Sunday about the story of Prince Pokoj changing the people of Croizante's hearts years back, the discussion at Sunday dinner had been all about Croizante. Nelia remembered being in the kitchen with her mother-in-law and listening to a rather long rant about how people so evil could not possibly change so quickly. She was certain that same opinion would make its way into this new rant that Nelia's message would cause. And it would end with Tafneya reiterating her opinion that a woman's place was with her husband.

Quietly, Nelia agreed – but not for every minute of every day of her life. *Just because I am here for a night, seeing the world, doesn't mean I've left my place next to my husband. Isn't his place next to me? And yet I wouldn't have considered him really having left his place when he went to war, though he was physically gone. He was loyal to me. Just as on the tax days, when he must travel north and stay for two days. I do not consider him 'gone from his place'. So, then, neither have I left my place next to him simply because I am in Croizante for one night.*

In the end, Nelia settled on writing that the Prince had offered for her to travel with his entourage (for she did not wish to sound too pompous and say she was actually traveling one-on-one with the Prince of the Kingdom, the Highest One over all other rulers. But even writing out the most unpretentious words she could think of made Nelia's heart race as she realized again who she was with. *Her.* Traveling with the Prince. As though his sister or friend!) and that they had settled in Croizante for the night because of some business the Prince had there.

"Ye ready, madam?" asked the old man, standing by now with a pigeon gripping his finger.

"Yes, sir," Nelia answered, handing the parchment over. She watched with fascination as the old man's gnarled fingers folded the paper, then wrapped it around the leg of the pigeon. Nelia smiled into the perfect circle of the pigeon's eye, in awe at the simplicity that stared back at her. With a quick twitch of the neck, the bird's attention was on something else. An animal so easily distracted made Nelia wonder if the bird would find its way to the landing post, but she'd seen it done before and it was the only way to get a message to Aaron.

She would have to have faith.

With a wink sent in Nelia's direction, the old man turned and climbed the rickety ladder leaning against the south wall, holding on with only one hand. Without looking, the man easily skipped the broken rung, unlatched the window and flung it open, all while keeping his stout body in balance.

"Aye, odlatywać lille fugl," the man growled. He pulled his finger back into his palm, and the bird flew off. For a minute Nelia held her breath, almost expecting the stupid creature to return, but nothing flew back through the window. "Ye got your wish, madam."

"How much do I owe you?"

The old man didn't answer till he was down the ladder, jumping an awkward, squatting jump from four rungs up. Nelia jerked forward to catch him, though she wasn't sure exactly how she would have done it. Her thoughts of heroism were unnecessary, though. The old man stuck his landing, then burst into gurgling laughter when he saw her flinch.

"Always good for a laugh," the old man said, still chuckling as he wobbled to the cash box. "So, over to Overge. I will get her back maybe in a week."

Nelia waited as he grumbled to himself in his dialect, one she'd never heard before and was at a loss to understand.

"One quadrans."

Nelia jerked her head up in surprise at the low fee.

"For a pretty girl and the Prince's guest," he said with a smile.

With the money paid, Nelia gave him a short curtsy and left the shop. Out in the street, she couldn't help looking back and found the man still watching her, still smiling.

The sun was about to set now; it was almost dinnertime, and she had yet to walk through Place de Pokoj. With a prayer that her mother-in-law would not catch word of any crude rumors sent heavenward, Nelia left her worries at the door of the post and marched forward. It was all she could do from so far away.

Chapter 9

black nails of
sorrow

A ncient tombs lined the north side of Place de Pokoj. Made of stone, standing upright with peaks at the top, they reminded Nelia of elfin hats. The trees crowding about the tombs had peaked points as well, along with vine-like branches that had made their way around the trees next to them, creating mystical-looking hammocks through the park. Round flower bushes covered in tiny purple flowers lined the packed-dirt paths, with large red-berry bushes placed every ten feet.

A deep rumble came from her stomach as she left behind the cemetery and stepped into the flower garden. Nelia wished she had another buttery biscuit with ham stuffed in the middle, but felt instantly selfish for her strong desire. She was becoming weak simply by knowing there was plenty of food waiting for her at the palace.

Too much abundance produces weakness, her grandfather used to say. Now Nelia could see just how true that statement was.

In penance, Nelia whispered a prayer of thanks for what she had and for what was waiting for her at the palace. There would be little available at home because of the dry season they were having, so she must be grateful for her moments of extra. Above all else, she must be thankful for what she had at the moment and enjoy the park's beauty.

The sky was turning purple, pink and crimson as she came to the center of the park, where a giant fountain threw water into the air in twelve arches. Each arch met in the middle where a large stone cross stood, a red light shining against it. Several benches surrounded the fountain but before Nelia sat, she noticed a smaller fountain to the right where children were running, shoving their mouth under a small spigot and getting a gush of clear water in return. As much as she enjoyed the lingering taste of the ham and mustard on her tongue, her throat begged her for a drink.

"Is it really clean water?" she asked a man standing by with a foolish grin on his face – the kind only proud parents had of small children when they did something new or adult-like.

"What? Oh, yes. Yes, it's clean water. Triven, come and show this lady how to get water. No, show her the big person one, and then you get some from the little one. Yes, there," the father said, his voice patient and sweet towards the little three-year-old that looked back for approval. Turning to Nelia, the father gestured with his head. "There you are. See the spigot just to the right? That's tall enough for you. Just do as the children do. Get your mouth right underneath and the water will trickle out."

Nelia obeyed, smiling at Triven, who watched her with wide eyes.

"Here, here," the little boy said, pointing with a chubby finger to the spigot the father had shown her. "Okay! One, two, fee!"

On three Nelia placed her open mouth underneath and was greeted with sweet, cool water. Direct from the mountain top – she was almost sure of it.

"Siiiiiii!" Triven shouted, jumping in the awkward, staggered two-footed way a three-year-old does.

The scene pulled her throat tightly together until she had no choice but to open her mouth and gasp for breath. From deep within her gut a barreling ache headed towards her throat, and her eyes started to blur from the tears in them. Quickly, Nelia swallowed hard to repair and replace the dam holding back her emotions, but with each breath, she only felt a horrendous sadness. She could feel the black, oily cloud around her, sinking its fingernails into her shoulders. In one last-ditch effort, Nelia placed her mouth back under the spigot and closed her ears to the gleeful noises of the small children around her. It was too much to hope that the children would disappear when she opened her eyes again, but reality didn't stop her from wishing.

Her wish was not granted.

With her mouth again under the spigot, Nelia concentrated on the sensation of nails digging into the flesh at her shoulders and swallowed. With steady gulps and a deliberate refusal to cry, Nelia finally felt herself calm down enough to stand up. When she did, she found Triven standing by, staring at her. He smiled shyly when she looked back, his brown eyes almost as dark as his pupils, reflecting Nelia back to herself.

"Hello."

"Hi."

The little voice was so sweet Nelia almost lost the small bit of control over herself. Again tears blurred her vision, but she refused to let them fall.

"Come now, Triven," the father of the boy called. He was walking towards them, holding out his large hand for the little boy to take. "Bye."

"Bye," Nelia answered, waving her finger at Triven before the boy turned away and gave all of his attention to his father.

Slowly the park was emptying of people. The sky was not yet very dark, but the colors of the streaks were getting deeper, signaling the finality of the evening. Nelia wasn't sure how safe Croizante was at night, but she felt no threat being in the park. The housemaid had told her she could call for a palace cab whenever she felt she needed it, but looking about at the quiet pathways and the calm people left, Nelia felt no fear. Calling a cab was for bothersome rich women, not for women like her. She would walk as she always did.

Walking was good for the soul, she told herself once again. For probably the one million and thirtieth time.

As the sound of the melodic fountain faded and the pathway turned to polished stone, Nelia found herself nearly alone. One young couple strolled through the park, circling as though being watched by a chaperone somewhere, along with a constable checking his watch every thirty seconds. The scene was endearing and memory-inducing. Chaperones had been all the rage as she was growing up. All the best girls had had them, to the point of girls taking a chaperone just about wherever they went, not just on dates. She had never had the funds or the family members to stand in as a chaperone. But the one nice thing Tafneya had done for her was to stand in as a chaperone for every date that Aaron and she had gone on so the townspeople of Overge would view their match as a respectable one. Remembering this, Nelia's heart towards her mother-in-law softened slightly. It had been a very kind gesture. Without it, there would be women in Overge who wouldn't consider the marriage valid, and who knew what they would try if they believed Nelia was not truly Aaron's wife.

Leaving the young lovebirds behind, Nelia passed under the green glass archway that led to a choice of four streets. Two looked residential, while the other two seemed to run more towards the town center. Nelia chose the one at the right, lined with shops closing and a few cafes.

Enough people were on the street that the town seemed safe even for a lone woman. Slowly she ambled along, looking through the windows of the shops: one selling fine, lace dresses, another selling beautiful confections that seemed almost too gorgeous to eat, and the last window framing shiny train engines and tin soldiers.

Nelia touched the glass of the last shop, her heart suddenly heavy, her body suddenly tired. There were often days like this when it seemed everything reminded her of Zayzay, but it was strange that she would be so melancholy only a few hours after being with the King. Again, it seemed her human heart was so frail and weak. Too weak to sustain itself alone with Aaron, which brought even more sadness to her. For a year now, she had wondered if she was good enough to stay with Aaron or if he would eventually leave her for another woman that could take the difficulties of life. Many other women lost their babies for different reasons and yet went on to have more. But she couldn't seem to get pregnant. Even after Dr. Wrathen had diagnosed her as barren, Tafneya claimed it was due to her weak constitution, her low state of humor.

What baby would want a mother with such low esteem of herself and who never smiled? Tafneya asked no one often.

"Babies are smarter than we give them credit for," Nelia murmured aloud, quoting her mother-in-law.

She backed away from the glass, away from the toys and her desire to buy one for a little boy dead more than two years now. Still, she couldn't seem to take her eyes away until a shout from further down the street caught her attention. A drunken shout – the kind she knew well.

Nelia squinted her eyes into the lamppost-lit street just as a tall, thin man stumbled out of a doorway and almost onto his backside in the middle of the street. He recovered quickly, as many drunks can who have drunk for many years. The man straightened himself, then hunched his shoulders, put up his fists, and took a swipe at someone whom Nelia couldn't yet see. Since watching men fight had been a secret passion of hers since high school, Nelia found herself almost smiling at this turn of luck. There was something about the primal energy, the way men concentrated so hard, the ripple that went through their muscles with each punch – all of it combined to make outstanding entertainment. Quickly she stepped into the doorway of a store, knowing that there were times men would stop if they saw a strange lady watching.

The drunk shouted in the local dialect, nothing that sounded remotely familiar to Nelia, as he straightened himself up again. A small, thin silhouette came into the light just then. A boy of about fourteen who growled at the drunk: a lecturing growl, the kind Nelia used to take on when speaking to her mother about her drinking habits.

The tall man didn't take too kindly to what the boy said – as most fathers wouldn't, in Nelia's experience – and got ready to take another swipe. The young boy was ready, but he had not the experience of his father. This was made clear when the father took a slow swipe with his right that the boy defended against, only to be clipped on the side of his jaw by his father's left hook.

Nelia gasped upon seeing the boy's neck flung to the side. For a moment she thought he might slump down into a heap, but within a few seconds, he righted himself. Nelia turned to watch the father, who seemed to show some pride in the boy getting up again. It helped the boy that his father didn't pursue hitting him while he recovered. The left hook had been enough to bring blood to his lips, but off-centered enough not to do too much harm. Just as Nelia felt some pity for the father – after all, he hadn't punched his son while he was down – the man let out a deep, gurgling, mocking laugh. The boy's cheeks turned scarlet.

When the drunken man staggered backward, the boy rolled back his shoulders and got ready for a real fight. A fight he would lose badly, for his father's eyes were now gleaming with the type of shame that led men to cruelty. As though to highlight her thoughts, a black shadow smoothed itself over the man's shoulder, practically salivating as it dripped malice around the man. With each passing second, the cloud had more control, the father, less.

Fear dominated the street. Nelia pressed her back against the building behind her, not wanting to be seen or heard, though she also wanted to be able to spring forward if the boy got into too much trouble with his father. And she was quite certain that he would. The man might be drunk, but he looked as though made of steel.

A hiss echoed from the corners of the street, sending a cold shiver down Nelia's spine. She could hear her Grandmama speaking quietly as she rolled bread dough between her hands.

"There was once a particularly dark and evil spirit upon my uncle. It was there for years, at first gray and then turning to a dark, gleaming black. In the beginning, only I saw it. Each time I pointed it out my mother or aunt would swipe at my head, the back of their hand knocking sense into me, as it were. Sense, ha!" Grandmama would always laugh at that part, her hands never deviating from the dough.

"They would have had more sense if they had listened to me," she would continue. "But no. He was the source of money, of food, and so we said nothing about the spirit. Translucent, then gray, then black. By the time it was dark as a shadow there was no more hitting me for saying something was there that they said was not, but hitting me for acknowledging that shadow instead of ignoring it. But you know, and certainly, they knew, that ignoring shadows that black only allows them to fester and dig their claws in. Uncle became angrier and angrier each time we looked at him, so we soon averted our eyes. I averted my eyes and had been since the moment he started visiting me in my room at night. But no one wanted to hear it. That was when the shadow started, and that was when the lard started coming in. Along with some meat and sugar and a new dress for auntie. When mama got a child in her belly uncle turned her out. Screaming and crying, I was. Hysterical. Didn't matter how much they hit my head. Over and over and over. Uncle shouted, and the shadow screeched and spat and drooled all over, but I didn't let up. That night, when I woke after being forced to drink a calming potion, uncle was there on top of me. The lamplight reflected his sneer and I saw the shadow moving and writhing, almost like a dog licking itself. But my uncle and his sidekick didn't know I'd snuck to the village to read the latest letter from the King. They didn't know I knew something. They didn't know I had carved a small cross. He found it in his back after ripping my nightgown from my chest. As he writhed in pain, I grabbed the slobbering black thing with my bare hands and wrestled it to the floor. Back and forth we went. I banged into the wall, then against the brick, but somehow or another I kept holding on, kneading this dough here. It was hard and cold. Cold as death. But still pliable like dough. The strangest thing I ever touched. After a time, I finally had the shadow molded into a pretzel in my hands. Then I threw it in the fire. Next day I was black and blue all over and uncle was hurting from his wound, but the black thing was gone."

Nelia would wait while Grandmama folded the bread over and over, then stretched it out into the shape of a leaf. Later Nelia would get to slash the dough eight times and spread the sugar water over the top of it. Once placed into the oven Grandmama would murmur into the light: "Almost threw my uncle in there as well, but… mercy… he was my brother's father."

Back to the present, Nelia watched the young boy dance closer to his drunken father, then dance back. A dirty flask appeared in the father's hands, its contents giving him the final courage his rage needed to beat his son into a pulp. Nelia swallowed back a scream, forcing her eyes to stay open, her feet at the ready to pull the boy away.

The minute the boy's first swing missed his father, three large shapes appeared on the street. Clearly men, though Nelia was uncertain if they were friend or foe.

Before the light even hit the strangers to the party, the boy tried another swipe at his father, his attention probably so focused on surviving that he didn't see the newcomers to the show. It would have been a perfect punch to the right side of the father's head, were it not for the strong arm that reached out and blocked the punch entirely.

The boy stood stunned. The father staggered back. The sharp whip of the night air whistled through the silent street. Two large arms reached from around the father and pulled him out of the light of the lamppost, where Nelia could barely see him or the other man. Though it didn't much matter: Prince Pokoj's voice had her turning back towards the boy.

She turned her head so quickly her temple grazed the corner of the building. The pain was sharp, exact, but left quickly enough with some rubbing. Once she was certain she wouldn't fall from disorientation, Nelia crept forward as a frog would. She felt a great need within her to hear what the Prince was saying. Why he was there and what would he do? Where would the grace lie? Insight into peaceful and pure justice would be something she could ponder the rest of her life.

"Are you all right? Do you hurt anywhere, Dantruel?" Prince Pokoj asked gently, his hand placed firmly on the boy's shoulders.

Dantruel turned to show the Prince his left ear, where Nelia caught a glimpse of dried blood that had once poured from it.

"My ribs, too."

"What happened?"

Nelia then noticed the energy vibrating from within Dantruel, making his hands and arms shake. Prince Pokoj placed both of his hands on the boy's shoulders and whispered something too low for Nelia to hear. The boy's eyes filled with tears that he angrily swiped away. She wasn't sure if the boy meant to try to push away the Prince's hands as well, but they barely budged. There was too much calm strength in them to be moved.

"Go now and see Xerxes at the palace. You are ready to train. I came just now from your mother's house, so she knows the time has come. But I want you to sleep near her tonight and report tomorrow night to sleep at the compound. Do you understand?"

The boy sniffed, then nodded. His jaws pulled shut, the muscles in his temples swelling with tension.

"And him?" Dantruel spat out, jerking his head toward his father. Nelia looked over to see the older man standing with his head bowed in either shame or sleep – she wasn't certain. One of Prince Pokoj's guards still held his arms back, though the hold was slack.

In Overge the father would receive fifty lashes for fighting while drunk, then he would stay in the deep cellar for two weeks for being drunk in public, though Mayor Billisborth would probably find a reason to keep him there longer. Perhaps the charge of simply interrupting his life of leisure would keep the drunk in the cellar another three weeks.

"I will deal with him."

"But you will not lash him," the boy said. It wasn't a question – more like an accusation. "He deserves lashes."

"Don't you all deserve something?" the Prince asked Dantruel.

"What of you? Do you deserve mercy at all times?"

"I deserve it more than him," Dantruel said, his shoulders shaking with anger and defiance.

But the anger did not dissuade the Prince, nor did it seem to change his patience.

"I understand your anger. His actions do not please me at all. Nor did the actions of his father please me. But my father gives every single person many chances to change themselves."

"Right lot of good change he did the last time. Only lasted about two years."

Prince Pokoj looked directly into Dantruel's eyes, unflinchingly, until the boy allowed calm to come over him.

"Do you know what day is today?" Prince Pokoj asked calmly.

The boy's face remained stone cold for a minute. Then another. Then, suddenly, the light flickered within them and his entire body went limp.

"Yes. He would have been nineteen. Don't you remember why your father only has three fingers on his left hand?"

"The old priest cut the middle one out 'cause he tried to hide my brother."

A muffled sob came from the drunken father, before the man of steel crumbled to the floor in a heap of sobbing.

"Your father is the reason the cry for change went up into the heavens and fell down in Niebo. Your father and four others were the only ones who cried out, who dared to cry out. They are the reason I came. And perhaps the reason you are alive. For you would have had your three years of testing, would you not?"

Dantruel glanced at his father, then nodded at the Prince.

"Forgiveness is not easy, Dantruel," the Prince said. "But when we understand the cycle of pain that people go through, we are able to reflect on something other than just ourselves. I'm not saying it's right that your father treats himself this way and then subsequently you and your mother in a poor manner. But there is deep pain within him that he must deal with, and that needs to be acknowledged. Just as much as the pain within you. Will you be at the tree tomorrow?"

Dantruel swallowed hard, closed his eyes, thought for a minute, then nodded.

"Good," Prince Pokoj said, clapping the boy on the shoulders – a clap that had the lad bending as though a springboard. "Off you go. I need to talk with your father. You won't see him for a while after tomorrow. I just want to let you know."

Dantruel paused in his steps. He glanced at his father, who was now quiet, kneeling on the ground, his head hung in shame. When Dantruel moved forward again, the drunken man said something in his dialect that had his boy nodding and again wiping away tears, but neither one of them moved towards each other. Instead, the moment passed and Dantruel moved out into the night towards the palace.

Prince Pokoj turned and looked in Nelia's direction, a broad smile on his lips.

"Come out now, Nelia," he said politely, teasingly.

Nelia straightened up, her knees groaning in protest at being bent up for so long. Quietly, she limped forward till she was under the lamp.

"Would you like Marvit to take you back?"

Nelia shook her head, warily eyeing the large guard with long, brown hair pulled back into a ponytail.

"I'd rather walk back with you, my lord."

"Very well. But it will be a moment."

With that, Prince Pokoj turned around and headed towards the kneeling man.

"Vincetruce, get up!"

Chapter 10

a purpose

"Yes, my lord," Vincetruce mumbled, his head still handing lower than his shoulders.

Nelia shook her head. She had never liked to receive her punishments, just or not, but her mother had punished her more if she were to hang her head too low. Lower one's eyes, of course; you must know your place, but never lower your head so low that it diminished you in the eyes of the Punisher. It would only make them want to punish you more. Strangely enough, it was true. She had seen the cruel light in people's eyes brighten at the groveling of others. Human nature was cruel, Nelia knew that. If one made themselves seem less than a bug, then the rest of the surrounding people would treat them as such. And what does one do eventually with a bug? One squashes it.

It was very good that Prince Pokoj was not anything like the men in her village who wore the gray mask over their eyes and doled out the punishments. She was curious, though, to see what kind of punishment the Prince would give out. He had spoken so highly of mercy, but what mercy was, specifically, Nelia could never get an answer to. It seemed to her that people who showed mercy ended up getting stomped on and respected less. But then, it was what the pastor always preached. The pastor wasn't someone who seemed able to dole out punishment other than verbal anyway.

"What happened, Vincetruce?" Prince Pokoj asked, his voice low. Almost compassionate. "Were you not able to do better than this after the last time we talked?"

"Lalle ne," Vincetruce said, before shaking his head and switching languages. "Yes. I was. But then I stopped... I just stopped so much."

"You stopped speaking to my father, and you stopped reading, and you stopped believing in yourself."

"It's difficult when life becomes busy."

Prince Pokoj raised his brows.

"Busy?"

Vincetruce shifted on his knees.

"Busy. Hard."

Prince Pokoj waved his guard farther away, then knelt before the man who just a few moments before had seemed ready to pound his son into the ground. He looked so pathetic that Nelia had almost forgotten he was the enemy. He *was* the enemy, she reminded herself, though it didn't seem like the Prince was treating him as one.

"Won't you stand up, Vincetruce?"

Again, with that gentle voice. Nelia hadn't heard anything like that voice since her grandfather had died. Or since the first few days after Zayzay had died. There was no memory other than fog for those first few days, but she could hear Aaron's voice, soft and melodic, saying something soothing. What it was, she didn't know. Her memory was too fuzzy, as though strong medication had influenced her mind during those days.

Vincetruce raised his head as he stood to his feet, though he didn't look towards the Prince. He looked far off. Right at Nelia. The surprise on his face would have been comical had he not inspired so much fear within her in the moments leading up to the Prince showing up. When the surprise faded, it was replaced with an inflexibility that Nelia had seen so many times in men who lived hard lives. Between his frame of steel and the scars around his bare arms and hands, Nelia knew he was a man who had worked the worst jobs in life. Aaron had a scar just like the curved one on Vincetruce's left bicep. It was from the wheat sickle. Vincetruce, like Aaron, seemed lucky to have his left arm.

"When life gets hard, you should come to me, Vincetruce. Instead, it looks like you went back to the bottle."

"Fate took away another baby from me. My wife goes between blaming it on the village leaving behind Krimaltin, and your father not caring enough for us."

"Yes." The Prince frowned. "I just came from speaking with Angeluxa. She seems confused and upset. I left a guard at your house for her. She needs guidance, Vincetruce, and your job is to be that guidance. You are the one who should remind her what the truth is. You should always stand behind her, holding her up. You should not care so much what she says, but be the one who catches her tears. She carried your daughter for nine months. The fever that took her away is not her fault and not your fault. You must tell her, remind her often, of how leaving behind Krimlatin left behind a life of fear and terror and death. My father has not given you anything but life."

"My daughter has no *life*," Vincetruce protested.

The Prince did not falter in his patience, as Nelia's Grandmama would have. She never had patience for doubt, for people believing the world should be perfect simply because the King was perfect. *We'll be perfect when you get perfect,* she used to say, laying the blame back on the person complaining.

The black cloud puffed out into the air again, oozing around Vincetruce's ankles. As he breathed in the cloud seemed to tighten, then stretch. The prince ignored the cloud completely, giving it no attention. It seemed to Nelia the wrong reaction to have to such a large cloud. The black magic did not work inside the castle and rarely appeared within the walls of Niebo, but the farther out of the walls, the more she saw grey forms. Nelia had always imagined the Prince would cut the shadows down each time he saw them, but he never did.

It was as though they weren't even worth that much consideration.

"The King cares very much for your daughter," Prince Pokoj said. "He cares very much for you and your son, and for Angeluxa. And he did not send that fever. That fever comes from bacteria that grows on the ground where the feces of cattle and other animals are not properly removed. Humidity encourages the bacteria to grow; rain and floods spread it further into the roadways, and then it comes to town through wheels, then feet, then hands. It's preventable, but difficult to stop once allowed to grow. And the King has set in place people who know how to prevent it. Unfortunately, the world is not perfect. And humans are not perfect. And we have yet to get to a point where everything works in unison."

"Also, the doctor wouldn't come to us or give us the medicine."

Prince Pokoj sighed.

"I have spoken to the Mayor about that. He will not change, so we have brought in people to talk to the villagers about changing him out. But we must find someone to run against him. And I believe that someone is you."

Vincetruce snapped his head up so quickly that Nelia flinched. She expected Vincetruce to be full of expectation and flattery at the suggestion that the Prince thought him good enough to run for mayor. Being a mayor made one practically royalty. But instead of flattered, Vincetruce seemed angry.

"Are you mocking me, sir?"

Nelia raised her brows at the lowering of Prince Pokoj's title, but the Prince said nothing. He didn't even blink. Mayor Billisworth would have taken the man to court to sue him for everything he had, but not Prince Pokoj. He took abuse without flinching, without getting angry. It confounded Nelia. She couldn't help but wait for the shoe to drop that would suddenly make Prince Pokoj snap. Just like everything else about him, she was certain it would be interesting to see.

"I might tease you when you are in a better mood, Vincetruce, but I do not mock. Ever. I have come here to find you and to start you on your journey, on the pathway that the King has set forth before you. Some things kept you from doing it before – that kept you from stepping into the right path, but now the time is right. You could always choose not to do what the King has prepared you to do, but there will be consequences, you know."

"Consequences for me?"

Prince Pokoj looked to the sky with a sad smile playing on his lips.

"Consequences for everyone. Each time someone chooses not to do what the King created them to do, there are consequences. Like Nelia's village. It's a small village lacking a science teacher. Her mayor is qualified to be one, but finds himself too important to do such a job. This has caused a greater problem with the water supply and the drainage system, because there is no one in Overge now who can manage the science of making those things right. There was a man whose skill is to be a doctor, so he studied it, over in Turkenshtoop, but after working for a few years he decided to set aside his medical degree and spend his life painting. Could he have done both things? Certainly. But he chose to do only one and spend the rest of his time fishing and taking care of himself. As a result, the fever came and took out about half the village. The King knew that this man could have saved his people, but he chose not to. The King asked this man to be a doctor for exactly that moment he could save people, but the man chose not to." Prince Pokoj shrugged. "There are always consequences."

"And what would the consequences be if I chose not to run for mayor?"

"I do not know the details. The King did not tell them to me. But perhaps a more ruthless mayor will win. Or perhaps nothing will ever change and generation upon generation will have to live in the separation of groups as you do now, where people with your blood do not receive the same care as the people with the Mayor's blood."

"Cities have had civil wars for less."

Prince Pokoj nodded. "True."

There was a silence for a moment.

"But running will be difficult. It will be easy for my opponent to focus on my downfalls, such as drunkenness and being seen in the street ready to fight my son."

"I never said that it would be easy. And I never said that you would win."

Vincetruce whipped his head around at that point.

"Winning is not necessarily the point. Showing people they shouldn't be living this way anymore, that things should be equal, is the point. Everyone should be treated fairly and the same. The King does not differentiate between the people in his kingdom. Neither should the people differentiate amongst themselves."

Vincetruce furrowed his brows at the same time Nelia felt herself doing the same.

"Yes, what is it?" Prince Pokoj asked, clamping his hand strongly on the man's shoulder, which made him sway at the unexpected movement. Nelia had almost forgotten that the man was very drunk; he held himself up so well under the gaze of the Prince. But now it was obvious again, and that observable sway made Vincetruce clear his throat, stamp his feet and visibly try to dig his heels into the ground to keep himself from moving.

"But if you appoint me to run, shouldn't I win?"

Prince Pokoj shook his head.

"People misconstrue this point all the time. Just because I ask you to do a job doesn't mean that you will forever have that job. Just because my father asks you to run for office or apply for a position or ask for something, it doesn't mean everything will work out exactly as you imagine it will."

"What, then, is the point?"

"First, obedience shows that you care about His Majesty the King and you trust that he has the best in mind for you. Second, there could be something bigger that must be worked on. In one circumstance, it could be that a person needs to gain confidence, or learn humility, or perhaps learn another lesson. Sometimes it is the people around you who need to learn a lesson from what will come of your obedience."

"In my case?"

"I can give you my thoughts, though the king has not told me the details about what will happen to you. But, knowing Croizante, I see that there is more for the people to learn. Like learning that a person can change, that putting a person down for mistakes they have made and never forgiving them or giving them a second chance will hurt not only the person they are prejudiced against, but themselves. They must learn that encouraging one to change, to become stronger, to become the person they are meant to be, allows everyone to become better. If you can become better, if you can get out of your ditch of depression and self-deprecation, can't someone else? The people of Croizante also need to hear the truth of what needs to change here.

Then, for you, I see that perhaps running for office will give you a purpose beyond what you give yourself. Running for office will give you a reason to get sober. But at the same time, you will get a lesson in humility."

Vincetruce widened his eyes at that last part. Nelia blew out a staggered breath and thought hard of whether she would obey.

"Public humility."

"More like public humiliation," Vincetruce mumbled.

"Do you deserve any less?"

The question surprised Nelia. Was this Prince Pokoj, the one who was so gracious and loving and humble and never put anyone down?

"I guess not."

"Listen, Vincetruce, if you run, if you obey, your success will be measured in how much you learn and grow from the experience. If you try to run without apologizing to your wife, without humbling yourself to your family, you will soon find yourself defending the indefensible: your previous actions. Because the journal will come after you as well as the people siding with your opponent. If you do not humble yourself, people will not learn that change is possible. They will not see beyond you as a non-perfect candidate to the issues that the village has, but they will only see you and the mistakes you have made and then have to defend either you or the current mayor – and not necessarily for the future you will bring, but for the mistakes you have made in the past. A disaster, basically. Plus, you will come away more hardened. If you win your ego will grow and your heart will be hardened. If you lose, you will become bitter."

"Not so good, the picture you paint," Vincetruce said.

"It is better if you humble yourself. Do you think that might be the main lesson you should learn?"

Vincetruce shrugged.

"I need my bed. I need to think."

"And talk to your wife?"

"And apologize to my son."

Prince Pokoj patted him on the shoulder again, gently this time.

"That's my good man. I'll be round tomorrow to talk to you again before I leave. Johan, walk back with him, will you?"

Johan stepped into the light, giving a barely perceptible nod to the Prince. Still, Vincetruce hesitated, looking at the ground before his Prince, his hips swaying a tiny bit as though to unlock his feet from the ground.

"Come, man, you need your rest," Prince Pokoj said, stepping in closer to Vincetruce. The rest of what he said did not arrive at Nelia's ears, and for that, she was slightly annoyed. The scene before her was almost as good as those novellas from the south that were played out at times in the village theater. She watched still, though she couldn't hear either the mumbling from Vincetruce that seemed to have tears along with it nor the Prince's strong words in an encouraging tone that made Nelia jealous. Then Prince Pokoj wrapped the drunken man in his arms and held him for a moment as though he was a father hugging a lost son. When they separated from each other, Vincetruce sucked in a deep breath and left with Johan, who stood steadily by.

Once Vincetruce left, Prince Pokoj turned to Nelia and held out his hand.

"Shall we go back to the palace? I'm sure the dinner guests are wondering where we are."

Nelia stepped out of the shadows with a smile.

"I'm quite certain they are wondering where you are, but not I. I told them I would eat in my room."

"And why is that, Nelia?"

Twilight glistened over the mountain village. Overhead a large, yellow moon hung low with a handful of twinkling stars glittering in the sky overhead. Prince Pokoj strolled confidently through the streets towards the palace. Looking ahead down the boulevard that was lined with trees now casting their immense shadows onto the street from the lampposts, Nelia saw the palace lit up with movement inside. Soft music wafted down from where the palace was nestled into the side of the mountain, along with a cool breeze. With the town now so quiet, Nelia could hear a waterfall in the distance, as well as bats finding their dinner.

"Will you come with me tomorrow?" Nelia asked. "To Overge, I mean."

"I will start the journey with you, but unfortunately I cannot make the entire journey."

"But you said that you wished to see Aaron."

"And I do," Prince Pokoj said, grinning at her. "But there are other things my father charged me with doing. And I must obey them."

They walked silently while Nelia gathered her feelings up from the ground. Knowing the Prince would leave her at some point during the day was not what she wished to hear. Being in the net of his safety was sweet; it caused her not to have to always look over her shoulder, which cooled her nerves.

"You're disappointed, Nelia?"

Nelia looked up to see herself becoming ever more encased in a sparkling bubble.

"Yes," she sighed. "I must admit that I am. I enjoy your presence."

Prince Pokoj did not reply at first but elected instead to continue walking through the town. They came along to the large gate at the road that would take them to the palace doors. The Prince did not attempt to walk through the gate, nor did he wave his hand impatiently for it to open. No. He stopped, his stature comfortably relaxed under the light, and called out to the guard smoking near the trees. Looking up and seeing Prince Pokoj, the guard beamed before shouting what sounded like an announcement to someone behind him. Within minutes, his colleagues poured out of the guardhouse like children scrambling to see the Christmas tree. The smoker laughed, mocking his friends in the local dialect. The fresh, direct way of these men made Nelia smile. They reminded her greatly of her grandfather and his friends. Overjoyed, happy men always made her smile. It seemed to her more genuine than when women teased each other. More innocent and better received.

She watched as the youngest soldier ran ahead of all the others, leaping over the small pile of sandbags and the trip arm lever that kept people from approaching the gatehouse. The scene reminded Nelia of Ivory's son until the last millimeter of the soldier's boot got caught on the lever. Within a split second, he was sprawled on the ground. His comrades were merciless in their laughter.

Nelia couldn't help but laugh as well. Even the boy, who rose with his face redder than when it had hit the ground, was laughing. Prince Pokoj was chuckling too, though he also was the one who held out his hand to the boy.

When someone called out what must have been a jab, the boy was quick to reply, his reply sending ripples of laughter through the soldiers and Prince Pokoj.

But within a minute, the event turned somber when the young soldier suddenly dropped to one knee and gave a low bow to Prince Pokoj. There he stayed for two minutes, the time of formal bowing in the kingdom of Niebo. When Prince Pokoj finally grabbed him with another hearty laugh, the two men hugged as though long-lost brothers. Nelia watched as the boy produced a picture of a baby from his jacket and the Prince once again showed his joy, giving the baby a special blessing.

The other soldiers were respectful for the sacred moment, but they weren't about to allow their youngest recruit to take all the time with the Prince. Soon they were jokingly shoving him aside. Even so, the young boy couldn't stop smiling. It was obvious he had got what he wanted and was content with that. He split the rest of the time between staring at the baby in the picture and paying attention to the jovial conversation around him. Each soldier practically lined up to hug their Prince, though they tried to pretend they were not. Nelia thought of kindergarteners lining up to see Kerstman, or Sankt Nicolaus, as the people here would call him. She covered her mouth to keep from giggling out loud. What separated them from the kindergarteners was that each soldier ended his encounter with the Prince by giving a deep and reverential bow.

After a few more jokes and blessings, Prince Pokoj took his leave of the soldiers and motioned to Nelia to join him. With a quick curtsy to the soldiers, Nelia rushed up to Prince Pokoj, who took her by the arm and walked through the gate with her. The soldiers barely looked at her, so occupied were they in talking amongst each other, which gave her hope that perhaps the whole town was too busy living right to spread rumors of her presence with the Prince.

"Now, Nelia, will you not come down to dinner with everyone?"

His voice was firm and yet so warm, enticing her to say yes. Yes. The very thought brought goosebumps to her arms; her heart skipped a beat, and all moisture left her mouth. Surely the guest list was full of nobility. She had survived the lunch with the King, but what made her think she could survive dinner unscathed with the nobility here in Croizante? It was too much to think about, all the things that could go wrong. Foolish mistakes, one after the other, appeared in her mind, so she quickly formed a rejection to the Prince – another action that caused her heart to skip a beat.

"I prefer my room, my lord," she finally stuttered out as they entered the palace. One of the ladies-in-waiting, sitting on a plush, velveteen bench near the door, stood when she saw Nelia. As though waiting specifically for her. "I would like some time to process the wonderful day I have had."

"I understand, Nelia," Prince Pokoj said, grasping her hand to kiss it lightly. "Rest peacefully. I will see you in the morning."

After a deep curtsy to the man who impressed her even above her husband, Nelia turned to the lady-in-waiting, who nodded slightly before heading to the stairs draped in thick, lush carpet. Nelia's mind was already on the savory feast she hoped was waiting for her in her room.

Chapter 11

meeting Zanderi

The next morning came, as all mornings do. The great exception was that for the second time in over a decade, Nelia awoke somewhere other than in her own sagging bed. Today she awoke in a plush, down-filled mattress that snuggled up to her hips and legs, and yet her back was not stiff or painful. She felt like a child in the wee hours of the morning, snuggling down into the warmth of a large bed and hoping perhaps there will be more time to sleep. With as little energy exerted as possible, Nelia focused on the heaviness of her body against the mattress, the way each bone lay in the warm bed, the coziness that enveloped every fiber of her being.

Was it not just yesterday that she had awoken in another strange bed? Where mice droppings were piled in the corner, and the curtains and blankets had been eaten away by moths? Having seen the mattress in that room wriggle slightly when touched, Nelia had opted for sleeping on the dusty floor with the mat she had brought from home and then left behind, not wanting any of the filth that clung to it from the hostel. Perhaps her accommodations would have bothered her on a different day, perhaps she might have bemoaned her inability to afford better any other day, but yesterday it hadn't mattered. Yesterday she had taken it all in with a sigh and a set jaw and left for her last hour-long journey as quickly as possible.

This morning, sunlight filtered in through the windows without hindrance. The glass within them was sparkling clean, not dingy from years of tobacco smoke and dirt as the ones from the day before. The plush, velvet curtains absorbed the light, allowing it to filter into the room only where they were not doubled in warm, red tones that spread across the bed and seemed to heat her more than the low fire and heavy quilts already did.

Nelia envisioned herself as a grand dame with all the time in the world to lie in her bed. She was not needed to cook or clean or do anything today at all. She was not needed to bake the bread or go out to her garden and chickens. And so, she would stay in the bed like a queen instead of setting her feet on the cold floor. The heavy bulk of three rich quilts weighed comfortably on her stomach. Lighting the kitchen fire had been her first job in the morning since her fifth birthday, which required her to wake up before anyone else. But today someone else had started the fire. Today she was still in bed and the sun seemed halfway overhead already.

Nelia closed her eyes again, then lazily opened them to the sunlight a few minutes later. Time seemed to stand still for a moment as her brain took in her surroundings each time she woke, then swirled them around to become even more beautiful in her dreams.

On her fifth or sixth time waking, the heavy door to the hallway opened and in wafted the scent of fresh tea and bacon.

Real bacon. From a hog.

Not the stuff the villagers in Overge were given at the mandatory meetings in the town square. The strips with centers too pink, like a crayon, and the fat part too mushy to be anything close to animal protein. Not to mention the smell. From experience, she knew there were at least two smells that, when fake, were obvious to the nose: banana and bacon.

Nelia frowned, her stomach turning at the memory of the last mandatory town meeting. She had squished as many pieces of fake pork as she could between two pieces of bread. Well, bread was a generous term when the mayor was no longer shy about showing the sawdust pieces in the bread loaves. If anyone complained, he made a spectacle of the person who thought the town was "made of gold, wealthy enough to feed the entire people for each meeting". When one man had once challenged aloud that there was no real reason for those meetings except to force them into compliance with new nonsense laws, that man was taken out and not seen from for another month. He returned from his time in the tower gaunt and mute.

Upon seeing him Nelia had wondered what it took to make a once strong man mute, but no answer ever came to her. An unknown fear kept her from asking her own husband or the mute man's wife. Curiosity killed the cat, as her grandmama used to say. The dark spirit that gripped her when she thought of that man convinced her that perhaps death would come to her should she find out. Death of the mind and soul, at the very least. And which was worse? After coming to grips with Zayzay's death, when she had just recently decided that life might be worth living, did she want to know what made it worth living only in silence?

When she saw the man or his wife now Nelia forced herself to swallow her thoughts back down into the pit of her stomach. At the last meeting, she had kept her eyes down, eating the fake bacon between two pieces of sawdust-bread and pushing aside her dread for the pains that would come the next day from the bread trying to make its way through her intestines. If she had a dog she could do as many at her table did and feed it to them. Though, only three months ago, Bettira's little mutt had fallen over and died midway through eating his third helping of the stuff. No one had proof, but of course, they all blamed the food.

"Good morning, Miss Nelia," rang a sweet voice from the corner. It was one of the maids from the evening before. The one who had merely stared at her when she'd admitted to having no luggage, not even a nightgown.

"Good morning," Nelia answered, noting that her voice was still rather dreamlike. And why shouldn't it be? Looking around, she felt like she was dreaming. Who would have ever guessed that she, Nelia Bitrovia, would wake up in a palace under velveteen curtains? Perhaps someone could have guessed that she might be a servant in such a place. Perhaps. Though not without changing her accent.

"Do you like bacon, madam? I brought you some, though not too much in case you dislike it. That Madame Buneburr abhors it, they tell me," the small woman said, imitating a rich woman's tone and accent on 'abhors'. "Which is all fine by me, since I'm allowed to eat whatever the guests do not eat. And when they do not even touch it, well! That is a treat. But whoever heard of a person who doesn't eat bacon? I no longer need it – not like when we were little lasses and mother always said that we needed fat on our bones. Still, I like it, and since it's cured I can keep it in my pocket wrapped with soft bread to bring home to my little ones, who love it as much as I do. Perhaps more!"

The maid dissolved into a fit of giggles at the suggestion. Nelia smiled, but her mind was too preoccupied with the idea the maid had just given her to laugh. Unfortunately, her lack of laughter caused a small, thin, snake-like gray cloud to move around the maid's bosom.

"I do like bacon," Nelia said, too late. When the maid only gave a nod in silence, Nelia changed her tone as she had seen the young women in Overge do when they were trying to get their lovers to buy them something grand or expensive. "I looooove bacon. It is probably one of my faaaaavorite things to eat. Really. I can't blame your children. They must think you are a saint! Able to keep that beautiful bacon wrapped up in your pocket without ever touching it just to give it to them! How you must looooove them!"

The maid blushed. The gray cloud loosened.

"What is your name?" Nelia asked, breathing a slight sigh of relief.

"Zanderi," the woman said. "And I do love them, yes, I do. I would do anything for them. Even when there wasn't much to be had, I did whatever I could for them. You know that around here, right after the Prince first came through and we stopped that horrific act, you know the one – well, things weren't so good. We had a few people move away. Rich ones. Come to find out it's all because they couldn't control us anymore. That's what my husband says, anyway. I'm not sure exactly why. I just know they left. And then there were the factories and the shops that sold us things that supposedly protected our children from getting picked. They moved away too. Then there was that whole ring of people, now I never knew about this until after they all left, but I am told that there was a whole market of paying someone off to take the name of your child out of the pot. Of course, that is just like some folks. But that's how so many rich people got to keep their kids. And how so many poor folks lost their babies. Though here in Croizante it isn't just about the money, you know. It's also about having the right eyes. If your eyes slant too much upwards than you are typically of Duwarant descent. See? I have about a quarter of Duwarant in me. My husband is over half. That is why our kids are pretty well accepted, though his grandmother and mother, who are full, were none too pleased that my husband married down. But they don't understand that times have changed and that being full Duwarant isn't supposed to matter as much anymore. It just isn't supposed to."

"Though I'm guessing it still does in many places, doesn't it?" Nelia asked. "That is much like in my town. There are some things that will never change. No matter how many things you contribute to society, the prejudice gets passed down like the flu."

"My husband says it passes through the blood, though I don't much agree with him because if that were true my children would be warring inside themselves all the time. Him, too. And I quite believe that the three-quarters of me would be killing off the one-quarter of me if it were in my blood. Don't you think? Then I'd be quite a mess, I suppose."

"Though perhaps our blood is wise enough not to fight against that which would kill the good parts as well. For how would you kill one-quarter of yourself? Cut off your arms or your legs? One ear, some fingers, and a breast?"

Zanderi smiled. The long, gray snake did not tighten, but it did not go away. Not for the first time in her life, Nelia wished her eyes weren't so open. Most people could not see the white or gray clouds;

they could only see it when the clouds were black, hence the name of Black Magic. But Nelia had been able to see them from the time she had been a small girl. A gift was what Grandmama called it, always asking her what she saw on who. A hoax for attention, Mother had called it.

"That's what I told him. We women think alike, we do. Sometimes I think a man probably would cut off one-quarter of himself if it were needed."

"Perhaps if needed, but not because his own blood was too ignorant to know what was good for the whole body."

That sounded too book-read. Nelia knew it the moment it was out of her mouth. Though she took a long time to read them, she had come to love to read books when Aaron was away to war. They helped her feel like she wasn't alone. Reading was not something any other friend or family member liked to do, and they often teased her when her language didn't quite match the intelligence 'they knew she really had'. Aaron always said that sounding knowledgeable and being knowledgeable were two different things. He always nodded her way when saying it.

The look on Zanderi's face gave away her emotions. The gray cloud also darkened slightly and seemed to hiss like a snake for a moment, though Nelia was willing to claim it was her own imagination. It didn't matter if the cloud hissed or not. What was certain was that she had lost points with Zanderi with that last statement. Or perhaps it was the culmination of all of her statements.

When the maid gave a curt nod, her lips pursed together, Nelia suspected she might leave. But Zanderi was more professional than that. She shut her mouth tight before hefting the wooden table up to the bed, where it sprouted legs suddenly. With a look of concentration that reminded Nelia of Zayzay carrying the milk to the table, Zanderi brought the tray over and carefully placed it in front of her. Nelia pushed her hips one by one up against the back of the bed, taking a deep breath in to clear Zayzay from her head. He would otherwise make her entire attitude drop to a low that would have her lying in bed all day. Thoughts of Zayzay brought on her the most danger of the Black Magic taking over. And once it came in, it was very difficult to get it to leave. She did not want the embarrassment of leaving black magic within this beautiful room.

Pushing aside her thoughts of her small son, Nelia focused on this first experience ever of having breakfast in bed. It was the kind of thing she read in the half-penny story papers or from snippets of eavesdropped conversations in town, but never had she before eaten in her bed. The wooden legs of the small table trapped her own legs underneath the breakfast, but she didn't feel at all claustrophobic. The excitement was too much to bother feeling the need to escape it. The warmth from the hot plates mixed with the cool breeze that entered through the open window was the perfect, cozy combination. To be sure, it was all she had ever envisioned and more.

Nelia smiled at her luck. Not even the day after giving birth to Zayzay had she been treated this nicely! Aaron had barely gotten home in time to see the little boy born. He fell asleep the moment the baby was pushed out and seen to be as perfect as babies can be, then slept for twelve hours as though he had been the one to do the work of birthing. Nelia had awoken with a tremendous hunger that was only half relieved by drinking her tea with a ration of sugar and a bowl of thin milk with hard bread. There was no other food, as she hadn't cooked while trying to birth her son.

Nelia lifted one cover, revealing a plate with about three pieces of bacon. The savory meat entered her watering mouth and almost instantly the fat dissolved against her tongue, leaving the toasted meat part to chew, which she did with glee. Nelia closed her eyes to fully enjoy the taste of the fattening meat, opening them to find Zanderi nodding with narrowed, thoughtful eyes.

"I can get ye some more," Zanderi said affirmatively. "Tea or coffee?"

"Coffee with cream and sugar," Nelia said, the wrapped tea bags already full of tea leaves having given her an idea. "Would you tell if I take the tea on my journey with me?"

Zanderi looked at her sharply for a moment, then broke into a smile. But the smile did not rise to her eyes and Nelia noticed the gray snake of air was wrapping itself around and around Zanderi's ankles. She would trip over her own pride soon, it seemed.

"You're like me, ain't you? Like I'd be if I became rich suddenly? You ain't got those precise manners of those women who were born with a golden spoon in their mouths. Of course you can take it with you! And look, I have sausages and pancakes, and sardines, and some juice. Would you like me to bring you more? Do you have children? I could wrap some up with bread if you wish. The only trick is getting past your dogs if you have them. They love bacon as well, you know. Do you know, once I waited on a lady who fed the bacon to her dog? Her dog! I almost cried out in pain, I did! But then I once gave some extra that'd been touched by a customer to my own dog. They have to eat too."

"But you make a good living here in the palace, don't you, Zanderi? I would think you have quite a nice salary."

Zanderi smiled politely as she uncovered a plate filled with eggs, a jar with jam spilling over and a cup of drumjing juice. Nelia's nose wrinkled at the smell. Too sweet for the morning. She never had liked that juice. Not that she had ever had it growing up, but the woman whose house she cleaned once in a while to earn money drank it all the time: Mrs. Viviez Xiu. She claimed to be a philanthropist, but in reality, she was a rich woman who liked to remind people what place they were supposed to inhabit. Nelia had been chosen from five other girls who had applied to clean her house. Mrs. Xiu made such a grand thing of it, as though it was a great honor. And being paid was the most humiliating experience. Mrs. Xiu always did it on the porch, speaking as loudly as she could to make sure as many people as were walking by could hear. She would run down half the list of things Nelia had cleaned or fixed for her, then make a grand exaggeration of how much she was paying so that 'those who have nothing might experience some relief in their expenses'. Every year Mrs. Xiu was nominated for and won the medal for philanthropy in Overge. Every single year.

"Would you like the drumjing juice, Zanderi?"

The young woman drew back, her eyes narrowed.

"I can't just drink or eat in front of you, my lady. No matter what kind of background you come from. And yes, I do make a good living here. I like my job and I do not aim to ruin it by taking my tea with a lady guest."

Nelia swallowed against the stinging rebuke. It widened within her a fear her mother had once told her was ridiculous: the fear of not knowing how to conduct herself. Her mother had called it ridiculous when Nelia had explained as a thirteen-year-old that she didn't know how to act if ever invited to the Mayor's house for dinner. Her mother had scoffed and said that since it would never happen it was a waste of energy to worry about it. If only her mother could see her now, in a palace where Nelia knew nothing of the customs. So, in fact, her fear was not so ridiculous.

This irrational fear was also the reason she had never gone to the open coffees at the school when Zayzay had started, and why she would never even try to win the tickets to the annual ball. Nelia knew she could handle herself on a farm and with the preacher or some of the other richer farmers, but her raw manners were evidence of her lower birth. No matter that they came from probably the same class – Zanderi saw a distinction between the two of them. And the smirk that played on Zanderi's lips was not something Nelia could read. Was she laughing at her, or was she wondering why Nelia was there in the first place?

Nelia sighed. She took a few bites of pancakes, refusing to look up to the maid. When Zanderi finally turned away, Nelia covered the drumjing juice up again, breathing once again through her nose. Even with the juice covered, Nelia felt as though the entire morning was dissolving into a catastrophe.

"I'm going home today, Zanderi," Nelia said in the most neutral tone available to her at that moment. "I would appreciate a bit more bacon to keep me moving through the day, and perhaps I will take one bacon sandwich as well. Although that ham sandwich from last night was delicious."

"I'll have Mrs. Funberie wrap a ham sandwich for you before you go. What time will you leave?"

"Are you trying to be rid of me?" Nelia asked, laughing, though Zanderi said nothing as she folded the blanket that had fallen onto the floor.

"Not to be rid of ye," Zanderi said, though her eyes said otherwise. "Just to be at the ready with a lunch pail for you and my chores done so I can get home at a right decent time."

"Are there times you don't get back home?"

"When a grand lady needs help with her packing and such, I have to stay and work on it. Some people prefer not to leave the palace until the last moment, so they leave at night, and some don't wish to go home at all. There was once a lady they assigned me to that took three days to get her things packed and gone on home," Zanderi said with a laugh. "Mrs. Funberie had to come herself and tell the lady that if she didn't leave, the mayor would have to start charging her room and board. 'Tis just like some grand madams, thinking they can stay or go anywhere they like and never pay for anything."

"What is the saying? 'When you are rich, you can leave your pocketbook at home because everything becomes free'."

"Seems that way," Zanderi said, shaking her head. "Doesn't seem right, though. When you are blessed with such a life, it seems you should share a bit with those of us born at the bottom. I'm waiting for the day the King turns things bottom-up. Hope I'm alive for it."

"Will he do that one day?"

"I was told he said as much long ago in one of them newspapers He sends out. We don't have a copy of the old ones here in Croizante, but a man who passes through selling tonics and medicines told me."

Nelia sipped her coffee; the rich, earthy taste mixed with real cream and real sugar was too delicious for her to pay close attention to what Zanderi was saying. The moment the dark liquid hit her tongue, it was all she thought of. Her mind was quite made up: more expensive coffee was worth it. Then she recanted. Perhaps it was that coffee not mixed with ground acorns was worth it.

Also, cream. Real cream. That made another difference.

Nelia smiled to herself. Two weeks. She needed to wait only two more weeks until she could wean their new young calf and drink the milk from their cow themselves. She took another sip. Cream. Real cream. In two weeks when all the milk would be for her and Aaron, with any leftovers sold in the market, she would feel like a queen every morning. When that day came, Nelia vowed to close her eyes and sip her acorn-coffee with cream and remember this moment right now.

"Try the scones," Zanderi prompted, though rather coldly. Nelia opened her eyes again and obeyed automatically. "Good, aren't they?"

"Very good," Nelia said, shoving more into her mouth. She was fully awake now, and her stomach wanted to be full again. It would be hard to wake up tomorrow in her own bed and teach her stomach to be content with crusts of bread left over from the night before.

Zanderi organized things around the room that were already organized as Nelia ate her full-fat sausage, fried egg and the other strips of bacon.

"What is the jam for?" she asked Zanderi as she carefully pushed the tray away, her stomach full to the top.

"Didn't you see the biscuits?"

Nelia stretched her arms and legs with a shudder.

"No, but it doesn't matter. I couldn't have fitted them in. I'm not quite sure my dress will fit now!"

Zanderi shook at the old dress with a raised brow. Some sparkles seemed to drop from the dress into a puddle on the floor. But the reminder that the sparkles existed at all made Nelia roll back her shoulders and lift her chin, though she was quite certain it made her look ridiculous. She was, after all, dressed in a borrowed nightgown with an old, tattered dress for herself to wear.

"I can pack the biscuits up for you," Zanderi suggested, busying herself with the tub that was off to the corner of the room. Nelia marveled as water came out of the spout with the turn of a wheel. All the way up to the sixth floor and over to that corner! Steam rose from the bath as it filled up. Not only did water appear magically, but it was already hot. If not for embarrassment at being ignorant, Nelia would have greatly loved to see what kind of operation downstairs made all of this possible. No matter what the cause of this magic, it would be too expensive to save her from getting water from the well each time they bathed or wished to drink.

"Would you like a packed picnic?" Zanderi asked again, her impatience slipping into view.

"A packed picnic would be wonderful," Nelia murmured, slipping behind the screen to take her borrowed nightgown off. Once out from under Zanderi's hearing Nelia mumbled, the words only a vibration to the outside world, "I am worthy. I am the King's."

Suddenly she felt as though the King's voice vibrated through her. She could once again feel his fingers on his chin and the burning through her body that his piercing eyes gave her. What was it he had said to her last?

Not from your womb, my child, but from a rock. Keep your eyes peeled all around you as you walk home, and you will find what you are searching for.

The memory caused such a swirl of emotions that Nelia had to steady herself before stepping out from behind the screen.

"Zanderi," Nelia said as she dipped herself into the warm water smelling of lavender. "Please pack a picnic for two. I plan to stop on my way home."

Zanderi nodded her head, before leaving with the mostly empty tray.

Chapter 12

one's place

Dressed, smelling of lavender and standing next to her packed picnic bundled up in a pail, Nelia looked over the room she had had the honor of spending the night in and sighed heavily. Somewhere in the distance, a church bell rang, the hour echoing off the sides of the mountains. Nelia counted, leaving the echoes to themselves, coming exactly to nine. Nine in the morning. She had never gotten such a late start to the day in all her life. Perhaps the only time had been when she was sick with a fever at fifteen.

Glimpsing herself in the long mirror. Nelia gave a small twirl and laughed for two reasons. The first was that she couldn't believe how well she looked. Refreshed. That was how she looked. It was the word that both her mother and Aaron's mother used when talking about the effects that Niebo had on a person, and they were right. Her skin still shone as though rubbed with diamond dust, her eyes were no longer dragged down by the puffy skin of exhaustion, she no longer looked malnourished, and the smile playing on her lips made her look like a woman who had nothing to lose. Who was she to look as though she had no care in the world?

She also laughed because she could not imagine her mother allowing her to sleep in and drag her feet in getting ready for the morning, even as a baby. Her mother used to brag about how she had been back to work in her city job the day after Nelia was born, with Nelia strapped to a board on her back. That memory brought Nelia's hand up to the back of her own head to the slightly flattened skull. Her grandmother always attributed it to the board Nelia had been strapped to for four months before her mother had given up the city to go home to Overge. Husbandless, but with a child. It had caused quite a stir amongst those who knew her mother.

"But you are none of that, Nelia," she told her reflection. "You will not go back to those downright awful identities you took on because you thought that taking them on would one day get them to accept you. They don't do anything but pull you down from the inside out. So, cast off those things! You are not a bastard. You are not stupid. You are not ugly. You are not worthless. You are not poor. You are not taking up space. You, Nelia, are a friend of the King. No, more than that. You are his daughter! And that is who you will be forevermore!"

The air glowed brighter around her the more she spoke. Nelia's smile became broader in the mirror and her skin sparkled as it had the day before at the palace. Even her eyes shone with wonder and splendor.

She looked like a whole new person. And the effect was dazzling.

"Madame," Zanderi called from the doorway. "Oh! What a difference a bath made for you!"

"It's not the bath, Zanderi, it's a new identity."

"As you wish," the maid answered, lowering her head in confusion.

"It is the identity of the King placed over me through my speaking of the words He gave me. You have an identity, too. You should go one day and find it."

Zanderi fiddled with the lampshade, rubbing away invisible dust from it.

"I know the King. I follow him."

"You've gone to see him?" Nelia asked, excited to have another person's story to hear.

"Gracious no!" answered Zanderi. "I know my place, and my place does not include the King's palace."

"But you've received an invitation?"

"Of course," Zanderi said with a shrug. "Doesn't everyone? It isn't anything special."

"I think getting a personalized letter from the King is a nice gesture and definitely means something."

Zanderi looked up then, her eyes fixed on Nelia's.

"I believe in the King and follow his ways and only his ways. But I don't believe in leaving one's place. There is still meaning in it. There is an order to things, like being born. You don't choose your parents, or the order you're born in. You take it all with a grain of salt. If we could all choose where we wanted to live, then we would all be in the palaces and not in the fields. I suspect that your place is in the fields; I just hope that you aren't so carried away with your visit to this palace that you neglect the fields you are to take care of. Because if all the farmers were to forget their fields then we would all starve. So, no, I have not gone. Yes, I do have an invitation. But I believe the King will reward me one day when I lie dying as he looks over my life and sees that I stayed in my place and did the things that were expected of me due to my birth."

Nelia said nothing. Was it not just yesterday that she had been standing in the palace, assuming that the entire invitation was a hoax and that she was about to get harassed and punished for thinking herself high and mighty enough to come to the palace? How quickly her entire view of the King and her own place in the world had changed.

"Are you ready to leave then, madam?" Zanderi asked coolly. "You know that the Prince already left?"

A zip of disappointment ran through Nelia, but with the discipline that a life of struggle brought, she kept from crying out or widening her eyes. Prince Pokoj had warned her he would not be with her all day. He must have had more pressing commitments to get to. Escorting her halfway home was not pressing.

"He told me he would go a little way with me," Nelia said, unable to help her tone of voice dipping into that which teenage girls use to make sure the other girls know not to mess with her. "But he knows best. I'll be fine on my own."

"There is one guard, you know," Zanderi said, taking on a superior stance in light of Nelia's disappointment. The competition between females in the air was fierce. It surprised Nelia how easily she felt pulled in to play the game, though she knew it came with no victory for either of them and would end up with one person hurt internally. She neither wanted to be left hurting nor to inflict pain on Zanderi. "And there is this."

Zanderi produced a small envelope. The letters were embossed with gold – and the red seal was broken.

"Well, I had to see if there was something indecent in the letter," Zanderi said in her defense, without being asked at all. Nelia thought of Zayzay and when he had been caught in the cookie jar. Human nature seemed to know when something was wrong, just as Prince Pokoj had said yesterday at the Gate of Croizante. "I can't be caught passing indecent notes between guests, you know. The palace has strict rules. It could ruin my reputation, being involved even a little bit in something like that."

The voice of Nelia's mother-in-law rang in her head.

'Cause the rest of us out here beyond the walls of Croizante need to learn a lesson from them, the people who used to throw their babies off a cliff!

Nelia shook off the thoughts. She didn't wish to think badly of Zanderi or Croizante. She knew Prince Pokoj did not, which was ultimately why she said nothing, gave no rebuke. With her mouth closed, she went to sit at the small vanity in the corner. The windows, cut into small, beveled diamonds, cast little rainbows across the desk and the letter.

Dearest sister Nelia,

I told you I would be with you for a little part of the journey today, but alas, I cannot. Not in body, anyway. In light of that, I wanted to remind you that I am with you always in Spirit. Do not assume the voice in the wind is against you. My father sees you always and I am with you always. I send with you your own personal guard. Sometimes you will see him, but sometimes you will not. Do not doubt, though, when you do not see him. And do not doubt that I am with you and that I am for you.

Remember to be on the lookout and trust what my father said to you.

You are loved, Nelia. Until we meet again face to face,

Adieu,

Prince Pokoj.

"You read it?" Nelia asked Zanderi, uncertain why she wanted a clarification, except that she felt rather powerful sitting at a vanity leafed in gold with someone else doing all the work around her.

Zanderi busied herself about the room, pretending she hadn't heard. Nelia waited in silence, a cold irritation grabbing hold of her. Before long, Zanderi squirmed. Then she nodded, her nose in the air. She knew as well as Nelia that there was no power in play here. Nelia had none. Neither did Zanderi. But upon further reflection, Nelia decided that wasn't actually quite true. Zanderi had the upper hand of having read the personal note, with Nelia not being able to do anything to punish her for doing so.

"Not sure why you need a note and not me. I got one three years ago and not one since. If you ask me, and of course no one does, I would say that the Prince should write one to everyone if he's going to write one at all. Don't we all deserve a note or two?"

"He would spend all his time writing, if he wrote a note to everyone just because he wished to write to one person."

Zanderi sniffed.

"Then perhaps it would be fairer if he wrote to no one."

Nelia resisted narrowing her eyes at the maid and her blatant selfishness.

"What did yours say then?"

"None of your business!" Zanderi exclaimed. "Though it was better than yours – I can say that much."

Nelia swallowed her stinging response. That strange desire to either hurt Zanderi was rising within her. She feared that if she spoke again, she would lose control.

Rising from the beautiful vanity, she caught sight of herself in the mirror and wondered if she had the strength to get home by herself. Suddenly she missed Aaron to the point of sadness. Neither the Prince nor Aaron would be traveling with her that day. End of story. She was alone.

But there was nothing to be done about it. Even if she were allowed to curl up on the bed and cry, she would still be in Croizante at the end of the day, and far from home. And she had no real need to call Aaron over to fetch her. He was busy in the fields trying to salvage a harvest from their dry dirt. She would have to go it alone, listening to the wind and keeping her eyes open for the right rock to look for.

Her heart swelled a bit. At least she still had a mystery to solve and keep her busy.

"Goodbye, Zanderi," Nelia said, giving the maid a slight curtsy.

"No reason to curtsy to me. I ain't nobody special."

"I was once told that everybody is somebody special, Zanderi. And I'm just beginning to think it might be true," Nelia said as she picked up the bundled-up pail. Without another word, for she couldn't think of anything to say that would bring a good response from the maid, Nelia walked to the great big door, opened it with as little show of effort as possible and walked away, trying not to trip or fall while still in Zanderi's view.

∼∼

The large hallway stretched before Nelia, leading to the grand staircase she had first come up the day before. The floors of the hallway were made of sanded wood, with small glass tiles lining the length of each side. The polished wood shone brightly when the sunlight hit it. The ceiling was at least three times her own height, and curved at the top. With each step of her boots, a click echoed through the tunnel, bringing to mind a monastery she had once seen when she was very little. There were doors along the right side with large, glistening windows to her left. At the end of the hallway, just as she had to turn to the right to descend the stairs, a very large tapestry covered the opposite wall.

Since there was no hurry in getting home, Nelia grabbed a few moments to herself to take a closer look at it. Yesterday, she had caught a glimpse and could have sworn it seemed hand sewn. At closer inspection, she found her impression proved true. Gliding her fingers lightly across the scene painted in thread, Nelia tried to contain her awe. No machine had touched this beautiful piece of art.

In the center of it stood a lady with her hair kept back under a scarf. She smiled a small smile at the child who wrapped his arms around her legs even as it appeared that a crowd encroached on her space. The boy was smiling too. Around the crown of the woman's head, there was stitching in gold thread, which shone with the light now touching it. In the background was a cross and clouds where translucent angels appeared. Or perhaps angels clothed in fog.

Upon stepping back, Nelia noticed the babies that lined the bottom of the tapestry and what looked like Prince Pokoj to the side, smiling and sitting amongst the babies as they crawled over him.

There was no telling how long Nelia stood there, soaking in the tapestry. There were no longer museums anywhere near Overge. The last time she had seen art, really, had been in fifth grade when they had traveled to Hunverilun to pay their taxes and sign the registry. The only art left in Overge was the statue in Upper Park. Mayor Billisborth had commissioned it a long time ago. Everyone with more education than Nelia had been very excited by the prospect of a true artist coming to their town. For weeks all they had spoken about was the statue and what the artist would sculpt. There had even been talk about building an art museum or at least an art exhibit.

But then the artist revealed his statue: three tall columns made of metal in the middle of the park. They didn't move; they barely shone. The artist said that the metal was supposed to have a matte finish, for it represented the sadness he felt in living in Overge.

Nelia couldn't blame him for that, though it offended many villagers. They especially felt their hospitality and money had been abused. Aaron said the artist shouldn't be paid, but Mayor Billisborth had paid him before the project was complete. Once that news came out, there were those who had to quickly change their opinions of the statue in order to justify their Mayor for being so short-sighted as to pay an artist before the work was even finished.

Politics was more than Nelia could comprehend.

She looked more closely at the tapestry with a sigh. She had forgotten how much she enjoyed fine craftsmanship. There had been a time when she had been able to make small tapestries, though they were nothing as great as this one. Still, had she had the money to sit and practice, perhaps she would have gotten better.

Perhaps not.

Turning to leave, Nelia soaked in the round, clear lightbulbs that lit the place up. Electricity was something Aaron had once told her about, but she had never seen it. Light that came out of nowhere was something she wasn't sure she would ever get used to. It made her bones quiver. It simply wasn't natural.

The shiny, marble banister was cold on her fingers as she balanced herself down the giant, polished wood steps. It took her two steps just to cross the steps and then descend once again. Leaving the palace behind weighed heavily on her. Before the century of Croizante having its gates closed and being steeped in the awful tradition of killing its own babies, it had been known for its intellectual kings and queens who built lavish libraries and encouraged inventors and thinkers. The greatest philosophers and some of the great writers had at one time stayed or lived in Croizante. Don Quinoteltual had stayed at this very palace, according to Grandmama.

Nelia sighed. How she wished she was young enough to run about the palace hallways, hiding and exploring. Surely there were hidden rooms and long-forgotten treasures lurking somewhere around here. At the bottom of the steps, her shoes sinking into the plush carpet, Nelia could envision herself and Aaron, dressed in fine clothes that they would never own, entering this grand place. She would be on his arm, a leather purse hanging from her shoulder and perhaps a fur shawl around her shoulders.

Or perhaps that was too much even for a dream.

The vision dissolved before she could get any more detail out of it. They didn't have the funds to go meandering about the countryside, staying at old palaces and visiting strange places just for the fun of it. Vacationing was not something people like them did.

"Madam, is there anything that I could get for you?"

Nelia nearly jumped out of her own skin at the sound of another human voice. She turned to find the housekeeper watching her. Remembering she had previously thought Zanderi to be kind as well, Nelia tried to keep a cool air. The impulse to rush to the woman as though she were her grandmama and take refuge at her bosom was buried away quickly.

"No, thank you. I have the lunch you had packed for me, and that is really all I need. I knew that the Prince has already left, there is no need to inform me, so I will be on my way."

The housekeeper smiled, the small lines around her mouth stretching out and disappearing as though they had never really been there. Behind the smile were small, white teeth lined up nicely with no twists to them at all. Though Nelia's own comment seemed silly once out of her mouth, there was no malice from the housekeeper. No retort came, as it might have from another woman.

"There is a guard waiting for you, though he said to take your time. He is at your command."

"My command?" Nelia said to no one in particular. She had no idea what to do with a guard. Would she have to give him orders like a puppy, or would he simply follow her and continue to do so until she gave him a specific task? And what kind of tasks, besides protection, was he willing to do? What kind of tasks would he try to do, and would he cease them if commanded?

Nelia stepped outside, her timidity heavy on her shoulders again.

She was going home, and although she was changed inside about how to look at herself, she was not so changed as to be able to confront the new authority she supposedly had. She felt no authority and did not understand what to do with it.

When the housekeeper drew her towards Igna, where the guard stood, Nelia cleared her throat by force and numbly stepped forward.

"I'm Nelia," she stuttered to the tall, young man.

"Nice to meet you, Nelia. I'm Hansutternam. Call me Hans. Place the pail here in the saddlebags. Igna is going with you as far as Trungulia. There she has to be given over to a man named Franz. He's been waiting thirty years for Igna."

"Thirty years?"

"Well, he's been waiting thirty years for the promises that the King has made him, and Igna is part of that promise. You might understand one day, but it isn't necessary. From Trungulia you will have to walk unless I find some other accommodations. It is only five miles from there to Overge, though."

It must have been the fat in the heavy breakfast that made her brain so foggy. Nelia could think of no other reason why she couldn't seem to understand the guard. Also, her limbs felt as heavy as lead, her heart suddenly overwhelmed, and every impulse within her was to curl up and sleep. The symptoms reminded her of that orange stuff her mother used to take to sleep at night.

"Yes. Ok. I know where Trungulia is, though I've never been there."

Hans smiled politely. Nelia's mind was too burdened to make a face as she normally would against the patronizing 'polite' smile.

"Up you go now," said Hans, gripping her at her small waist and lifting her to the saddle as though she were made of feathers. She couldn't help blushing at the contact, though Hans didn't seem to take notice of it. His fingers didn't try to stroke her sides at all, not even when he surely felt that there was no corset underneath, no slip and no cotton gown. She couldn't afford any of them, which didn't normally matter since she never before had a need for a strange man to lift her onto a horse.

Lowest of the low.

The words echoed in her head. She could still see Exelyee's disdain as she walked by, advising her sister to keep a good grip on her purse as she followed Nelia's trail with her eyes. Nelia had never worked at the brothel; she cleaned the storefronts of it and the other building on that road. Being out there every morning led to rumors, but the worst had come when someone had found out that her mother had worked at a brothel a long time ago. Not the one in Overge, but that didn't matter so much.

If Nelia hadn't been lucky enough to marry Aaron, those rumors about her being a gutter woman would have made her unemployable. No one knew what Aaron was doing, marrying her, but there they had it. When Aaron left for the war it became difficult to go to the market without being harassed, either by women telling her how repugnant she was or men propositioning a visit to her bedroom.

But all the rumors started to die off once Aaron came back. Mostly because none of the other husbands wanted trouble with Aaron – especially after he got home from war with that rather shocking scar on his face and the stories of how he got it. As the story went – by word of his army friends, for Aaron wouldn't speak a word about it – Aaron had been in the middle of a ring of six enemies and fought till the death of all six of them, as though made of supernatural substance. What kept the story alive was that there were more than two witnesses who had watched as he fought off the last three.

Chapter 13

dirty beggar

R eady to go, then?"

Nelia looked up, her face again flushing hot with being caught daydreaming.

"Yes," she croaked out, looking down to fuss with arranging her skirts and the blanket around her. The morning was crisp, though she barely noticed, for her insides were still burning from her ridiculous emotions.

"Madam, this is a present from the palace," the housekeeper said, appearing at Igna's side as though out of vapor. Nelia looked down to find a neatly-folded, homespun shawl in purple. "You will need it, I think. The fog is descending fast down the mountain. Though I do not think there will be rain, the air will be damp, and we do not wish you to get sick upon leaving here."

"A gift? For me?"

The hasty words were out before Nelia could think. Bullying at school had taught her to not react with words: that reaction would get her into trouble more often than not. But that, along with many other lessons, had never stuck to her brain.

Before shifting in her saddle to reach down, Nelia brushed away the faint red that was beginning to clot the air in front of her face. Luckily for her, the cold air had already made her cheeks and nose red. Unhappily for her, she had to move dangerously far to the left in order to bend down far enough to reach the shawl. Even with the housekeeper standing on her tiptoes and stretching her arm up as far as she could, Nelia had to stretch her side in ways she thought would bring about a cramp or possibly send her flying to her doom. Luckily for both of the women, Igna was well-trained and stayed steadily in place. Grasping the shawl, Nelia pulled her back and stomach muscles in with all her might, managing to get back upright – though out of breath due to the spasms flaring up around her middle. If ever there was evidence that she was no longer the young filly she had once been, she had it today.

"Are you all right, Madam?"

"Yes," Nelia said, the words puffing out into the morning air, then hanging as white smoke for a moment before dispersing.

"Madam, we can wait a bit before leaving," Hans said, coming around the back of Igna, his large hand running alongside Igna's backside to keep her from startling. His eyes were round with concern, his voice devoid of any coercion.

"No, I need to get home. I thank you for the shawl," Nelia said, huffing less, though her muscles still flared in anger. "Thank you for your hospitality."

The housekeeper gave a small curtsy before turning back towards the palace. Surely there was always something for a woman of that stature to do, more than be held up in small talk with a guest she didn't know.

"Hey-ho!" called Hans, as he slipped himself onto a large, brown mare, who gave a long snort before she stepped grandly towards the gate. Never before had Nelia seen a horse march so smartly for anything other than a show parade.

"Come, now, Igna," she murmured anxiously, though it was unnecessary. Igna stepped forward in line with the right flank of Hans' horse.

"What's her name?" Nelia asked, looking for small talk to pass the time with Hans. She still wasn't certain what it meant that he was 'at her command'. Being on equal footing would be much more to her liking.

"Ferulia. She's a grand mare, she is."

A shout from the guards at the gate to Hans stopped the conversation between him and Nelia, though she didn't much mind. Thinking the soldiers would remember her, Nelia nodded and smiled at them, but they took no notice of her. It hurt her pride, she couldn't deny that, but she also couldn't deny the fact that the night had been quite dark and with the Prince, who would have noticed her? She told herself she had no reason to dwell on the slight to her female ego. Why would she want attention from strange men, anyway? To point it out to her husband? None of the women from Overge would bother listening to her brag, much less believe her. The only reason left, then, was to boost her waning confidence.

She shook her head at herself, just then noticing three beggars sitting outside at the gate. They must not have been there last night, for she couldn't imagine the Prince ignoring them. One was an ancient-looking woman with a leathery face who seemed to chew incessantly on her lips with her toothless gums; her pale green eyes gaze directed straight at Nelia. The two of them locked eyes for a moment but Nelia pulled away quickly, not wanting to stop to speak to her. Much to her distress, the old woman excitedly stood up, sending up a dingy, greenish cloud from around her feet, and called out strange words to Nelia. Nelia could only focus on the greenish cloud. She had seen that poisonous gas before, but she couldn't remember what it represented. Nelia pointedly turned her attention away from the crazy, shouting old woman.

The other two beggars were men. One with a missing leg and the other fairly young, but with the empty look of one who took too much ophenoidas – whether smoked in the pipe or crushed and snorted, Nelia couldn't tell. Neither could she see if he was one who poked at his skin like Schzuten in Overge, who sat in a greasy black cloud on the banks of the creek and poked himself over and over and over again.

Hans slowed the horses to a stop, to Nelia's dismay. She squirmed in the saddle, then squinted beyond the trees as the wife of Mayor BIllisborth often did when she didn't wish to speak with anyone. Out of the corner of her eye, she watched Hans lower himself off Ferulia, but Nelia stayed where she was.

Beggars made her very uncomfortable. Twice a beggar had chased her away after she offered them food instead of money. Another time, a beggar had assaulted her with a blunt knife for walking too close to his 'home' that was invisible to the naked eye along the path. The worst time, though, had been when Schzuten went crazy and ran about the town pinching women in the buttocks and squeezing their breasts. There had been so much screaming and mayhem that many of the women in the market, Nelia included, had ended up falling and almost being trampled. She had been pregnant then, though thankfully she hadn't lost Zayzay at that moment.

Now that the horses weren't walking, Nelia took the opportunity to unfold the shawl and wrap it around her head and shoulders. With something to keep her occupied, she hoped that neither the beggars nor Hans would call on her for anything. She had no money, though she had some food. But it would be rather unfair for a poor woman like her to feel obligated to give food to those who begged at the gates of the palace of Croizante, would it not?

"A small aandenkenri for you, my dear?"

Nelia took in a deep breath before looking down. The old woman looked back at her, the black pools in the center of her eyes slightly foggy, though not so much that Nelia doubted she couldn't see at all.

"Thank you."

Nelia answered but made no move to take the small parcel in the old woman's hands. They were so dirty that she could not help but hesitate. If dirty people carried plague or fever, what were the chances of the small parcel also carrying those germs?

Nelia also saw the woman's fingers. Gnarled, red, and frostbitten, most of the fingernails had fallen off. A strange click sounded in Nelia's chest. She couldn't help but allow her eyes to travel from the woman's fingers up her arms, which were covered in dirty rags that literally hung in torn pieces. It was impossible to know when the woman had last taken a bath or changed her clothes, but the smell surrounding her gave an idea. A black cloth –Nelia couldn't tell whether it was clean or dirty, though she assumed well enough – protected the woman's neck from the wind, and ten or twelve clips held up her thin, salt-and-pepper hair. Each clip hosted two or three lice at any given time.

How was it that little boys could not withstand the plagues and fevers that swept through the lands, but dirty old women could?

Nelia's heart balled up tightly in her chest. The block of ice it became turned her insides freezing cold. She shivered, though there was no wind and the sun now shone enough for her face to feel its weak rays.

"Take it, young lady. A small aandenkenri. For you. He told me to give it to you."

Nelia, who had taken her eyes away from the lice crawling about the woman's clips to the horizon where she could see the downslope of the mountain, brought her gaze suddenly back to the old woman. The woman smiled, showing the last three teeth left in her mouth, protruding from her gums like stalactites and stalagmites. One great yank seemed all they needed to take them from their lonely places in her otherwise empty gums.

"Who told you to give it to me?"

"He did. You know. His voice comes in the wind and today I listened. Yes, today I listened. Not always do I listen. No. Some days I say, 'Go away for I cannot listen today.' Or perhaps I will tell him, I say to the wind, 'I am not worthy that you should speak to me, see? I have failed in so many things.' That's what I say sometimes, I do. But not today. I saw Prince Pokoj coming out of the sunrise. Just like that." Her old, gnarled fingers flicked together in a silent snap. "He arose on his white horse and for a moment I was still. Like a statue, I was. I could not decide. One voice told me to shout, to run, to screech. Another told me to stay still and hope to just watch him pass. I followed the second voice. Too many times, I screech and then people run away or try to put me back to the tower. I don't like the tower. I like the earth.

The sun. The moon."

"You saw the prince leave the palace today?"

The old woman nodded her small head. Nelia saw that she could see the distinct shape of the skull underneath the frail skin – skin so fragile and thin that it seemed a strong wind could peel it away to reveal the bones. It made her think of the museum that had come through Overge: the traveling museum of shrunken heads. They weren't to be handled, for they were frail, or so the man with the large black hat had told them all. But he had had them out on display for three farthings. She had only been eight at the time and had never owned a farthing, but she was smart enough to know not to ask Mother for one, much less three, to see some shrunken heads.

She had hated watching the girls talk about the display on the playground, not knowing what they were talking about. Each time she would attempt to join their conversation, the girls would move away saying that they had signed a pledge not to spoil it for those who hadn't seen it yet. Never mind that they knew she would never be able to see it.

The day the man had left the town with his red covered wagons, Nelia was taking the clean laundry back to the rich part of town. After dropping everything off and gathering all the money, she sucked in the confidence to run after the caravan and ask to see the skulls. She was certain the man wouldn't refuse if she had the money. He had that metallic cloud hovering around his heart that was there any time a person was in love with wealth. Running through the woods, Nelia thought she had lost them when suddenly she caught sight of the last red wagon lumbering along. There were shouts back and forth from each wagon and a call to be careful, when suddenly the wagon hit a tree root and seemed to fly about three feet in the air before landing again. That was when a string of curses hit the air, along with a great puff of black smoke that went up before showering back down. It settled around the wheels of the wagons – a place Nelia had never thought to look for it before, and the reason she now always searched for a cloud near a person's feet.

The curses grew hysterical; then there was the sound of a leather whip against flesh and a loud cry. That was when Nelia stopped running towards the wagons and instead sought shelter. Adults. Bad moods. Whips. She knew better than to approach the caravan. Her chance of seeing the skulls disappeared in a puff.

Just as she tried to throw herself into a hollow tree, Nelia's foot rolled on something and she too went flying.

"Zstrovitch!" she cursed, immediately ducking her head, though neither her mother nor Grandmama were there to hit her for the naughty word.

Pain emanated from her right knee where it had kissed the rotting tree trunk. She rubbed it as her father had once taught her to do, only to find her fingers sticky with blood and the sting of touching raw skin zinging up to her head, causing more curses to fall from her tongue like drool.

"Zstrovtich, castrunico, falenktu!"

In a fury, Nelia stood up, but again her left foot rolled. That time it was her bottom that stung. Before she could curse again or cry, her eyes landed on a white ball smiling at her without lips. It was a small, rounded skull the size of a baby, but with the features of an adult. It took her about fifteen minutes of staring at it before finally picking it up, mostly because she expected it to come alive at any moment. When she finally did pick it up, she held it far away for a long while, just in case the jaws tried to snap at her fingers. After a few moments of stillness, Nelia quickly put the shrunken head into the empty laundry bag and ran home with it, her right knee stinging and bleeding the whole way home.

It was a week later that she dared to touch it again, after hiding it under a rock in the dry garden. Gathering her courage by cursing herself for her cowardice, Nelia plucked the skull up and turned it around in her hands. Even through the grime the garden dirt had left behind, Nelia could see the tiny screws at the temple and jawline. And though it looked like bone from far away, it was actually made of clay – able to be crushed by an eight-year-old and a hard rock. At least that part was fun, along with knowing her friends had wasted their money and she hadn't. Never mind that luck, not sense, had prevented her from spending it.

This was what Nelia thought as she reached out and took the small parcel from the old woman. She took it between her index finger and her thumb, trying hard not to imagine the germs now crawling up her hand.

"It is for you. He said to give it to you."

"Prince Pokoj gave it to you for me?"

The old woman pulled her head away in great shock.

"No! Not the Prince. I see the prince and he talks to me and only me. And maybe Ralf, here. Him, too. No! I told you, he told me in the wind. When I hear the wind talk, I listen. No, no, sometimes I don't listen. But today I listened!"

At that, the old woman smacked her lips as her shoulders seemed to stoop in fatigue. Nelia placed the parcel down between Igna's mane and the top pommel of the saddle. Everything within her screamed for her to wipe her fingers on something, to somehow get some of the germs off, but there was nothing. Just Igna. Nelia settled for rubbing her index and thumb together lightly, as though rubbing the germs into each other might kill them.

"Are you cold?" Nelia asked, though she wasn't certain why she did so. Her heart felt no sympathy for the woman in any real way. But a gift was a gift, and she felt she had to do something. Before the woman answered, she picked a louse crawling down her cheek and popped it between her nail-less fingers. Pushing through her disgust, Nelia lifted her new shawl from around her shoulders.

"Here, please take this. It will keep you warm."

The woman looked up and shook her head.

"I have, I have. That woman, she does come every winter. That's when she does give me new one. See? Is right here."

The shawl drew away from the woman's neck, revealing a deep red that lay against her skin. Nelia swallowed and tried not to wonder if the black that was visible was dirt or the color of a different piece of clothing. She didn't wish to find out.

"Okay, now, you go. See? Hans is going. Hi, Hans, hi."

Hans' horse marched backward just as smartly as it marched forward.

"Hello, Meigh, how are you? Why are you back out here?"

Meigh waved her hand around, shaking her head as though the gesture might cause her to think of a better answer. That gesture, the same as Nelia's Grandmama would make when she was thinking, caused her heart to crack. Slightly.

Meigh could have been her grandma, given the circumstances. They had almost lost their house three times. What would have happened to them? Mother had said that Nelia would have worked on her back – something Nelia, at nine years old, hadn't understood the meaning of at the time.

"I have house. Yes, yes. I keep promise to Prince Pokoj. And he came see me. But me, I am lonely in house. I come here, talk to people, see things and listen to wind."

"You are not getting into any trouble?"

Meigh laughed a childish giggle, her three teeth again the only thing Nelia could see.

"Sometimes! Sometimes, I get into trouble. You know, the kind of trouble that makes my head spin and not hear the wind. But I try not to. My daughter, she come to get me sometime. And I go sometime, someday. But, you know? I'm okay. Okay."

"All right, Meigh. I'm giving you this before I go."

Hans handed a basket to the woman, who took it with a look of childish glee on her face.

"Jam?"

"And lots of it, Meigh. I will see you again."

"Yes, yes."

The old woman already had her back turned on them when she answered. She hobbled back to a certain spot indented by her rump sitting there throughout the morning, still giggling over the basket. She swung it near to Ralf, who grunted and held up his own, too busy stuffing venison into his mouth to answer with words.

"Off we go then?" Hans asked, not waiting for an answer before shouting 'hey-ho!' to his horse, who marched on ahead. Nelia placed the shawl back over her head, trying not to think about the germs she had contracted, determined to find some soap before eating again that day.

Chapter 14

a strange song

They rode silently down the mountain for the next three hours. Just as the housekeeper had said, the fog had descended the mountain. At one point, Nelia could barely see Hans ahead of her. The slight outline of his figure and the swish of his horse's tail were what kept her from panicking.

The wind whistled around her, soothing her thoughts into bits of nothingness. Nestled deep into her woolen shawl, Nelia spent most of the descent in a haze, rethinking the last two days. Though she could see the tip of her breath swirl into the fog as a thin, white smoke, she did not feel cold at all. Partly because of her semi-embarrassment at her thoughts of disgust concerning the old woman.

All her life Nelia had considered herself someone who was at the lowest of all the levels in society, except for that of a beggar. Not that she wouldn't ever become one – she could at any moment. When Aaron had taken longer than other men in coming home from the war, she had thought she might have to, so uncertain was she that her mother-in-law wouldn't kick her out of their small cottage.

But that same thought, one only heard by herself and yet meant to help her feel a kind of atonement, was contradicted almost immediately. She wouldn't have become a beggar; she would have worked first. She had experience in many things. Namely, housekeeping, gardening and canning. In Aaron's absence, she had picked brusnica berries. That was hard work, and she didn't like it at all, but in spite of her feelings she had become good at it. Aaron didn't like that she did it once he got back, and especially after she became pregnant. It did get to the point where it became difficult to bend over to get the berries.

Also, there were the summers she had worked the beer telks during the county festivals. There she had met Aaron for the second time. It was there that he had asked her to go out with him.

Nelia shrugged her shoulders to herself. There would be plenty of things she could do to not become a beggar. Besides, she didn't drink alcohol, and she never experimented with ophenoidas. Never. And that seemed to be what brought all beggars together. That, and possibly a loss of the mind.

What about losing Zayzay?

Nelia looked up, only to find she was still alone. The words were so loud in her ear she thought someone had said them. Perhaps Hans, though it sounded nothing like his voice. But Hans was well ahead of her, scouting out the path before them. She could see the round rump of his horse and little else.

What if you lost Zayzay and Aaron?

The idea startled her. Not that she never thought of losing Aaron. Him going to war had forced her to think of losing him only one year after their marriage. And when the fever had come and she had again thought of losing him. She had thought of dying herself when that damn fever came.

So, what about losing Zayzay and Aaron? What was that question supposed to point to? Or was her mind playing tricks on her? Was the stress of the last two days finally getting to her?

Nelia pulled the shawl off her head, the cool air hitting her warm hair and instantly lowering her body temperature. For a moment she focused only on the steaming sensation that her hair was giving off and the strange buzzing noise around her. Then the wind blew past her, and again she heard a voice.

Who is to say you would not have become a drunk?

Ah. Nelia drew her shoulders together to bring her discomfort and judgment a bit closer to her heart. Perhaps she could squeeze it out of herself. If Aaron and Zayzay had died, how could she be so certain she would not have ended up drinking?

Well, Nelia answered herself with a nod, there was no proof she wouldn't have. And had she become a drunk just as her mother had, then she probably would have ended up on the streets. Still, she liked to think she was smarter than that. At least, a little smarter.

That thought consoled her for two minutes until she shifted her skirts and the dull red of the paper wrapped around the parcel that the old woman had given her caught her eye. Nelia picked it up and turned it around in her hands. The parcel could fit in the palm of her hands; it was so small. The red paper around it was a used, rather dirty red napkin. The shape of what was inside was indistinguishable. Sitting against the pommel of the saddle, the present just looked like a lump; a very out-of-place object against such a beautiful saddle, though Nelia mused that the parcel and its looks were just good enough for her.

The buzzing sound around them grew louder, almost as though there might be beehives nearby, but Nelia ignored it. Anything could be lurking behind the fog, but she had Hans to help protect her.

Slowly she picked up the parcel and held it in the middle of her left palm. It wasn't heavy. It wasn't light. It didn't jingle when she nudged it, nor did it add to the buzzing sound around her.

Though the germs terrified her, Nelia couldn't resist eventually opening it up. The contents couldn't possibly be dirtier than the used napkin. This is what she told herself as she commanded her fingers to unwrap the filthy layers. To her surprise, the red part was just one wrapping. The red covered an orange, less dirty napkin, which covered an almost new bit of blue napkin. The colors of Croizante. The old woman must have gotten the napkins out of the palace trash – a thought that made Nelia's stomach roll.

Slowly, Nelia peeled away the blue napkin covering until a tiny charm in the shape of a baby bottle tumbled out onto her palm.

The charm was a shiny gold color, though from the chipping on the corner Nelia knew it was anything but actual gold. Still, it was pretty, gleaming against her skin. The clip that would hold it in place on a chain was loose, telling the story of how it had ended up in Meigh's hands. Nelia turned the charm between her index and her thumb in wonder. Whatever had made that woman give this to her, she couldn't imagine. Because she was a woman of child-bearing years?

But no, it couldn't only be that. She had rambled as though only half possessing her mind, but she'd said that the wind had said to give it to her. The wind.

Nelia jerked her head up as she watched the wind make a U-turn and come back to blow gently against her face. *The wind*. Was that where that question about Aaron and Zayzay had come from? Or was it her subconscious? Or... was it the King? He told her that she would hear His voice through the wind, after all.

Before she could answer her own questions, the buzzing in the air became louder, more music-like. Almost like a mixture of crickets and grasshoppers. Maybe the dry climate was driving the grasshoppers down the road to other crops. Unfortunately, that might mean they were going towards Overge. A bad, bad omen. The last time they had come they had eaten every single crop and left nothing for the people. That had been a very difficult winter.

Hans stopped ahead of her and turned his head towards the east. He got off his horse, his robe whipping around him, seemingly lifted by the wind as the sound persisted. Nelia slid from her horse, her ears and mind concentrating on the surrounding terrain.

There were no birds. The trees were actually bare, their leaves having dropped already. The cold air, the barren landscape, indicated that the sound could not be from crickets or grasshoppers, Nelia realized. She ripped the shawl fully from her body to better hear the sounds. Grasshoppers would have moved on already. She came around her horse to stand near Hans, uncertain whether or not the noise was a warning of danger.

A small distance away Hans stood tall next to his horse, facing the east, where a small road led away into a denser area of the woods. Nelia crept closer, her ears picking up more beings, more voices, more noises joining what was already overpowering her senses. Still, she could not see any other living thing around them. No birds, no insects, nothing.

"Hans?" she asked, her voice timid compared to the noises that were starting to rise together in what she could only describe as a song. Hans turned to her, his head cocked slightly, the most utmost peace and reverence on his face. "You know – you know what this is? What is it?"

Nelia's shoulders blades popped off the cavity of her back chest as her body fell into itself. Her chest caved inward to allow the joints of her shoulders to displace and almost overlap before her heart, which she found to be beating faster and faster in anticipation. But of what?

Was it the anticipation of war? Perhaps a soldier like Hans would find the anticipation of war something to give reverence to? No, surely not. Surely not war. When war had threatened her and her family, there had been a different feeling within her. A feeling of deep darkness. This ball of energy within her middle, this faster pulse in her heart, was not fear of a dark pit of uncertainty.

This feeling was the same as what she had felt upon meeting the King.

The notes of the loudest noise rose to a pitch that she had never heard before. It did not pain her ears, and yet she felt she could not get away from it. If she focused too much on the unusualness of the note Nelia felt her body become agitated, but when she allowed the noise, the song, to flow over her as though a soft waterfall, she found the pressure within herself lessened.

In slow, steady motions, Nelia's knees gave way, bringing her whole body to the soft forest floor. At that very moment, Hans knelt on one knee, though with more grace than she. Nelia watched him and felt the stirrings of envy, but the emotion had no grip on her. When envy could not possess her, curiosity replaced it as she watched Hans' lips start to move. She could hear nothing above the music and when she tried to strain to hear it, the peace within her lifted. It was only a slight lift, but it was enough to make her stop trying and simply listen. That kind of peace was not something she wished to let go of.

Her ears filled with the noise, which became sweeter by the second. There was a harmony she could hear now, with a louder, deeper drumline beat.

Upon her knees, Nelia dared to lift her head, then her eyes, up to the sky, and wept silently without knowing why.

"There goes... there goes... the prince... above all others..."

Nelia scanned the treetops, her tears rolling down her cheeks, looking for the voice. That voice. Among all the others.

But there was no one else but Hans and her.

And suddenly a breeze filled in the crevices between her, Hans and the horses, and it seemed that the decibel of the noise immediately lowered. Her ears practically pulled from her head trying to pick up the sound, able to catch some harmonies, but the drumbeat was all but gone.

"King of... all kings... the prince... saved the world."

Hans rose and gave a salute. Nelia stood with trembling legs. Unable to hold her shawl so tightly and keep her balance, the material slipped to the ground; her foot caught on a tree root and almost threw her into the sprawling bushes.

"Shall we go?"

Nelia knew she looked as bewildered as she felt, but it wasn't just her near fall into a thorny bush that had her agitated. As much as she was prone to pass by through life without too many questions, knowing that she was expected above all to move forward every day despite the good or bad that had happened the day or even the moment before, Nelia prepared herself to dig her heels down into the dirt this time. Yanking her shawl up to wrap it over her head and out of the way of her feet, Nelia raised her eyes to the guard and shook her head.

"Do you truly think I will leave this place without an explanation?"

"Of what?"

"Of that – that – that noise!"

"Noise?" Hans asked as he pulled himself up onto his horse in one graceful, swift motion.

"That noise! What made it? There are no birds here, and no insects that I can see. It was as loud as the cicadas in the summer, but I saw nothing. The ground is still already starting to freeze here, so how could there be life out here right now? And yet, there was that noise. Oh, no. Don't tell me you didn't hear it! Why did you get off your horse if you didn't hear it? I don't believe you, and I won't go on before you tell me what or who made that noise. Are we in trouble? Are we walking the wrong way?"

Hans laughed, genuinely unaffected by her fears. Less than unaffected – he seemed to bubble with an inexplicable joy.

"Of course I heard the songs. They are songs, not noise. And I allowed you to hear the songs because I felt that you needed to hear them. Besides, I like to kneel in respect, so I wanted you to hear so they would also affect you. Does it not make you want to give your all?"

Nelia stared at him, then nodded slowly. That was a good way to describe the chain of emotion within her.

"What made the noise?" she whispered, wanting to know and yet knowing that the answer could change the course of her life for forever.

"The trees, the rocks, the water, the dirt, the flowers, the grass. They all sang out to the Prince, for he went down that way to a village. Have you not read the passage that 'in the absence of people praising, the rocks and mountains will cry out'? He must have passed by close to here because there were a few rocks crying out, asking that he sit with them to rest his feet, but Prince Pokoj was unable to. He never has as much time as people claim he does. But you can't blame the rocks for trying. It is an honor among them to have the Prince sit on them or stand near them, or even rest his boots on them. The trees gave out the drumbeat, their branches beating against the songs of the rocks and dirt. And, as you can probably guess, the grass gave harmony. There are few flowers among them here that I see, though I heard them. Most are still underground or just seedlings, and are very difficult to hear."

Chapter 15

love and mercy

Nelia closed her mouth, which had slid open as Hans spoke. Slowly she allowed the spit to wet her mouth, then swallowed before walking back to Igna, who waited patiently where Nelia left her. She had to stand on a rock to mount her horse again, wondering the entire time if the rocks would throw her off because she wasn't the prince. She was quite a poor substitute, to be sure.

"Come on, now, Nelia. Do you need help?"

"No," Nelia said sharply. "Of course not. As long as this rock doesn't shout and make me fall from scaring the wits out of me."

"It is only the Prince and the King who received the shouts of the rocks and trees," Hans said.

"Of course," Nelia said. "Certainly."

Her pride now at stake, Nelia tried to jump, but only got as far as throwing her shoulders against the saddle. Igna snorted as though laughing. Nelia would have hit the poor horse if she weren't busy enough already trying to mount it. Beating her horse would only make her a fool. More of a fool, at this point.

"Umf!"

The air left her lungs with a jolt as she jumped again, throwing herself harder up towards the horse instead of directly at the saddle. At least this time she managed to grab the horn. With her left arm almost halfway over the other side, all Nelia had to do was shimmy upwards, though it proved more difficult in real life than in her head.

She couldn't see him with her face squished against the leather saddle, but Nelia imagined Hans was sitting atop his horse, shaking his head. That was what Aaron would have done; she was certain of it.

"Got it," Nelia grunted in satisfaction, as her left leg finally found its way over the saddle. At that point, she had to lift her body up and gather up her skirts. Which, again, proved more difficult, for her thirty-something-year-old body had gained quite a few bruises and sore muscles in the last two days. And those same muscles now seemed to refuse to work at all.

"Shall we be off now?" asked Hans, his horse coming alongside Igna, who again snorted. Though she had quietly endured the humiliation her own rider had brought upon herself, Igna seemed ready to move onto other, more dignified actions. Nelia felt very much alone in the middle of the woods at that moment. Not even her horse was on her side.

With a shrug, Nelia settled back into her saddle and was careful not to look Hans in the eye too closely.

"I've never ridden a horse before today. We only had a donkey at home."

Hans gave her a broad smile, which she saw, but she wouldn't dare lift her eyes to meet his golden ones.

"When I started working for the Prince, he gave me a horse that must have been about twenty hands high and told me to get on it. But there was no saddle. I knew it was for laughs and such, like a friendly hazing between men, but I never thought it would end up being as funny as it was. At one point in my struggle, I realized that I had a choice to make, which was the point of the exercise: to learn to laugh at myself and let the good-natured teasing go, or to get angry and humiliated at a simple gag."

"Yes, yes," Nelia answered, waving her hand dismissively. "I need to learn to laugh more."

For a minute, Hans' only response was to allow his horse to turn towards the less-traveled road and give a bow. A bowing horse. Nelia stared in surprise. When Igna moved forward, Nelia braced herself for the bow by clutching Igna's mane and squeezing her thighs hard around Igna's middle. Sliding forward off her horse was not something she was willing to put herself through. No, she decided, she would not dismount Igna until forced to or once arrived at home. As though sensing her rider's fear, Igna simply nodded her head and followed Hans.

Nelia tried to make herself look a bit straighter, a bit more sophisticated sitting in the saddle, though she knew that would be hard to pull off after the scene she had made getting back on Igna. Still, she had to grasp at whatever dignity she had left, though it was quickly vanishing.

"I think you passed that small test with flying colors, Nelia. You don't give yourself enough credit. I, for one, have never seen a woman with so much stamina and humor for herself. Your ability to laugh at yourself is higher than most women I know or have encountered. I wasn't telling you that story because there is some moral in there for you to learn. I wouldn't do that, because I think you already know it. I am commending you for your ability to keep moving forward even when things don't line up in your favor. Climbing onto a horse that is too high for you can be humiliating, but you kept trying. I've known a few women and some men who would have allowed the humiliation to get to them and either yelled or acted indignantly. The truth is, we all have obstacles that we must get over, but we were given a sense of humor for a reason. There is also a reason that laughter is said to be the best medicine. When we take everything so seriously, when we hold on to our humiliation and allow it to settle in our bones, we eventually see the consequences."

A slight rose-tinted cloud hovered the air in front of Nelia's eyes as she listened to Hans. She knew the rose cloud was seeping into her cheeks. Its warmth caressed her cheeks, but she didn't move to wipe it away. He was complimenting her in the most real way she had heard in years, and she was determined not to ignore it or to let it go.

Such a strange decision for her. Her audience with the King must have changed her heart more than she gave him credit for.

Since Hans didn't seem to need a reply, Nelia didn't give him one. Instead, she let go of Igna's reigns and engrossed herself in the task of sitting in the saddle without falling out. But that thought made her feel guilty. For Igna. Though the horse couldn't read her thoughts, Nelia found herself stroking the long neck anyway. It wouldn't be the horse's fault if she fell off. Certainly not. It would be her own clumsy fault. And only because she wasn't paying attention or because she tried to do something ridiculous, for Igna was the gentlest, most even-paced horse she could imagine.

"You are being kind to me, aren't you, girl?'

Igna snorted, though she kept her eyes straight ahead. Nelia watched as the thin fog lifted from the ground, like a knot of threads being pulled apart slowly and diligently by someone like her Grandmama. Grandmama never wasted thread – or anything, for that matter. Mother used to mutter under her breath about Grandmama being overbearing in her desire to never make trash, even as Mother would be throwing something away. Once, late at night and well-hidden around the corner in their small house, Nelia had watched her mother throw away a broken bowl, then take it out of the garbage while muttering about the horrible habits her mother had instilled in her, before throwing the bowl away again, against her self-given advice. Nelia had stayed near the edge of the living room as her mother poured herself a glass of wine, all the while staring at the garbage bin, before pulling the bowl out again. The whole act had repeated itself before Nelia got bored and put herself to bed. The next morning the glue had still been drying in the cracks between the pieces of the bowl. It had held for another two years, before shattering one day when Nelia tripped while stirring the butter and sugar for a cake.

When the threads of fog finally lifted past Nelia's nose, she noticed the new terrain they were riding in. She should have gathered from the slight downward angle that they were leaving the mountain, but she hadn't bothered thinking about it. Now they were approaching the territory that she was familiar with: trees lined up along fields with small cottages nestled here and there. The road wasn't too narrow, nor was it too wide. In the distance, she heard one of those strange new contraptions that some weekend salesman had tried to convince someone in her village to buy: a mechanical planter. The man had said it ran on manure somehow, which turned most people off from even wanting to know more about it.

Nelia laughed at the memory. People like her and Aaron who were around manure all their lives didn't get too excited to be handling it just to make a machine go. It didn't keep those in town from lecturing all the farmers the next Sunday for not caring enough about the environment that they lived in. Nelia couldn't quite understand why, but the affluent people in the town always seemed to think it was the poor who used too much fuel – that it was the poor making the skies gray at night when the only chimneys that were constantly gushing out smoke were those of the rich.

"Does it matter?"

Aaron's voice was loud within her. Nelia shook her head. Her eye caught on the small, still wispy black cloud hovering near her.

Aaron and his favorite phrase. Nothing should matter to her, she supposed. Or perhaps it was *what* mattered to her that most bothered Aaron. What would he rather have bother her? She wasn't sure. But he most assuredly didn't like to hear from her about how much the rich bothered her. If she got too enthusiastic in her criticism, Aaron would salute her as though a general in the revolution and call her 'comrade'. But that wasn't what she wanted. She knew well enough that what General Cuxitre had implemented in Cjaultrounj or what General Ussontunich had done over in Kztrighrichen had gone from an interesting idea to a deadly one. That wasn't the kind of revolution she wanted. She didn't want blood in the streets.

She just wanted justice. And to wipe the smirks off some of their faces. Being rich didn't make you smart. Mostly, being rich just set you apart from the real world, it seemed. And she wished there was a way to say that to them that would hurt... just enough.

"*Love... mercy.*"

That wasn't Aaron's voice. He was a kind man. A loving man – in his own way. But she had never heard him speak about mercy except for a few of his stories from the war. And love? That was a word shown in his actions, he had told her long ago, not a word to be said too often lest it lose its meaning. Nelia snorted. Men were funny folk, but then he'd probably learned that little phrase from his mother.

"Is it I who should have love and mercy?" Nelia asked aloud as the breeze picked up. "I wonder if what I extend can be counted as mercy since I have no power for it to truly be withheld. Even if I wanted to be unmerciful, there is no power in it."

There was no more wind. Not a sound.

No matter. It wasn't like she had expected the wind to speak to her. That would be slightly crazy. To temper her embarrassment, Nelia focused on the sensation of her hips going up and down with the sway of Igna. With each step, they got closer to the place where Nelia would leave her. And strangely enough, that made her sad. As much as she felt at first that this large horse was snickering at her, always resisting her, Igna seemed now almost like a part of her. There was a small part of her offended that she didn't get to keep her.

Still, leaving Igna also meant she was close enough to home to walk. Possibly five or six miles. She remembered her father-in-law saying Trungulia was about that far away. Nelia knew she could walk five miles in less than two hours, which meant she would be home before dusk. A jolt of happiness zipped through her at the idea of being back where everything was familiar.

A few weeks ago, all she had desired was to leave home. It was all she could think of. Each morning she had counted backward the number of weeks or days left before she got to leave. Aaron had mumbled one morning that it seemed she was all too happy to leave him behind for adventure. To that she had given no reply because, in a way, it was true. She had been all too happy to leave. Things between them hadn't been the same since that strange quarrel a few weeks before she had received the invitation. During that first week after their argument, Nelia had struggled every hour, it seemed, against the desire to run into the woods and never look back. She had entertained the dream that there was a town somewhere close by where she could start over and magically find a suitable job which would allow her to leave her husband and that whole life behind. But she never ran.

Not that she couldn't. Divorce was still law in Overge. Her own mother-in-law would probably pay her to leave Aaron alone. Though jobs were scarce, Nelia knew she would find something eventually – but then living all by herself, with only herself to take care of, seemed sad and lonely and... final.

She hadn't left. She hadn't run away. But the fight between them had still bothered her for days on end. What was most frustrating to her was that the entire incident didn't seem to affect him in the least. And yet all of it, scene by scene, stuck to *her* like feathers to hot wax.

The climax of the dispute had swirled around in her mind over and over and over again until she'd thought maybe she would need those pills her mother used to take just to fall asleep. Those words just wouldn't go away: "Honestly, Nelia. Why do you talk as though you know anything about anything?"

Of all their brawls, this one had cut Nelia to her very core, changing something within her that she couldn't quite place. They had had fights with more yelling and screaming and harsher words said, but Aaron had never ever, not once, been so personal in his insults as he was that day. Perhaps it was the tone of voice; perhaps it was because she'd felt her idea for draining the field was ingenious and hadn't realized just how much her pride hinged on him being proud of her for coming up with it. All this she had thought during the days afterward, but it was of little consolation to her. She could admit that her pride leaned too heavily on his acceptance of the idea, but soothing her pride was not a solution that would take away her hurt and anger.

Yes, it had been her pride that Aaron had crushed when he'd barely listened to her idea, treating her as though she was one of those women who talked nonsense all the time just to fill in the silence. She was nothing like those women. More than crushed pride, though, was the insult to her intelligence. Insulting her intelligence was not new. People had done that to her plenty during her life. However, never had one of those people been Aaron.

Pushing away her pride after two weeks, or rather, her crushed pride, Nelia had thought more on her idea and again become convinced of the likelihood of it working. So, twice more she'd tried to speak to him about it. After all, she had convinced herself, Aaron should be allowed bad days. With the bad weather and the further talk of taxation and the house always in need of repair, it was possible that her husband had met a breaking point that day. Trying to think the best of him, she proposed her idea again. The first time she'd barely got a few words out of her mouth before Aaron had brushed aside the idea with his fingers and walked forward to shake their neighbor's hand.

It was the last time she tried, though, that ended up hurting the most. True, she had hijacked the moment that Mr. Grunseler had come over to talk about catching more rainwater between their two farms, but it had seemed a good idea to pull someone neutral into the conversation – someone who might see the good in her idea.

What had irritated Aaron the most, or at least the moment that she'd noticed Aaron was not just annoyed but angry, was when Mr. Grunseler started asking her questions as though her idea might just work if they could get to the gritty details of the plan. She had left the conversation satisfied with finally being heard... until that night at dinner.

How she could have been so ignorant of her husband's ego, she still didn't know. Pride, again, most likely. She was proud of her idea, and the way Mr. Grunseler had validated her opinion only puffed her up a bit more. She was so filled with pride that she ignored the angry swirl of red and yellow fog around Aaron's feet. It wasn't until he walked into the house with that fog clutching at his chest and turning a rotten shade of green that she realized something was very amiss. And when Aaron ignored her, Nelia realized that things were worse than ever before.

Though she tried to ignore the green fog swirling about, setting his dinner before him with a smile and a greeting, when Aaron finally started speaking to her it was to inform her that he had never been more irritated with her in his life, that she had embarrassed him and stepped out of bounds. Then came the worst: "Had I known you would be such a disgrace to me and our neighbors, I would have thought twice about marrying you in the first place." After that he added the last bit about her thinking she knew anything about farming and drainage.

Yes, Nelia thought as she sat on Igna with fresh tears streaming silently down her cheeks, it was the worst row they had had as a couple. It had been worse than her mother's slaps; worse than her grandmama's sighs; worse than the fact that her father was never around to discipline, slap or even yell at her. The silence was worse than anything until the night Aaron left her with those words hanging in the air, filling her lungs and threatening to choke her to death.

But it wasn't like them to sleep on the sofa. (Mostly because they had no sofa.) And Aaron would never have stood for being thrown out of his own bedroom. So, to avoid her husband Nelia had spent the evening darning socks and her apron and towels – all the darning in the entire house. Three years' worth of darning, in fact, since it was her most dreaded chore.

After two days Aaron came back from the fields and kissed her lightly on the shoulder. And four days after that, as he stood outside the doorway of the house, his hat in his hands, looking out into the distance for rain, he admitted that he and Mr. Grunseler would implement a version of her idea. Mind, not the idea as she had said it. They had made significant improvements to her concept. That part he emphasized with a squint of his eyes as he pretended to search for rain in a cloudless sky.

Nelia stood with her hands dripping suds, staring out the small, dirty window near her sink, unable to look at her husband.

"I'm glad you two might have found a solution to the drainage problem. Perhaps we will have more crops to handle then next year."

Aaron grunted but said nothing else. Nelia stood frozen in time at the sink, the water cooling by the second. When she finally gathered the courage to turn and face her husband, she found the doorway empty. The only thing left was a trail of translucent red droplets hanging heavily in the air. They were so low that Nelia knew Aaron had left long before she turned. Red droplets of shame fell in the air quite a bit slower than people would imagine.

Chapter 16

awakening from the daydream

"H o!" cried out Hans.

Igna obeyed immediately, the sudden movement jerking Nelia to attention and causing a nerve in her neck to pinch painfully. She couldn't tell how long the past had consumed her thoughts. Maybe a few minutes. Perhaps an hour. As though waking from a lazy afternoon nap, Nelia rubbed her eyes and tried to clear the muddle from her brain.

Leave the stones behind…

She looked to the left and right, the sensitive nerve clicking and tingling with each worthless movement. Except for the faded, wooden sign that hung from one rusted bolt announcing their entrance into Trungulia, Nelia saw nothing else. No one was around, and Hans was too far ahead to whisper to her. There were leaves on the trees here – they were far enough down the mountain, on almost the same elevation as Overge – and there were birds, but never before had Nelia heard a bird speak to her. The thought made her ponder the possibility. With all the strange things she had already witnessed on this journey, perhaps it wasn't an irrational idea after all. Once a boy had told her he heard horses whispering in real words. She hadn't believed him at the time, but after the last two days she believed he might have told the truth.

Nelia laughed at herself, now pondering the possibility that the child was telling the truth. Surely animals didn't talk.

But the more she thought of it, the more her doubts grew. Though many did not believe her, she could see the black magic before it turned black, when it was just a heart sickness. Shame she could pick up and hold in her fingers.

No one ever believed her when she told them her secret, just as no one probably ever believed the boy. Perhaps no one believed them because they weren't supposed to believe. Perhaps if everyone knew all the quirky and strange talents each person had, no one would get on with their lives. Surely it would just be one more thing to be jealous of or go to war over. She wondered if there was a place where it rained garnets of shame all the time. Would an army invade such a place, with no regard to the people there?

Nelia shook her head; if others could see the droplets of shame that turned into glistening red stones, there would surely have been wars. Lucky for mankind, most people could not see the gemstones of shame.

The first time Nelia remembered telling an adult what she could see, she must have been about eight. Nelia remembered standing in the garden with a pink dress on that was too long for her short legs, with the waistband tucked at the back with safety pins to give it some shape. When Old Lady Myrtle came out of her house that morning, Nelia had stopped playing with her dolls and stood watching her for a long time. At first the yellow smoke swirling around the woman fascinated Nelia. She stood transfixed as it drifted around her, expanding and tightening on what seemed like a whim. But then, without warning, something ominous about the smoke gripped her heart. Nelia remembered the chill that had spread over her chest, pressing hard on her lungs until she gasped. The pressure seemed to mount, urging her to warn the old lady, but she was too afraid. When she realized that her feet were stuck to the ground and wouldn't budge until she warned Old Lady Myrtle, Nelia finally shouted at her that the yellow smoke of plague was creeping around her. The admission released the pressure from Nelia's chest, but instead of thanking her as Nelia had thought she might, Old Lady Myrtle accused her of being a liar. The old woman ran at her with a wooden paddle, sending Nelia flying into the woods to escape an unmerited spanking. Luckily for her, the old woman gave up easily. Unluckily for her, a spanking from her mother awaited her at home. Not even her mother believed her when Nelia cried that she didn't want Old Lady Myrtle to get sick and die, that she was trying to help her.

"You are a liar and a thief!" screamed Old Lady Myrtle the next time Nelia came out to play. "Why would anyone trust anything a piece of garbage has to say? Go away!"

A shudder rolled down her spine at the memory.

"Nelia! Are you getting down to stretch your legs a bit? This is the end of the road for Igna. If you want to say goodbye you can, but you will have to get off, eventually."

Nelia looked down slowly, babying her neck. Hans' voice startled her out of her memories, but his words kicked her in the stomach. In a whoosh the wind in her lungs left her body, leaving her feeling dizzy. All because it was time to give up Igna. He might as well have asked her to give up her house. Igna was her safe place in her journey home. And once safety was tasted, it was hard to give it up.

Yet give Igna up she must. This she knew immediately when she saw an old man with bowed legs hobbling towards them; the smile on his face was so radiant it out-glowed the sun. She could not keep Igna, for she was not her horse, and yet her heavy body did not lift from the saddle. Even when Igna snorted, shaking her long neck as though to jiggle Nelia off herself, Nelia's body did not respond.

"Go' mornin'," the man said, still smiling so widely that Nelia's cold heart started melting in the glare. "Igna, sh'is, nah?"

"That's right," Hans said, holding out his hand to introduce himself to the man, who said his name was Ebidaihah. The two men continued their exchange, while Igna kept snorting and shaking her head.

Time to get down. Walk on your own two feet, Nelia.

Her legs became unglued at those words, though not because she found them particularly inspiring. Rather the opposite. The words lit a fire of resentment within her that had her jumping down from the tall horse without thinking, almost twisting her ankle as she landed.

"Damn horse, who needs you anyway?" Nelia muttered. "Walk on my *own* two feet, you say, do you? I've been walking on my *own* two feet since the day I was born: you should know that if you're all-knowing and such. But then, maybe you aren't so all-knowing. Maybe not."

With a loud huff, Nelia marched in the direction of the small town. It wasn't until she was in the center of the two-cross-streets town that the line of black smudged against the sidewalks caught Nelia's eyes. She stopped mid-stomp and stared. Almost every building was boarded up.

Looking up to the windows, she saw the yellow flowers giving the 'all clear' sign to anyone traveling through, but the absolute silence of the town gave away the death toll.

The Plague.

"Your own two feet," Nelia muttered again, though half of her anger was now replaced by a sudden sadness.

Death. Loss. The very definition of the past few years of her life. She had lost everything that meant the most to her in her life except for Aaron. And sometimes she thought maybe she had lost Aaron in the worst way imaginable: having him still around and yet not truly her own.

Are you willing to love him?

Nelia scoffed, the dryness air in her throat coming up like mothballs out of a closet. The bitter taste was almost the same as well, just mixed with dirt from the empty town.

"What about him loving me?" she asked to no one and yet to the one that suddenly mattered most to her. "Is he willing to love me?"

I'm asking you... about you... Not about him. About you.

But Nelia persisted in her question.

"Am I so hard to love?"

The question might as well have come out of the stars, for all she knew. It was never a question she had dared to ask out loud, but there it was. She saw the last few letters, all in smooth, black ink, falling to the ground with a heaviness that reminded her of lead.

"Am I so hard to love?"

The repeated words didn't bother to materialize physically, as though they themselves pitied the level she was sinking to. She smudged the letters that piled on the ground into the dust with her boot and wiped her eyes quickly. Though the town seemed empty, she certainly didn't want some stranger from only three miles away from her in-laws seeing her pathetic words and tears. Who knew who her mother-in-law knew?

You can cry.

"Don't want to."

You have to... feel to love. Allow yourself... to feel.

Nelia hung her head as she slowly walked to an empty bench and sat down. The entire town seemed empty. Looking down the street from where she'd come, Nelia saw that even Igna was now gone. Hans was nowhere in sight, and neither was the blighter who had taken Igna from her.

She was alone.

"I always feel alone," she admitted. "Especially since Zayzay left me. And Aaron left me emotionally."

War... loss...

"Yes, he lost quite a few friends in the war. And his brother, but he came home to me and we had Zayzay and we were happy."

Happy? Were you?

Nelia's spine stiffened at the accusation. Normally she wouldn't dare be so bold or truthful. She never let any of her friends, if they could be called such, know just how distant she and Aaron had continued to be after he came home. It was the trauma of war, perhaps. Or possibly something she had done. There was always the possibility that it was his manifest regret at marrying her in the first place. That old, heavy thought brought her shoulders slumping. To be fair, she had never understood why Aaron had married her. Love wasn't really something farmers dealt with. Once she'd asked him if he married her because he felt sorry for her. Instead of answering, he had changed the subject and later told her to never bring it up again. He said he would ignore the question if she dared ask a second time.

Zayzay coming along had taken the focus off the holes appearing in their marriage and instead shone a light on them as a family. Having Zayzay helped solidify their need to work harder to support themselves as a family. Zayzay's birth also forced Aaron to reconcile with his parents, for they would need them to help with the baby and they needed the stability of knowing his parents wouldn't kick them off the land. For a while, Zayzay had brought them all together, helping each one of them realize there were more people in the world affected by their decisions than just themselves.

For four years Nelia hadn't waivered on whether she was worth anything. Her son needed her, and that was enough.

But then Zayzay had died.

"I'm just a piece of garbage," Nelia said, repeating Old Lady Myrtle.

Who told you that?

"You should know. Old Lady Myrtle. And my classmates. And pretty much everyone who looks sideways at me or who won't let me into their mom clubs or who won't bother to give their condolences on losing my child. They just think I'm garbage. They hardly acknowledge me. Only the people at church say hello. And even they never invite me to tea unless it's for charitable reasons."

Do you... think you're garbage?

"No. Maybe. Well, usually I guess I do," Nelia answered the wind, though the air felt hot and dry and still. Yet she heard the voice in it and knew she had to answer it, even if she looked as crazy as Barbarane, the woman who twirled in the center of Overge shouting about the sky falling.

"It isn't so much about thinking, though. It's more a matter of how I feel. They make me feel like I'm worthless. Sometimes Aaron makes me feel like I'm not worthy to be his wife. Maybe... well, maybe I wasn't worthy of being Zayzay's mother. Sometimes... sometimes..." Nelia lowered her voice, not wanting anyone else to hear what she was going to say next. "Sometimes I think it was better that he did go with the plague. At least he wasn't old enough to understand how people felt about me, and then about him because of me. He didn't have time to learn to hate me or misunderstand me. I would have made his life miserable, really. Once he started school, what if he wasn't good at it, like me? They would have laughed at him and made fun of his mother being a dunce. I think about that sometimes."

Dust coated her throat and her tear ducts, keeping any moisture from escaping. But that didn't matter. Her tears for herself had dried up years ago. Perhaps she would have cried for Zayzay one more time, for her heart twisted each time she spoke of him. Her arms ached to hold him again, playfully spank his bottom, tease him with a wild raspberry or hide until he found her, then tickle him until he gasped for breath. 'Miss' wasn't the right word. It didn't encompass half of what she felt.

In that moment, right there on the hot bench, her throat screaming for a drop of water, Nelia found herself unraveling, like an over-washed pullover.

But what is the truth?

"Truth? About what? Ah, yes. Truth over feelings. As my grandpa used to say. Is that it? What is the truth? Well, I guess they are right in some sense of the word. I'm not born worthy of their friendship or admittance into a club. Not by the standards they go with."

Are those the standards… by which they should live?

"I haven't read your letters in years, though those are not the standards we learn at school. But everyone knows no one follows the standards. Everyone knows that the only people who must follow the law are those of us who live under the line of standard wealth."

Who are you? By law?

"A citizen of your kingdom," Nelia said, her eyes widening at the truth of her words. Never before had she thought about who the law said she was, instead of who those around her village said she was. By law, she was a citizen in the kingdom of Niebo, and that meant that she had an inheritance along with certain rights. Just like those with money. A citizen of Niebo didn't need to have money to have rights. By the law, under the King, they were all equal.

Nelia almost laughed aloud at the truth, but too quickly her laughter turned into a grimace. What use was truth if no one around you lived it?

You live it.

"As though that will change anything," she scoffed.

The wind didn't answer for a few minutes. When it did, all she heard was, *Who is Aaron?*

"Again with Aaron? He's a citizen of your kingdom as well, of course. But what happens when a citizen of your kingdom hurts another citizen of your kingdom? Is there punishment? He should at least apologize. We've been distant for so long and yet…"

Nelia allowed her voice to fade away. The words disappeared into the dry air. There was no need for any reply from the wind. Already her mind zoomed towards the inevitable questions: have you ever hurt Aaron? A marriage is comprised of two people, is it not? Aren't you the one who pulled away after Zayzay's death, even refusing to go away for a weekend with Aaron, lecturing him about the cost of going away and how irresponsible he was to even dare to suggest it?

"Yes," Nelia admitted to the voice in her head. "And he told me it was irresponsible of me to allow my mind to disintegrate into nothing. And I got mad. I threw that plate against the wall and told him to shut up and mind his own business."

Nelia's bones shivered at the memory of the plate crashing against the wall. Never before had she seen black magic come out of someone's nostrils. It had so frightened her that she'd jumped away from herself, thinking perhaps fire would come out next. Throwing the plate was to make Aaron mad, as angry as her, but she didn't want to burn him up like a dragon protecting a princess.

Of course, dragons were from fairytales, so it was ridiculous for her to jump away. Strangely enough, her anger had dissipated to make room for her fear, and she had found herself staring with wide eyes at her husband as though seeing him there for the first time.

And what she saw had frightened her even more than the black magic, because Aaron was standing in the doorway, his body practically blocking all the light from the fireplace in the next room, a warm, orange glow all around him with tears running down his cheeks.

"But that was three months after Zayzay died. He should have given me more time. It's been two years now and we've had better times. I even apologized for throwing that plate," Nelia insisted, her body rocking back and forth in the dry air as the sun beat down on her. "I'm sure I apologized. Yes! I apologized a day later when Aaron finally came home. He just kissed me gently on the cheek and said nothing. But things were okay. They were okay after that."

The wind whistled by, but no words reached her ears.

"I do love Aaron. In my particular way. I'm just... tired of life being like this. I'm not sure what the purpose of any of this is. My childhood, meeting Aaron, him going to war, him coming home, having Zayzay, Zayzay leaving us."

In the midst of it, I'm with you.

Those words brought a memory of her grandpa to Nelia's mind. He was rocking slowly in his handmade rocking chair, sitting next to a low fire though it was a blistering day out, his unfilled pipe clasped between his teeth. Though he had quit tobacco thirty years before, he never could rock in his chair without a pipe between his teeth.

The memory was so thick that Nelia could reach out and touch the wispy, white hairs of her grandpa as he rocked backward. Feeling her fingers, he stopped to give her a grin, his wrinkled face contracting into a folded fan. As his eyelid fell to give her a slow wink, it revealed the only spot on his face that the sun had never hit. It was the only place that revealed to the world how much clearer his coloring was than hers.

"Remember that day? That day you found me just like this after school?"

Her grandpa's words vibrated against her inner ears as though he were still alive, sitting right there in front of her.

"Yes," she said, trying to swallow to help her dry throat. "I was probably eight and wanted to know why some kids at school wouldn't play with me. I asked you if you loved me even though I couldn't read. My teacher had placed me in the corner and told the rest of the class that she understood why my father never showed up to see me. 'Why would he want to attach himself to a stupid girl?' were her exact words."

"And I told you what?"

Again, Nelia swallowed. The hot air caused the image of her grandpa to waver. She widened her eyes to keep the image before her, but before she could find the ability to speak through her dry throat, her grandpa was fading into the dust.

"A child is not a mirror reflecting the failings of a parent."

Nelia stared at the empty street as the memory of her grandfather continued speaking.

"You were not a reflection of your father's failings, nor are you a reflection of my goodness or my failing," he said, bringing Nelia's attention back to him. "You are a new creature, Nelia, with your own goodness and your own failings. And even still you are not a reflection of any one thing you did well or did wrong, but a conglomerate of everything. You have a bit of your daddy in you, whoever he might be, and a bit of your dear mother and a bit of me and Grandmama, but all those small parts only make up a fraction of the big whole of you."

The dry air had already caused her lips to crack, and when she smiled at the memory Nelia felt them fight against the pull of her cheeks. Though she hadn't fully understood what her grandpa had said that day, his words had comforted her. Thinking again about Zayzay, Nelia knew the truth was that she wasn't happy he had died. It hadn't been better for him or her that the plague took him. Had he lived to face the challenges of going to school where people would judge him for who his mother was, Nelia would have gladly faced them if it meant being able to hold him in her arms at night and watch him grow into a man.

"I miss my boy," she cried, tears still refusing to come out, but the heaviness on her chest enough to cause her to gasp as though weeping.

Though it seemed her lungs had a mind of their own, with some grit and determination Nelia got herself under control. She refused to sit and weep. What was the use of it, anyway? A headache was all that it would gain her. Besides, she was so close to home and yet still hours away. The sun was high enough now that if she started walking, she might be home before it set. Going along the road after sunset wasn't recommended. She'd never done it without Aaron. Not since he came back from war, at least.

With one more gulp of air, Nelia straightened up. Gathering her wits was what she was used to doing – something she had witnessed her mother and grandmama do many times over the years. Even her mother-in-law didn't allow herself time to cry. Poor farming folk didn't have the luxury of mourning for too long.

"Perhaps that's why death seems to affect our hearts more than city folks," mused Nelia to herself as she dug into her pockets for a sandwich. But it was empty. All the food that the housekeeper had packed for her was still in the saddlebags on Igna, who was now owned by a bow-legged old man. Hunger tightened around her middle. While filling her belly had felt so good yesterday, today she regretted it. Had she kept it half empty, she would feel only the dull gnawing, not the sharp pain.

Nelia saluted the sun to keep its rays out of her eyes for a moment to scan the horizon. There was nothing but a handful of sagging, dilapidated houses. Two smaller roads were visible, probably leading to farms or possibly other houses, and the one large intersection where a broken sign read: *Overge, 5 miles.* The arrow point was broken off, but Nelia was almost certain which way her village was. It was only one road going in the direction of the sun, and she was convinced that her village was to the west. Almost certain.

Nelia hesitated and looked around one last time for Hans. He had said that he would walk with her to Overge, had he not? The memories from that morning were fuzzy. Had he said that before they'd stopped to talk to the dirty beggars, or afterward? She couldn't quite pinpoint the specific memory in her head. It was possible she'd wished it instead of him saying it. Aaron's voice, accusing her of making up her own memories, echoed in her head. Aaron often complained she did this. True or not, a cloud of desperation started to gather around her ankles at the thought of being alone. Alone with her thoughts.

The skin on her arms heated at the thought of her longing for a strange man to be by her side as she walked home. A wave of rolling heat swept slowly through her body and the pink cloud of shame started descending, surrounding her shoulders and chest first. The hair on the back of her neck pricked up and the wall around her heart squeezed tighter. Was she as weak as all that? She had traveled on her own to the King; why was it that she felt weak and unable to walk a few miles home? All her life she had rejected the idea that she needed a man, just as her mother had taught her. Mother had always scoffed at the idea of women needing men. From that seed had grown an entire forest in Nelia's heart and soul. While Aaron was gone she had done everything alone. But somehow, somewhere she had become weak.

Who was she? The question repeated in her head.

Aaron might be angry, seeing her walk up the lane alone.

The thought made her look up, defiance rising within her. Who was Aaron to be angry about her being alone? He could have accompanied her. And why would he prefer her walking with a strange man? Did he never fear that she and a strange man might fall into temptation if left alone?

Or perhaps he didn't think a man would want her.

Nelia snorted in the air and started walking. No, she would not wait. She was not a woman to wait around for a man to help her, especially when he had left without even telling her goodbye. One working so closely with the King and Prince Pokoj should have better manners than that.

Nelia kept walking, her steps becoming more of a march the longer she allowed the thoughts to swirl in her mind.

Not that Aaron's manner should affect her decision at all. She was a strong woman, used to doing things on her own. It was wavering like this that caused the intellectual women who came giving their lectures every few months to doubt that the women of Overge were on board with female independence. Nelia hadn't bothered going after the first one, when she had been eighteen and so excited to be a part of a group that included only women. But she had left the lecture so insulted that these soft, thin women thought the women of Overge weak that she'd almost stood up and screamed at them. Still, as much as she was indignant at their lack of knowledge and sympathy for the working women of Overge, Nelia felt the tug to be a part of their group. Strangely, as most things turned out in Overge, the women who never worked but whose husbands did had formed a chapter. And that chapter excluded anyone unable to pay the dues in full.

"Well," Nelia muttered, slowly walking down the street, trying to keep her head lifted high. "I am Nelia. I do not belong to the Females Together network, but that doesn't mean I'm not a strong woman. Unlike most of those women, I worked three jobs while pregnant to keep from having to sell the farm to my neighbor and face the humiliation of having lost everything from my in-laws. I am the woman who went fishing by herself while Aaron was away so I could eat, defying the unspoken rules of Overge that claimed fishing was a man's sport. I took the scythe and cut the wheat one year because my father-in-law said he was too busy, and no other woman would let their husband help me."

Nelia marched forward, her energy renewed for about four minutes before she realized that while she should not linger, she also shouldn't walk too quickly and tire out before getting home. At the starting point she was five miles away from Overge, but her home was a mile down the road that diverged from the entrance to the village. And once there, it was possible that she would find the place empty, since Aaron had said he would eat dinner with his parents while she was gone.

A breeze rushed through the trees, blowing away her busy thoughts, allowing her to loosen her shoulders and relax more. It didn't matter what Aaron had done or would do in the next few hours, she decided. It was good enough for her that she even wanted to go home. And that was what she would focus on, for things would be better going forward. She could feel it.

Chapter 17

stones of shame

A little way out, Nelia turned to look at Trungulia once more. It appeared that the sad, empty town stood squarely in the middle of a strange desert valley that ended by sloping upwards again towards green needle trees. Nelia turned towards home again, smiling at the green around her. Somewhere close to her a brook bubbled, which meant there would be many animals lingering about. For the first time that day Nelia heard grasshoppers talking and birds singing to one another. The sun still had a few hours to shine, but the air was already cooler than it had been when she'd sat in misery on that empty porch in Trungulia. Nelia was grateful for the woolen shawl, wrapping it loosely over her head to keep her head warm. After a few minutes, she felt overly warm but refused to take the shawl off. In an odd way, it made her feel safer.

Rest…

Nelia almost laughed.

"What for?" she asked. "I just started walking."

Rest…

"I don't want to be lazy. My grandmama made me fight against that inclination all my life and I will keep fighting it, your majesty," she answered the wind. "I can't rest."

Pockets.

Instinctively Nelia stuck her hands into her pockets, even though she knew there was nothing in them. There never was, because the fabric of them was so thin that if any object was slightly heavy, it ended up ripping a hole in the pocket instead of the pocket holding it. Her fingers grazed the lines of stitching where she had sewn the fabric back together or placed another layer on top to strengthen the pocket. Her rough finger pads traced those lines with a hint of amusement. Several times in the last year she had thought of closing the pockets up altogether, but not having a refuge for her hands made her anxious.

As she shoved her fingers deeper into the thin pockets, Nelia found an almost secret pocket that she had unintentionally made by patching two pieces of fabric together without paying enough attention to the seams. Nelia frowned at that. She had used to sew better when Grandmama was still alive. Mostly because Grandmama would have insisted she do a better job.

Only two fingers fitted through the hole, but they immediately touched something small and smooth. Actually, four little objects, one on top of the other. They were as hard as rocks, but light enough and small enough not to be noticed.

Nelia slowed her pace as she gently pulled the objects out of the pocket. When her eyes caught the reds and pinks of the stones, she stopped in the middle of the road, too surprised to continue walking.

They were Aaron's garnets of shame.

Her mind raced back to the day the droplets had appeared. It was as though she were watching one of those moving picture shows projected onto the cool, green trees of the ever-thickening forest. She was even wearing the same dress, since her other dress still had a hole in it from sitting too close to the fire one evening.

As usual, Nelia felt hot, pink air surround her face at the memory of almost catching herself on fire. To be fair, she had practically fallen asleep sitting up, but that didn't erase her embarrassment from being so careless.

Leave the stones… behind.

Nelia sat heavily on a large boulder, dropping her right hand down to immediately obey, as she always did when told what to do, when suddenly she stopped.

Why was she obeying so readily? Why should she get rid of the stones?

Unable to stop herself from looking again, Nelia held them up to the light of the sun, which was now low enough not to hurt her eyes too much. Still, she didn't look directly at it. Grandpa had told her it would blind her. She held the stones before it to see if they were translucent. Sure enough, they created the prettiest pink light that sparkled across her hand, turning her skin into something completely different. Something pretty. Something shiny. Something that had never been there before.

Hypnotized by the light, Nelia sat looking at it when suddenly the wind moved sharply towards her.

Well? Are you going to leave them behind?

For the first time, Nelia heard a voice in the wind. Distinctly. It was clearly the King's voice. Not a whirling sound, or the rustle of leaves and air. It was His voice. Clear as day.

Leaping to her feet, Nelia looked around, gripping her fists tighter together, keeping the semi-precious stones safe in her hands. Of course, no one was near her.

The stone's coolness against her palms was at the forefront of her mind as she looked around. She couldn't take her focus off the cool hardness against her calloused skin as she sat back down on the boulder. But once there, one stone started to heat up. At first she thought it was the natural way of things, the stone heating up as it sat against her warm skin, but that didn't seem right. The heat was more intense, more intentional, and somehow it ignited an anger from deep within her.

"I shouldn't have to leave them behind. He should apologize, and then I can give them back. Or I can keep them to remind him. Or to remind me not to cause trouble, because that's what he thought I was doing. So I'll keep them to remind him of our quarrel and remind me that men don't want to be spoken to."

Is that the truth?

"Yes," Nelia answered, all the stones now picking up the heat from her hand and transmitting it back to her skin. She focused on the warmth for a moment, but the question of truth came back to her, piercing her in the heart. She breathed in hard as a long, gray stick of thick air came straight through her chest. The sight of it made her stomach roll. It was the first time she had ever seen that type of black magic, but not the first time she had felt that roll in her stomach.

You are lying.

She didn't need the King to tell her that; the hard knots in her stomach had already made it perfectly clear. She had never been too good at lying. Though there were times in her life when she stuck by her lies, there had never been a lie she had told that hadn't come with that same sickening feeling in her gut.

"That quarrel was mostly his fault. It was his immaturity and inability to see me as more than his wife who cooks and cleans. That was all on him."

But the unforgiveness is all on you…

"Why should I forgive him?" Nelia cried out, her voice picking up passion with every word. The stones burned hotter now, and she almost wished she could let go, but now her fingers wouldn't open. Down deep inside her, she knew that they would burn into her flesh and stay inside her hands if she didn't let go, but it seemed as though her fingers and her brain could no longer connect. "He hurt me! He sees me as less than even I see myself!"

No, it isn't about you. His reaction was about how he sees himself.
The words hit Nelia in the gut.

"No," she answered, almost pleading. "No, Aaron has good self-esteem. He knows he is better than me. His mother reminds him often."

But you solved a problem he thought three years on how to fix.

"He shouldn't have reacted like that. He should have more humility. It would be the first time in my life I had accomplished something worth bragging about. Why can't he be like Pamurrun's husband, who gloats about how wonderful and smart his wife is?"

Aaron is a different man. And Xingsu isn't perfect.

Nelia cried out in horror as the smell of burning flesh sprang from her palms. The pain was almost worse than childbirth. The stones were sinking slowly into her hands, taking their time to burn away the flesh, muscle, nerves, and ligaments. In a fit of pain, she glared at her hands and willed her fingers to open, but they refused. Instead, they glowed orange hot and trembled at the damage the stones were doing, helpless to stop the burning.

"Get them off me!" she screamed to the voice, to the King.

Only you can…

The rage and confusion were so much that Nelia thought she might die on the spot – until suddenly the solution was clear.

"I forgive him!" she screamed. "It isn't worth hanging on to this anger produced on false terms!"

Her scream echoed through the forest behind her and zipped down the road, before making a turn and coming right back to smack her in the chest. The impact on her heart was enough to force her fingers to release the stones, which fell to the ground and were immediately swallowed up by the dirt.

Tears streamed down Nelia's cheeks as she held out her damaged hands to the earth, the throbbing pain still very much a part of her thoughts, though Aaron dominated above the pain.

"I love him," she whispered, choking on the truth. "Sometimes I just don't know how to love him."

Give me your hands, child.

Nelia held out her hands, palms down, weeping on the boulder that sat only a few miles from her home and husband. All her energy was gone. All her *everything* felt gone. Just yesterday she had felt like a cleaned-up person, but now she felt like an empty vessel.

Quietly she sobbed by herself, holding her palms out. Certainly she was a sight to see, though that thought was too fleeting to make any lasting change. Only when she felt the pulsing nerves in her hands calm, like a machine slowly shutting down, did Nelia look up, certain her hands had fallen away completely. But being left with only arms wouldn't have ended the pain; it would only have moved the pain to her wrists.

Slowly, she attempted to curl her fingers closed and found that she could without pain. Instead of the burning, her palms felt light, fluffy and cool – as though she was holding whipped cream, though there was nothing there.

Nelia's head started spinning as time slowed and came to a stop in front of her. A panting sound that echoed through the branches of the trees struck her with fear until she realized that it was her own breathing. She stumbled a few steps forward, in shock. Or maybe awe. Had she truly screamed out to the air? Had she actually forgiven her husband?

And for what?

The rough bark of the cedar tree against her cheek was cooler than her skin and helped ground her in reality. She was there. Really. She was still away from home. And the last few minutes had happened. Though the sun was moving lower in the sky, there was still sufficient light. Her head now feeling permanent on her neck, Nelia dared to hold her palms up in front of her face and look. Though there was no more pain and no wound, she could make out the round marks. They were slightly red, healed scars. Permanent. Aaron would be asking her where they had come from.

She sighed and rubbed her worn cheeks that were still wet with her own salty tears across the tree trunk as she tried to organize the sequence of events, both physical and within her heart.

The heaviness she usually bore for her husband was mostly gone, though she wasn't as stupid as to think that everything at home would be magical from now on. Aaron had not changed. And nothing had eradicated the same old habits between the two of them.

Nelia switched to her right cheek scratching against the bark. Her body felt so light and airy, she thought perhaps she might fly all the rest of the way home. Was she so worn out that she was drifting out of her body? No. No one floated out of their body out of the weakness of fatigue. Only once in her life had she witnessed such a thing, when Major Rhinestucher had seen a carriage trample his son's body right in front of him. Nelia had witnessed the entire incident. She was seven at the time and in the plaza, watching in fascination as a strange foreigner convinced men to pay him for moving green cups around. The men had to guess which cup held the marble and always lost. Up until the screams started vibrating through the streets, Nelia was on a winning streak of 4-1 in her head.

She wasn't supposed to be there. Mother had sent her on an errand to drop off the clean laundry at the rich folks' houses and surely expected her back by then, and yet there she was, hiding behind the green-bricked columns of the city hall, watching shenanigans, as her grandmother would call them.

When the screaming started she didn't look at first. It sounded like those screams from the dancing ladies late on Saturday evenings. She'd seen them once going home when Mother was trying to sell jars of apple butter house to house. After that night Mother had switched to laundry. Nelia remembered not liking seeing the ladies screeching like owls, though every other movement of their body had indicated they were laughing. She also hadn't liked seeing their thighs exposed and their chests piled up like mountains of mashed potatoes. Instead of turning to see these women now, Nelia kept her eye on the marble. But when even the man moving the cups looked up to see what the commotion was about, Nelia finally looked as well.

At that very moment the two horses, their eyes wide and wild, pushed a small boy down to the ground, sending him flying like he weighed nothing more than paper and pounding him into the dirt with their hooves. It seemed to Nelia that the boy never had a chance of even knowing what was happening before he was shoved into the mud. When the wheels of the carriage bumped violently as they drove over the small body, Nelia vomited. The full contents of her stomach lurched out from her throat just as the carriage jumped into the air and crashed onto its side, the driver flying forward until his body smacked into the brick wall of the courthouse.

It was all over in a matter of minutes. As Nelia wiped her mouth, sidestepping the mess on the ground, she saw Major Rhinestucher. His dark face looked an ashen green. His mouth was locked in a permanent scream of horror, though his body didn't seem to respond at all. That was when she realized why. As everyone else ran about, shoving him towards the trampled remains of his son, his spirit floated above his body, hanging in midair as though on a coat hook. Nelia watched with her mouth open as the spirit hung low, watching the scene with deadened eyes, before jerking left and right, up and down, then dropping back into the Major's body like a popped balloon.

Though blood ran down the street and the town was in chaos, Nelia could not move. She watched the Major, with his large, bulging arms, slowly push everyone around him as though they were flies and shove forward towards his son. With a gentleness she didn't think was possible from a man of such might, the Major picked up what remained of the boy. All four of his limbs wilted down from the Major's arms. Nelia saw one hand dangling, barely attached by white, string-like components. From there and other places, blood dripped rhythmically with the slow gait of the Major. When Nelia looked at the boy's face – Carter had been his name – another sudden purge of her belly shot out. Carter's head was covered in both blood and dirt, one eye bulging out of the socket, his mouth hanging open in a silent scream.

That image haunted her forever. It wasn't until later, almost four years, that she would remember seeing the Major's spirit lift from his body. She dreamed it one night – the same night that the town buried Major Rhinestucher, who had been found one morning over the side of the cliff. No one knew if it was an accident or purposefully done, but Nelia knew. She knew the Major had died the day his son died. His face had remained a permanent greenish-gray color from that moment until he left this earth.

Nelia took in a deep breath. Where the bark of the tree had felt good, now her skin felt raw and wet. She touched her fingers to the spot, expecting blood but only finding tears. Each time she remembered poor Carter and Mayor Rhinestucher she cried. Every fiber within her urged Nelia to sit on the ground and release a good sob before falling into a blissful, dreamless sleep. That was what she might do if at home, but it was not something she could do here in the middle of nowhere.

Chapter 18

a baby from a rock

The sun was still making its way across the sky, and she still needed to get home before it set. If she appeared in the doorway after dark, she would rightly receive an angry lecture from her husband. No woman was safe alone after dark outside of town. Not these days.

But before she got any further than two or three steps, a strange sound stopped her. Then it came again: the sound of a cat, as though in pain.

A cat! Pushing off the trunk of the tree, Nelia felt slightly rejuvenated. Excitement and happiness dared to flow through her suddenly. Though she loved cats and yearned for them to let her hold them, most had a distinct dislike for her. The only one who had ever showed her love was Moonbeam, and he had died four months ago. He had been her companion for seven years, while all the other cats ignored or disdained her. Grandmama said it was because of her natural smell. Mother said since they were smart creatures, they avoided stupid ones.

When Moonbeam was old enough to prowl about the house on his own, the first thing he had done was to seek Nelia's bed and curl up on the pillow. Aaron had been home from war then, and she was ready to give birth to Zayzay. And though she was about to welcome her own bundle of joy into her arms, it overjoyed Nelia to the point of crying to see that a cat liked her. Aaron teased her for it and his mother scoffed and rolled her eyes, but they didn't understand that to her it was a good omen; an omen that her baby wouldn't reject her but would welcome her as a mother.

"Here, kitty, kitty," Nelia called out, crouching down to see better along the darkening forest floor.

Every vibration of the ground, every leaf that fluttered and every stalk that billowed had Nelia turning that way, but she found no cat. Still, there came another cry. This time closer.

There was a distinct temperature drop already, only four tree-lines into the forest. The dusk was denser, and the air was heavier. Across the way to the right, Nelia caught sight of a mouse skittering away. She waited, hoping the cat wouldn't be far behind, but nothing ran after the mouse. She stepped farther in, though only silence greeted her.

"I should go home," Nelia muttered to herself, even as she took more steps inside. "'Why are you late?' 'Well... I thought I heard a cat.' 'A cat, Nelia?'"

Nelia stopped imitating the conversation between her and Aaron and stood still. There it was again. A mew. A cry. It was getting fainter. But now she could hear the pain in the sound. The desolation. No wonder the cat hadn't chased after the mouse; something was wrong.

Afraid she might step on the poor creature, Nelia knotted up her skirt and lowered herself to the earth. Crawling around with her hands skimming the damp, dirt floor, Nelia continued slightly to the left. All the while she held her breath, silently praying for the wounded cat to cry again.

Just as she was about to shuffle forward another step, there was a sharp cry from near her hand. Even though she had been searching for the cat now for about ten minutes, she still jumped nearly out of her skin to hear it so close by.

"Come now," Nelia murmured, now on her knees and feeling about in the leaves for the animal. She saw no green eyes peering out at her, which made her heart sink. Perhaps it was too late to save the creature.

Her heart wrenched. It was too late to walk away. She couldn't let the cat die by itself now. It almost felt like her destiny to be the one to look after it, even if but for a few moments.

"Come on, little kitty," Nelia cooed, her palms sweeping to the right and then the left. Suddenly her left palm felt something clammy that moved at her touch.

It wasn't fur she felt, and she wasn't sure if the coolness was blood or skin. But could a cat somehow have pulled so much fur off?

"Wah!"

This cry was sharp and had a familiar sound to it. Then came gurgles and whimpers.

"No!" Nelia cried, her slow brain finally catching up. Jumping to her feet, she bent over and began brushing any leaf and branch away near her. It was the foot that she saw first; that was what her hand had touched. Again, something moved as Nelia moved the poor covering of leaves away, revealing a naked baby leg. Knowing where the foot was, Nelia then scooped her hand underneath where she could calculate the body lay and swiftly brought the bundle to her chest.

The child screamed in fright, but it didn't have much energy to continue. The skin on the poor body was clammy, covered in goosebumps and swollen in several places where insects had feasted on the baby's blood.

"Hush now, little one," Nelia murmured, holding the child as close against her chest as she could. She dared not yet look at the baby's face and risk falling and twisting a knee or ankle. They still had a bit of a walk to go to get home. Home. Where Aaron waited for her.

"And what will I say to him, do you think, little one?" Nelia asked, as the sun became brighter now, and they stepped onto the side of the road. With a sigh of relief, Nelia saw they were alone still and that her shawl was still next to the boulder. "Well, never mind that. For now, let's get those leaves off you."

She knelt down gently, leaning against the boulder for support. When she pulled the baby away from her chest, it let out a pathetic howl that dissipated into a whimper.

"Numi, numi yaldati," Nelia sang quietly. The baby kept its eyes closed but whimpered into silence. "Numi numi nim."

Gently she peeled the leaves from the baby's body, revealing more bites and scratches. A soiled diaper drooped off the malnourished body, but Nelia could find some hope in that. At least he wasn't so dehydrated as to need the hospital.

It was a boy. About six months old perhaps. Nelia rolled the child into her shawl. He allowed her to handle him without so much as a cry or whimper. Then she tightly wrapped the warm cloth around and around the body until he was snug and safe. Between the shawl and her arms, the baby soon relaxed and fell into a deep sleep.

It was time to get home. She had someone else now to care for, someone who needed food and water sooner than she did. And suddenly, what had seemed like a long walk just half an hour before now seemed too short to conjure up an explanation that Aaron would believe.

Chapter 19

new wine skins

G oing somewhere fast, are we?"
Nelia twisted her body sharply to the right at the voice, though she realized who it was before she saw his face.

"Hans."

He was not too far from the four black marks on the ground where the stones had been swallowed up, sitting majestically atop his horse.

"Where did you go off to?" he asked, laughing. "I turned around and suddenly you weren't there."

Nelia nodded down the road.

"I had to start getting home," she answered, not about to mention anything about thinking he had abandoned her on purpose. There was a throb in her palms as the baby squirmed in his dreams, but Nelia was not about to tell Hans about the stones either.

She heard the guard slip down from his horse and approach her from the right. Though her first instinct was to hide the baby, she knew it was futile. There was nowhere to hide such a bundle. But she also knew that if Hans were to take the baby, he would have to pry it out of her cold, dead fingers.

"What have you got there?" asked Hans. "Is it a boy or a girl?"

"A boy."

Her quick answer was one thing, but it seemed quite a different thing to see Hans' lack of surprise that she was holding a baby at all. It sent a chill down her arms.

"Why are you not surprised? Do you think many women find babies along the forest floor every day?"

"Was he deeply in? I had the impression that he would be lying down next to the rock, easy to find and all."

Hans said this without looking at her, instead opting to keep his eyes locked on the boy. He placed his large fingers in between the tiny ones and instinctively they grabbed a hold, pulsing with the willingness to keep living. Nelia was pleased to see such strength in the baby – a baby she was already considering her own. For the first time in years, her arms were full again, and she would do anything to keep them that way.

"What will your husband say?" Hans asked. He straightened up and fell into step alongside Nelia. "Will he allow you to keep him?"

"Aaron? I don't see why not," Nelia answered, though her heart was not so confident as her words. She knew her husband, and she knew he was not a hard man. He would not send the baby back to die in the forest. "There is no place for the baby to go. Someone put him there to die."

"Or to be found."

Nelia stopped walking for a moment to look Hans squarely in the eyes, but then walked on without speaking again. His words stayed with her as they passed tree after tree, minute after minute. Her arms began to feel heavy, but Nelia ignored the discomfort. She wasn't about to complain about holding a live baby in her arms.

"We are almost to your home, are we not?" Hans asked, there pace having brought them already quite far.

Nelia looked about her and, seeing the crossroads at the end of the horizon, nodded.

"Not too far. There, at the crossroads, I will turn to the right. The town is just to the left and a little way more. My house is off down that road, then down another and nestled into a grove of trees you can't yet see."

"You don't live in town then?"

"No," Nelia answered, surprised he would think such a thing.

"I grew up in a town," Hans offered, as though that might answer her surprise. "I always wondered about the kids who got to run about barefoot in the summer. Gah, I was jealous of them."

"Jealous? Of not wearing shoes?"

"Yes! They got to run about in the fresh air. I had to run about in the muck. A few summers I would go to the harbors, but then it got so dangerous even my absent mother thought it wasn't a place for me. One summer, at seventeen, I walked out of town and kept walking till a man offered me a job. It was in the forest cutting trees and I loved it. Never looked back after that."

Hans took in a deep breath. He seemed at home in the forest, though it was clearing up into fields the closer they got to the crossroads. Nelia glanced down to the left, where the trees opened up to a field that was half withered and half prosperous. A little farther down, she could make out a large house with smoke coming out of the chimney and wondered if she should go there instead of her own house. Perhaps her husband would be there. But then he wouldn't *really* think she wasn't coming home today, would he?

She shook the thoughts away as the baby boy rubbed his head into her breasts, moving towards her as though to suckle, but gave up before really trying. Stress sent pinpricks down her arms and legs. Time was pressing. This baby needed food. She took a deep breath in, already noticing her lungs being weighed down. Nelia inhaled again, trying to stay calm while getting the necessary oxygen.

The little boy squirmed uneasily and opened his eyes in search of the one guilty of disturbing his sleep. It was the first time she saw his pupils. For a moment they stared at each other, her deep brown ones into the lake of his golden-brown. There was no fear in his eyes, though she obviously would look nothing like his mother. There was no recognition either, which was to be expected. What Nelia hadn't expected, but what she saw, was the baby drinking her in, almost like he was sizing her up. And what he decided at the moment was that she was enough.

This she realized when he yawned sleepily, shuffled his fists about in the snug cocoon she'd made for him with her shawl, then settled back into a blissful slumber. Safety was his number-one concern, it seemed, and safety was what he felt with her.

"Well, then, here we are," said Hans. "At the crossroads. So, do we turn to the right now?"

Nelia looked up in surprise at being already at the point in the road where the crude wooden sign announced Overge just one mile to the left.

"You don't have to come with me," Nelia said, nodding down the road. "I know where I am well enough."

"Nonsense," announced Hans as he led his horse to the right. "Remind me to unpack your things when we get to your house."

"What things?"

Hans looked at her in a quick double-take, as though to be certain she was serious. Nelia saw him do this from the corner of her eye, but could not take her own off the precious face of the sleeping baby she held. There was a small doubt within her that he was real. To make certain she was not going crazy or making the entire incident up, Nelia vowed to keep her eyes on the baby until she got home and had Aaron confirm his existence by holding the child himself.

"I brought all the things you left on Igna. To be honest, I almost forgot to get them. It was the old gentleman who came hobbling after me yelling that I needed to go back. I almost ignored him; I was so concerned about finding you again. But when he told me you had left your bundles, I decided to go back and get them. I would have felt badly if I'd left them behind and later found out you had something valuable there."

"Nothing valuable," Nelia answered. "Everything I own really is on my back. There is some food, though."

"Food is valuable enough, do you not think?" asked Hans. "Oh, but wait! I have some fresh milk in wineskins. Never used wineskins, you know, but I don't know what else to call them. Apparently, that is how one sells milk around here."

"Not in Overge," Nelia said with a giggle. "We sell milk in glass bottles."

"Well, that is what the old man gave me, saying he felt it necessary."

"Perhaps it is goat's milk. I've heard some places store goat's milk in wineskins."

"And what, really, would be the difference?" asked Hans, stopping a moment to take something from his horse.

A release of laughter rose out of Nelia from the depths of somewhere she didn't feel too often.

"I don't honestly know," Nelia said, her words, caught in the laughter, tumbled over themselves until she noticed they were hitting the baby too forcefully. She quieted herself and left the laughter behind. Now that she wasn't afraid it would leave her completely, setting it aside was not so heavy an effort. And she knew laughter would not leave her completely, for a baby always brought laughter. They couldn't help it. "Perhaps those who started the practice had reasons for it, but I do not know what they could have been."

"Well, look at that," mused Hans, with such awe that Nelia felt compelled to turn around. She found Hans standing next to his horse, holding a wineskin – but instead of the usual large, round cork top, this wineskin had a small seal that looked to be made of supple material and in the shape of a teat.

"Is that a joke?" Nelia couldn't say any more. It seemed surreal what she was seeing.

"I don't think so. The old man was talking on and on about how all the children in his parts used to drink goat's milk and grew to be large and strong, but that they had all moved away. He kept making the skins for the goat's milk, but the new people in the town refused to give it to their children once they were weaned from their mother. I forget now what he said they drank instead; I was quite worried I wasn't going to find you, so I only half-listened to the man. Anyway, he insisted over and over again that I take this. He gave me about ten of them. He said they don't even have to be kept in the cold stones of the cellar. He says the udder keeps the milk cool so as not to sour."

Nelia looked at Hans, hoping he could see the question in her eyes but also hoping that he wouldn't ask in words.

Her prayer was answered. Hans said no more, but approached the baby and gently placed the supple material near the little boy's mouth. The baby moved away at the cool touch on his lips, but when a large drop of milk fell on his tongue, he immediately understood. The entirety of his being changed demeanor. He strained his neck, searching for more of the sweet nectar, though he didn't seem able or willing to open his eyes.

Hans placed the full of the rubbery material in the boy's mouth and gasped in awe as the baby instinctively suckled at the milk.

"Amazing," he murmured.

"Just wait till you have one of your own. It is even more amazing to watch them search for their mother's milk only hours after exiting her womb," Nelia said, watching with relief as the boy suckled down his dinner.

"Well, I will have to wait until I find a woman worthy of that job," he said, his smile broad and teasing.

Nelia pushed him gently with her elbow. What a freeing sensation it was to have a younger-brother type to tease. They both watched the baby drink until the wineskin was half gone. Feeling like a cad, but not knowing when the baby had last eaten, Nelia gently took the milk away, giving him her knuckle to suck on to quiet his protests.

"Why not let him have it all?" asked Hans, holding the milk up as though weighing how much the baby boy had eaten.

"If his stomach has been empty for a long while, he could vomit up the milk. Just gets to be too much for an overly empty tummy."

"You know this by experience?"

Nelia nodded.

"Both personally and as a mother. There's nothing worse than watching precious food come back out of you because you didn't have the patience to wait."

Hans peered down the road, then clicked his tongue at his horse and took up walking again. Nelia followed, so satisfied with the bundle in her arms that she couldn't contain her own smile.

"Do you hear that?" Nelia asked after they had walked in silence for a few steps.

The crickets were coming out, singing the night into being.

Hans sighed as he looked around. The sun was at eye level now, spreading pink and orange fluff through the sky, and it seemed to sing its own glory. Somewhere in the distance, birds sang to their young, and in the wheat fields something Nelia had never heard before was also chattering a song.

"Those aren't crickets," Hans said as the wooden fence that ran around Nelia and Aaron's rented property came into view. Just one hundred meters away was the pothole-ridden dirt road that would coil through a smattering of trees before opening into a field and then revealing her cottage along another line of pine trees. Nelia's heart almost burst at the sight of it. Partly with happiness and partly with nerves.

That was when she heard the long grass singing. Hans was right. The sound was not that of crickets chirping or birds singing; it was the grass, rocks, flowers, and trees.

Chapter 20

home again

The singing was in her language this time, the language she had spoken as a child with her grandparents. And in that language, she heard the long grass singing and shouting, "All hail the glorious Prince. For He is worthy of our praise! All hail! All hail!"

It took but one exchanged glance with Hans for Nelia and him to both start at a quicker pace.

"It's Prince Pokoj!" Nelia said, her heart beating wildly. "Is he at my house?"

"He was at least here!" grinned Hans, slowing when he realized his long step was more than Nelia could keep up with. "Come here, this way. Step up onto my hands and I'll lift you onto the saddle. I'll trot alongside, and we'll get there quicker. Hopefully, he won't have left before we get there."

Nelia scurried, leaning into Hans so fully that her breasts pressed up against his shoulders in a most embarrassing and unbecoming way. This she realized later when thinking on her day while in the warmth of her own bed. Her uncorseted breasts. When later she admitted her shame to her husband over the incident, Aaron only grinned a rather knowing grin and laughed. Her face turned red – she could see it reflected in their dirty kitchen window – but the baby crying saved her from having to think on it further. It wasn't but five minutes later that Aaron joined her in comforting their new son and kissed away her worry of acting improperly in public with a Prince's guard.

"You were in a hurry to see me, love," he said, his lips still close to her cheeks. "And to me, that is all that matters. Whether you innocently press your breasts up against a man who knows better than to take advantage of you is not anything I'm worried about. You are my overly innocent girl, and with that can come some inadvertent breast pressing."

With that said, Aaron moved around to press his chest against hers, causing her to laugh and erasing all her shame.

But while sitting atop the horse, Nelia did not so much as realize what she had done. She had no thought about it. Hans did not pause or twitch or turn red. He didn't react at all unusually, and so Nelia did not think she had done anything wrong. All she could think about at that moment was getting home. The idea of seeing Aaron again caused her heart to pulse in double time, but the possibility of seeing the Prince again made her heart skip beats. And if both men were together?

Before that thought could cause anxiety, she shook it from her head. Aaron and the Prince together? No. Perhaps if the Prince hadn't specifically asked her if she wanted Aaron to go to war again, then cold fear wouldn't be spreading over her chest at him possibly being there, at her house. It had been hypothetical at the time, but still... he had asked her, and now there was evidence that he passed this way. Right near her house.

No. She did not want Aaron to go to war. Though if Aaron had to go to war again, at least she would have a son to keep her company. She would not be so lonely. On the other hand, she would also not be free to pick up whatever work she could for them to be able to eat.

Her body moved rhythmically up and down, left and right, as Hans led his horse down the road, avoiding the potholes to keep the horse from stumbling. The movement was relaxing. Nelia could understand how it was that people became obsessed with riding horses. They were so different from donkeys. She could almost have relaxed and fallen asleep with the baby boy, if it were not for the singing.

The sound along the dirt road was glorious. Exactly as Nelia imagined an opera would sound like, though possibly prettier than an opera. One could not compare the sound of grass singing with the singing of a human. Nelia was almost certain of that. Though she had never heard an opera singer, she had heard the women at church who believed themselves to be talented. They had nice voices that could carry a tune much better than she could. But after listening to the grass sing and the boulders give bass while the trees strummed and hummed on backup, Nelia couldn't imagine anything else coming even close to the perfect sound she heard at that moment.

The baby stirred slowly in her arms, then stirred more frantically. His eyes popped open, revealing an intensity she had seen before on Zayzay. Then the tiny body squirmed again and a pathetic squeal, like a tiny piglet, came out. Nelia smiled and lifted him into an upright position. With accustomed hands, she patted his back and sang him something made up from her heart about a baby left in the woods who might save her life. About halfway through the song, several large bubbles came out both ends of him and then all was quiet.

"The Prince is here," Hans said, suddenly.

Nelia looked up with a start and found herself to be just on the cusp of her own driveway that led directly to her house.

In her tiny house, a light hung from the ceiling in the living room, allowing the travelers to see through the glass windows and deep into the house. Nelia was about to ask exactly how Hans knew the Prince was still here if she could see no one through the windows, but laughter floating out from behind the house answered her unspoken question. Then the magnificent horses standing to the side of the house came into view, each eating from a grain pail. Next to the house there stood a guard at attention. Another guard leaned against the shed.

"He is here," Nelia said, more to herself than anyone else. Though her heart skipped around joyously in her chest for a moment, the next moment it was sinking. Her house was not a place that should receive a prince.

As Hans and she approached the house, Nelia wasn't able to rip her eyes from watching the other guards. The one at attention didn't flinch; he didn't even look to see who was coming. The other one near the shed looked them both over, sending a nod of greeting to Hans. Out of nowhere a man who looked more like a commander walked towards them with a grim look on his face, his brow raised.

"Who is that?" Nelia asked, but Hans was too busy adjusting his stance to take notice of her question. At one hundred yards out, Hans halted, stood at attention, and waited for the commanding officer to finish the approach.

"At ease, Hans. Where have you been?"

"Dropping Igna at her new owner, sir. And escorting Miss Nelia back to her house, sir."

"I didn't plan on seeing you coming here," the officer said, giving Nelia a grim, though not unfriendly look. "I thought you had another assignment after leaving Igna."

"Just to make sure Miss Nelia came home safely," Hans answered.

"Right. At ease then, soldier. Go on and deposit the lady with her husband. Then bring your horse to eat some supper before we have to be off. Unless the Prince tells you otherwise, you will spend the next few days with us."

At that, the officer raised his eyes again to Nelia. He seemed to think twice about something he was about to say, then started again with his voice lower. "There will be another assignment soon, but first we must see if the nation of Kzenigurben will continue to be our ally or if they have changed their minds and will go with the black magic."

"Shall we influence their decisions, sir?"

The commanding officer almost started laughing, though he checked himself quicker than anyone Nelia had ever seen. He cleared his throat loudly, then stepped out of the way to let Nelia pass through, still atop the horse. He gave her a slight nod, his only action of recognition towards her. Nelia gave him a weak smile. Suddenly, her muscles tingled as though about to fall asleep. She was glad to be sitting on a horse. Slowly they passed by her house, each place lacking paint or needing repair painfully perceptible as she moved past the tiny dwelling. It had not been built as a house, but as a resting stop on the far end of the land for when the cattle or sheep came to graze on this end. A slap-together addition allowed them to be cozy yet comfortable. But that addition was already pulling away from the main area of the building. She wasn't certain how much longer the house would last, though she had no idea where they would go if ever if came undone altogether.

Looking down at the nameless baby in her arms, the vivid memory of bringing Zayzay home overtook her senses. That day, with Zayzay cuddled against her chest, she had stood in the same place and thought the same thing about her house. For the first few hours of being home she had fussed about how they would all fit together, but once night fell and exhaustion smoothed over her like butter on bread she had found herself grateful for the cradle near her bed. There Zayzay had slept, murmured and cried during his first night at home, and there he had died just four years later. That was not something she had ever regretted.

The new baby wiggled, then opened his eyes. This time though, as he yawned, and a bubble burst forth from his stomach, he didn't settle back into slumber. Wide awake now, he fixed his eyes straight on Nelia, never wavering as he rose and fell in her arms in rhythm with the horse's gait.

They turned the corner of her house and immediately Nelia's heart slammed into her lungs. There, just a few yards away, she saw her large husband leaning against a newly-painted fence. The one that separated the corral from the hog pen. Next to her husband stood the Prince in his regal uniform, his hair sleeked back and his lips in a wide yet comfortable smile. They both looked up as she and Hans came closer. Aaron's large smile was directed straight at her. She hadn't seen him smile like that since their wedding day.

At the fluttering of her heart, Nelia smiled back, then raised her arms a bit higher to show Aaron the baby. A shadow crossed over his eyes. He exchanged a look with the Prince, who seemed to give a gesture that told Aaron to move forward in greeting his wife – and to welcome the child. A gesture that seemed like a commander reassuring his recruit.

At that analogy in her head, Nelia's shoulders sank. It seemed very possible that one of her greatest fears was about to be realized: Aaron would go off to war again. And how many men went off to war and came home alive and in one piece more than once? She knew of no one. The only man in their village that had gone more than once and was still alive had come home with only one leg and half a hand.

"Hello, Vackerlik," Aaron greeted her, his smile wobbling for a second. As though fate would have her fall in love with him over again, his hair flopped over into his eyes, giving him the same look he had had the first time he'd invited her to walk with him. "Mi ez winzig klein ding?"

Before Nelia could properly answer, her husband's large hands were underneath her hips, picking her up off the horse as though she weighed nothing. There had been no reason to doubt his strength, and yet a strange sense of relief flooded through her. So much did his touch of her affect her that she felt as though she might cry. But out of gladness. Never in her life had that happened. And yet it had happened just the other day with the King, had it not?

Nelia sniffed. It was yet to be seen if she was changed for the better. Or even permanently. Or if Aaron would find her newly-found emotions to be annoying. It was yet to be seen if she would find *herself* to be annoying. Feelings, after all, could be a nuisance.

"I found him on my way home. He was crying," she said by way of explaining, propping the nameless baby up for Aaron to see. Without waiting for an invitation, Aaron tugged the small, underweight thing out of her arms and held him so closely that for the first time she wondered if he missed holding a child as much as she did. Did men's arms ache when their little ones were taken away? Why had she forever thought that was a female symptom of grief?

Before the tears could roll down her cheeks, Nelia busied herself with trying to find another wine bag full of goat's milk. Not that it was needed. When she discreetly absorbed her tears with the end of her sleeve and turned around, she found the baby boy staring straight up into Aaron's eyes, with one slender fist holding tightly to her husband's nose.

"I was resting for a bit, sitting on a boulder near the side of the road when I heard a cry like a cat in pain," Nelia started to explain again. At the mention of a cat, Aaron gave her a look that said he was happier the noise had turned out to be a baby and not a cat. "Aaron! I must get another cat anyway, so why not rescue one who has no home? I need a cat to catch the mice who seem to think the larder is their house and our food theirs."

"Would you prefer a cat or a son, Aaron?" boomed a voice from behind her. Nelia turned at once and gave the man one of her awkward curtsies.

"I've never seen a woman give you a curtsy," Aaron teased the Prince.

"That's because I wouldn't dare bring an uncouth man like you into a room with ladies," the Prince jabbed back with a laugh.

The jovial attitude between the two men was strange. It put her on the outside of something intimate. Never had she ever seen Aaron interact like such a friend. Almost like a brother. And to the Prince! It must be true, then, that the trenches bonded men together in ways nothing else could.

"I don't dare think my kind of curtsy brings the honor that you deserve, my Prince," she said, feeling suddenly shy in the middle of three men. Four, if she were to count the baby. Which made her stop suddenly. "And just how did you know the baby was a boy?"

"He told me a boy was coming," Aaron said, his voice back to its baritone. "I just didn't realize what a winzig he would be. Looks like maybe he's in need of a change. Do you have any nappies, Nelia?"

The joy in Aaron's face was something to behold. Nelia stood transfixed by it for a moment or two before answering about the nappies. She couldn't seem to recall a time when he was so happy. Not even when Zayzay had been alive, though surely that would have been the last. The problem was that she hadn't thought to record the moment in her brain, foolishly thinking there would be more and more days of joy and laughter with such a beautiful child in their possession. Before the black plague, she had never thought Zayzay might die. Days of joy are something a person can take for granted when their child is healthy and alive.

"I believe there are quite a few in the trunk with all of Zayzay's things," Nelia answered, the lump in her throat making it difficult to speak.

"Can I put some clothes on him from whatever is in there?" Aaron asked.

It shouldn't have been difficult to answer him, and yet Nelia hesitated. She shoved her hands in her pockets, though they offered her no source of comfort. Still, the gesture reminded her that she was going to forgive her husband. And that she had given up those stones that reminded her of past grievances. Did that not also mean moving on in other things too?

She could not forget Zayzay. He was not a stone or a past grievance. But she could also not deny her husband his joy. Nor should she lose the joy she had discovered when she had picked up this baby simply because her husband shared those same feelings. If she were going to question his feelings for Zayzay due to his reaction to the new baby, should she not question her own joy at holding the baby?

Or, instead of questioning and feeling jealousy for a child now long gone, perhaps she should look towards the future and hold on to the joy of a child who needed them.

"Yes, Aaron," she answered, quietly and precisely. "There are many things in the trunk. You may put anything on him that you wish."

Aaron smiled, kissed her nose, then walked back to the house with the nameless child still in his arms. Nelia turned to the Prince, wishing she could present her confusing emotions to him but feeling that she should not bother him with petty thoughts and differences.

"So, you found what my father wished for you to find," the Princes said, his smile still genuine.

Nelia couldn't help feeling caught off-guard. Genuine smiles were so rare in her town.

"Did he truly mean for me to find the child?"

"Why wouldn't he? The child needs a family. I don't know all the details, but it seems that the mother hid him from the father, who tends to drink and hit his wife. One night she became afraid that the man would kill their son, and so she hid him. My father kept the wolves away for you to find him. He knows you. He knew that you would not pass up the cry of a child," Prince Pokoj said, adding with a wry smile, "or that of a cat."

The horizon was lighting up with pinks and oranges, colors she hadn't seen on her land for a long time.

"Aaron seems happy. And not a bit surprised. I spent too much energy on these last few miles worrying about what he would think of me bringing home an unknown child."

"Were you worried he would not accept any other child but his own?"

Nelia looked the Prince directly in the eyes, wavering on whether to tell the truth to a man who seemed to be more intimate friends with her husband than with her, though that had not been how she felt back at the castle. Or perhaps she still felt that close to him, felt the desire for him to be her closest friend, and this was a bit of jealousy on her part.

"It was a surprise to see you here," Nelia said, ignoring the last question, which she saw did not get past the Prince at all.

"I told you I wished to meet with your husband again."

"But you did not say it would be now. Why did you not leave with me then?" Nelia paused, thought for a second, then decided to go ahead with the real question burning within her. "Why did you go a different way this morning and leave me with Hans?"

Prince Pokoj playfully pinched her chin, sending a puff of golden sparkles into the atmosphere. Joy. Happiness. She had seen those emotions before. But a very long time ago. She wondered if those emotions came off her chin or his fingers. Probably his, she decided.

"You had something to attend to, as did I."

Still, the Prince smiled. Nelia stared blankly back at him for a second before recalling what had happened along the journey. Had that been just that same day that she had sat on the deserted bench in that awful town? Had it been just a few hours before that the stones had been burning her flesh and she had been desperately trying to shake them loose from her? It seemed an entire age had passed since those happenings.

She felt very exhausted suddenly.

"Yes, Prince Pokoj, you are correct. I did have a few things to attend to."

"And you did well in attending to them, Nelia," he said, dipping his face to meet her eyes again. "I mean that. Listen to me when I say these next words: I am proud of what you faced today and the decisions you made. They are not easy, but you have shown yourself to be not only courageous but also softhearted; willing to forgive and move forward; willing to love something or someone more than yourself. I'm proud of you."

Tears sprang to her eyes. Nelia twisted her mouth to keep them from falling, but the Prince smoothed out her lips, touching them gently with his fingers.

"It's good to feel emotion, Nelia. It means that your heart is softened again. And a soften heart can do more good for the kingdom than a hardened one. Let them fall, for they are tears of gratitude, respect, and love. And that love and respect is not just for your King and his discipline, but also for yourself. That's the good kind of pride."

With all of her muscles softened, her tears rolled down without hindrance. She counted one, two, three, four, five, six, with a seventh rolling down a moment later, just for good measure. It was then that her mouth was free to smile, and her heart settled into measured beats.

"Will you stay for supper, my Prince?" Nelia asked, just as she heard footsteps behind her.

"Yes! Stay for supper!" boomed Aaron, holding the nameless child in the crook of his elbow as though a sack of flour. The child stared out into the world with interest, raising his small hands when he caught sight of the Prince.

"I forgot about that onesie," Nelia whispered, her heart suddenly lurching before she commanded it to settle. "Zayzay wore it the day we went on that picnic. But he must have been only three months old, and this baby seems about six months."

Aaron's lips pressed against her temple, an action that brought her heart back down to a normal beat. She raised her arms to take the baby back, for holding a child was something she would never pass up, but the baby was set on being held by the Prince. She dropped her arms with a smile as the baby boy squirmed and squealed, holding out his arms and lurching forward as though to throw himself into Prince Pokoj's arms.

Chapter 21

a final blessing

"Come here, little one," the Prince said, placing his gloved hands around the baby's stomach and lifting him easily from Aaron. For a man who had never been a father, the Prince seemed perfectly comfortable holding a squirming child.

And yet, Nelia noticed that the squirming and whining stopped immediately. Once the baby was in the arms of the Prince, he was quiet and content, his large eyes looking about, peacefully taking in the whole of his new home.

"He quite likes you," Aaron said, wrapping his large arm around Nelia's thin shoulders. "I remember all the children and babies liking you in each village we went into."

"It's a talent," the Prince answered with a smile.

"Will you stay for supper then?" Nelia inquired, noticing that she felt at home under Aaron's arm. The strangeness between them seemed to have evaporated, shifting their relationship back into the lane it had been in before Zayzay had died.

"Alas, I cannot," Prince Pokoj answered. "I'm wanted in Kzenigurben. My father has business for me there. And on the way, I may try to stop in Belbinse. Do you remember that town?"

Nelia felt Aaron's arm stiffen. A gurgling came from his throat, but no true words.

"Yes, you do then. I want to pass by and see how the rebuilding is going. Many people came out of their bomb shelters after the war. All the ruling class was more or less wiped out."

"By their own pride and stupidity," Aaron said through gritted teeth.

Prince Pokoj looked up from staring at the baby, looking Aaron right in the eyes.

"Peace, Aaron," he commanded, and immediately Aaron's arm went limp on her shoulders again. "There is no reason to hold a grudge. We forgive, and we move on. The people who are alive today are not the ones who warred against us. For the most part, anyway."

"When will you come again?" Nelia asked, wishing to change the subject for Aaron's sake.

The Prince heaved a large sigh and smiled.

"Soon. You know I will come soon. But you are always welcome to come back and visit. Hans! Did you unload Lady Nelia's things?"

Aaron looked down at her with raised brows, his eyes teasing her at the noble title the Prince gave her.

"It, well, it seems he calls everyone 'lady', regardless of whether they are one," Nelia stuttered, the red cloud again shifting around her body.

"Yes," said Aaron, smiling. "Human protocol has never deterred Prince Pokoj from doing what he knows is right. If he gives you a title, it is because he sees you as deserving."

"Listen to your husband," Prince Pokoj said, looking back down at the baby, who cooed up at him, swiping at his nose and grabbing onto the tassels from his coat. "But I cannot leave with this child still nameless. He is worthy of a name."

"Do you know what his mother named him?" Nelia asked.

"You are his mother now," the Prince said. "The woman who gave birth to him is no longer living." He paused as Nelia digested the information. "What shall you name him? I will bless him with his name and be off. Yes. See? My commanding officer is already gathering our horses and things. So, Aaron, how will you christen your son?"

"Anatole Itxaropen," Aaron replied without hesitation.

Nelia drew back to look him fully in the face. Surprise mixed with pure joy raced through her veins. She felt hot, then cold, then as though floating on a cloud of sheer happiness.

"Anatole Itxaropen, I bless you in the name of the King. May you grow in peace and prosper to your fullest potential."

Prince Pokoj made the sign of the cross over the child – who grimaced with a half giggle when he couldn't catch the royal fingers in his own small hands – then handed the baby back to Nelia, who wasn't sure she had the strength to hold him, though the minute he was back in her arms her muscles reacted properly. Silently, she watched as Prince Pokoj took from his pocket a large gold coin and pressed it against the baby's stomach. Then he took out a tripled-pointed knot made of sanded cypress wood. Anatole immediately put it into his mouth, but made a face and dropped it when the royal fingers came into his view again.

"And this I will give to you," the Prince said, taking out a small, gleaming box. He handed it to Aaron, who didn't dare take his eyes from Prince Pokoj. Nelia peered at the box, which was painted a shiny black with silver brackets on each corner. The strange thing was that there seemed to be no top or bottom. There was no line at all that would indicate where the box would open from.

"Ah, you see it, don't you, Nelia? That there is no opening? If you were to want to open it, you could. Inside is the plan that is perfect for Anatole's life. The plan that he should follow should he choose to follow me and my father. If you were to open it yourself, though, the plan would turn to dust, and you would never find out what was inside. Anatole could still find his future by coming to my father – not to worry about that, for my father does not blame the children for their parents' misgivings. But I would ask that you do not open it yourself, but leave it for Anatole. Things will work out best that way."

"Does everyone have a box?" Nelia asked, surprised by the zing of jealousy zipping through her.

Prince Pokoj smiled and pinched her chin in a brotherly fashion.

"No, but everyone does have the best plan for them. You opened yours on the way here – at least part of it."

"I didn't!"

"But you did, Nelia. The old woman gave it to you. Part of your plan is to bring this boy up in the best way you know how. He needs a mother and a father: you and Aaron. The other part of your plan will unfold, and already is unfolding, as you move along now under the peace that you brought back with you from visiting my father."

"And you, Aaron," Prince Pokoj said, turning his gaze back to Nelia's husband. "You know what you are to do. You knew long ago, but have strayed. And you know you have not been honest when you told your bride you did not believe in my father. So, I ask that you get back on your pathway and move forward. There is much work to be done, and you are needed. Raise the boy well, treat your wife well, and I will see you in a year's time."

Aaron jerked his head into a halting nod, then saluted the Prince with a tap of his booted heels.

Prince Pokoj shook Aaron's hand heartily, then pulled him in for a hug between brothers. With Nelia he was gentler, wrapping her in his arms and embracing her lightly so as not to squish Anatole. Then he kissed her tear-ridden cheeks, pinched those of Anatole, and mounted his horse with a flourish.

Nelia was too overcome with emotion to say anything as the other soldiers mounted their horses and flanked Prince Pokoj. Nothing in all her life had stirred her to such a passion of pride as that moment.

Sniffing back her tears, Nelia waved at the men, then buried her head into little Anatole once they were gone from sight. In the background once again the flowers and the rocks sang while the trees played background music. So full was her spirit that Nelia couldn't speak at all.

"You met Prince Pokoj, then," Aaron said, gently running his fingers through her hair. "I'm sorry I told you I didn't believe anymore. I do. It's just that life hit me so hard after the war, and especially after Zayzay died. I didn't know what to do with myself, really. We'll believe together now, and we'll fight together now. Each month we'll go to read the letters, and together we will stand up to those in Overge who don't want to do what is right."

"That won't be easy at all, Aaron," Nelia replied, unable to smooth the worry from her face. "That isn't at all what I thought we would do. That isn't at all what I've ever wanted to do."

"It is, though, Nelia. You've always been a fighter, one to question and challenge the unjust. But you've never had anyone behind you to encourage you in the fight. Now you'll have it, though. Now you'll have me."

"I… I don't quite know what to say, Aaron. I'm not sure I'm the woman you are painting with your words."

The air between them stirred. Nelia watched a pink cloud of love, not of shame, swirl until it slowly encircled all three of them.

"Come inside, my bride," Aaron said, guiding her by the small of her back. "I know we aren't perfect and there is much to smooth out, but I have faith we can do it. And for the moment we can share in feeding this young winzig something to fatten him up. Between the two of us, we'll have him looking healthy. He'll fit into our family as our son before anyone can dare criticize our taking him on."

Nelia narrowed her eyes at Aaron, about to complain about his mother, when he suddenly laughed.

"Yes, Nelia, I know. There will be much complaining, but no one ever said life would be trial-free. Let's just try to enjoy the moments without insults when we have them."

Before she could answer, Aaron swept her up in the air and into his arms. She shrieked first with the fright of possibly letting go of the baby, then with laughter when Anatole proved to enjoy the change of pace. The three of them entered the small house, its air now purged of stilted silence. Now, it was rose-colored and filled with the sweet smell of flowers.

"Anatole and Nelia, my two loves," declared Aaron loudly. "Welcome home!"

Lexicon

Chapter 1
Page 9 Helestau Mare- Big Pond ROMANIAN
Page 10 Klinous- made up word for their money
Page 11 Nic Nie Robić- do-nothing person POLISH
Page 11: Kostspielig- expensive GERMAN

Chapter 2
Page 17   Pokoj- Peace CZECH
Minunate- Wonderful ROMANIAN
Rechter- Judge or Ruler DUTCH
Chansagwan- Counselor KOREAN
Bapa kekekalan- Eternal Father MALAY
Sostenitore- Supporter ITALIAN
Umeluleki- Counselor ZULU
Frälsare- Savior SWEDISH
Joh-Eun- Good KOREAN
Muwaja- One SWAHILI
Jumala- God FINNISH
Mwenye Nguvu- Mighty SWAHILI

Chapter 4
Page 39 Síochán- peace GAELIC
Page 45 dzin-gin POLISH

Chapter 5
Page 59 Skutta- hop SWEDISH
Page 59 Snurr- spinning, spin SWEDISH

Chapter 6
Page 63: Niebo- sky POLISH

Chapter 9
Page 83 odlatywać fly away POLISH
Page 83 lille fugl- little bird NORWEGIAN
Page 84: quadrans was a Roman bronze coin very low in value.

Chapter 10
Page 97: Lalle ne: indeed, certainly HAUSA

Chapter 13
Page 130: Zstrovtich, castrunico, falenktu made up swear words

Chapter 14
Page 132: Brusnica- cranberry CROATIAN
Page 133: telk- tent ESTONIAN

Chapter 18
Page 169: Numi numi is a Hebrew lullaby

Chapter 20
Page 181: Mi ez:-what is HUNGARIAN
Winzig klein- tiny GERMAN
Ding- thing GERMAN

Chapter 21
Page 88: Anatole- Rising sun, rising light HEBREW
Page 88: Itxaropen- Hope, expectation BASQUE

about the author

Kat grew up mostly in the Midwest. Being asthmatic while living on a horse farm, she tended to stay inside during much of the haying, which eventually, led to her acting out stories to pass the time. That in turn led to writing them. Any time the hay was not being harvested she was outside playing. Mostly 'war' with her older brother.

Being an author, along with 'world traveler', was the only thing she wished to ever be paid to do, though she has succumbed to working other jobs such as retail and waitressing. She wasn't half bad at being a waitress but retail she found rather boring.

After living in Ireland, Spain and France she now resides in Texas with her three girls and her husband, who stalwartly puts up with all the ladies in the house.

Kat views life as one story after another. Each person has their story and each one is valid. Even if presented in fiction, there is something to be learned from each and every one.

Watch for more stories coming from Kat Caldwell and Ladwell Publishing.

Follow Kat:
on Instagram: katcaldwell.author
on Facebook: katcaldwellauthor- Pencils&Lipstick
on Tiktok: pencilsandlipstick

Find more on katcaldwell.com and lifefictionandhappiness.com

other books and novels
by the author

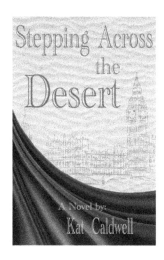

Five years ago, a servant from her father's house sold Rowena as a slave. Now, a stranger at her master's table will change her destiny again.

Christophe knew that taking a woman across the desert would be dangerous. What he didn't know was how much it would affect his heart.

Once again in London, Rowena must decide on whether to accept her past and move on with her future, or run away from it all.

You'll never get stuck in your journaling process with *A New Way to Journal.*

With 36 prompts to keep you digging deeper about yourself and your view of the world, along with extra questions at the end meant for posterity's sake, *A New Way to Journal.* will reset your desire to journal.

This journal is set up as a three-month journal if you write out three prompts a week, but with a space to write the date, you can feel free to go at your own pace.

LADWELL
PUBLISHING

CPSIA information can be obtained
at www.ICGtesting.com
Printed in the USA
BVHW031717311019
562607BV00001B/13/P